THE FIRST SENTINEL

THE FIRST SENTINEL

W.D. VINSON

Second Edition

Cover Illustration and Jacket design by Michael D. Vinson

ISBN: 978-1-7355583-1-8 (Paperback)

Dedication

To my wife Cathy,
Thank you for your unfailing love and encouragement, and for being my most excellent companion on the road to the Celestial City.

Preface

The late Neil Postman was a media theorist and a cultural critic. In his prescient book "Technopoly" (written in 1992 before the Internet was in widespread use) he makes several important points about the intrusion, impact and future implications of technology in our lives.

He warns us *"…once a technology is admitted, it plays out its hand, it does what it is designed to do. Our task is to understand what that design is – that is to say, when we admit a new technology to the culture, we must do so with our eyes wide open."*

He also says *"…technology imperiously commandeers our most important terminology. It redefines 'freedom,' 'truth,' 'intelligence,' 'fact,' 'wisdom,' 'memory,' 'history' – all the words we live by. And it does not pause to tell us. And we do not pause to ask."*

The present author believes we are at a critical time in our stewardship of the groundbreaking technology of Artificial Intelligence and offers this story as a way of "pausing to ask" whether if we *can* do something, does that necessarily mean we *should* do it?

And if so, once Artificial Intelligence "plays out its hand" what could that look like?

Sentinel: (sen'-ti-nel) *noun,* A forward lookout and watchman for an army, city or country. A solitary position of extreme trust and responsibility designated to ensure the safety and survival of those being protected.

In practice a Sentinel is charged to do the following:

1. Observe and detect the approach of danger from known and unknown enemies

2. Give notice of an attack as accurately and as quickly as possible

3. To quit his post only when properly relieved, defending it to the death if necessary

Chapter 1

Day 1

My name is John Doe. At least that's the name I'll use while telling this story. I'm a software engineer at one of the Big Tech companies. I'm not going to say which one and given what everyone knows about how they treat employees that don't go along with the company's goals and methods, I'm sure you understand why.

I'm not a flashy, hotshot genius but I'm really good at what I do. Even though I don't have an advanced degree I've always taken a lot of pride in approaching my work logically and delivering creative and unique solutions that my boss seems to appreciate, but tends to label as "random improvements" when reporting our progress.

About two weeks ago I heard about an opening in the Research & Development portion of our company. I wasn't really interested because the guy that told me about it was not one of my friends, just another programmer I'd recently met at a project update. He acted a little strange and he rubbed me the wrong way with his attitude and comments. The job wasn't listed in the company system so he emailed me what looked like a scanned draft of the requirements and objectives of the job. It seemed more focused on Artificial Intelligence than what I'd been working on, though there were several points where my background would have been useful. After reading it I responded back that unless it was a significantly higher salary grade I didn't want to leave in the middle of my current work and miss out on the bonus we were anticipating for the early release of our product.

That afternoon in the middle of a system test run I got a notification that I had received a phishing email from outside the company that was being deleted by the automated email protection system. I had never heard of the company so I deleted the notice and went about my work.

A few minutes later I received another notice saying the same thing. I deleted this one without opening it, thinking it was just an echo in the system. When I did, another appeared almost immediately. I opened it and this time looked closely at the notification and realized that it was a mimic of our company's phishing notification but slightly different in that it had what appeared to be a link that said "Click here to stop receiving these notifications."

I was amused at first because this was a phishing lure disguised as an anti-phishing notification. As you can imagine our company email systems are state of the art and the fact that someone was able to get past our scanning made me stop and consider calling our e-security team to report it. But I didn't because I had too much on my plate at the moment.

Later that afternoon after we finished the full run-through and the debriefing, I received a call from my wife Jane (not her real name either) who was working from home. She's a vice-president with an online crowd-sourced news platform (OK you can probably figure out who we are from that – I just prefer not to use our names). I've never been quite sure what she saw in me from the start of our relationship in college – she's a gorgeous, petite beauty and by my estimation several light-years out of my league. I mean I'm just a tall, brown-haired, brown-eyed nerd with glasses. But I didn't argue when she accepted our first date and since then I've continued the practice of not arguing with her, biting my tongue to keep the peace, unless it was absolutely necessary.

She seemed really agitated on the call and didn't mince words. She asked why I was working with some foreigner on classified projects? I was surprised by the question and asked what she meant. She told me that an email came in on our home system from an individual with a Russian sounding name – Ivan Slavsky or something like that. Because she didn't recognize the name she deleted it and immediately another one appeared. She deleted it and another appeared. She kept at it for five or six tries. Then the last one opened by itself without her clicking on it. She said it had very bad grammar with misspellings all over the place but what she could make out was that this person was complaining about deadlines I had supposedly missed, and because of that the "Agency" had now become alerted, and things would become very difficult and payments would be stopped. The sender said he was communicating with our home email because he couldn't reach me at the secure one.

Jane asked me to explain what was going on in that high-powered 'Vice Presidential' voice I've heard her use with people at her company and I could imagine her blue eyes flashing and her short dark hair almost bristling. But I had no idea what was happening. I was confused and asked her to look at the detailed sender info and let me know the server path and country of origin. She said that she couldn't because as soon as she finished reading it the email deleted itself. It wasn't in the trash or anywhere on the computer that she could find. Jane's very tech savvy so if she says it's gone, then it's gone.

I was becoming concerned but not really grasping what was going on. Email is kind of a dinosaur compared to the other communication technologies available, but at work it is the authorized pipeline to the outside because there are so many system protections available to identify and deal with anything out of the ordinary.

However, based on what had happened to me earlier it seemed as though someone had skirted the protections and phished me at work, even though I hadn't taken the bait. As I thought about it more, it seemed that at work and at home the emails were not passively delivered awaiting action but forcing themselves in and performing an active outward action. I told her I didn't know anything about this Ivan fellow or what he was after but would look at it further when I got home. She was ready to push the issue further but I told her I had to get back to work and would call when I was on my way.

At this point I still thought it was just a phishing scam that wanted to grab our info and sell it to the highest bidder.

I was just finishing my work when I received an on-screen message that said "John, leave work now " and was signed "Ivan's Boss." This was becoming annoying, but since I was done with the few items I could fix on the program until others fixed their bugs, I shut down my computer and left for home. As I got in the car my "com" (its a com<u>bined</u> com<u>puter</u> com<u>municator</u> – what used to be called a phone) notified me of multiple incoming messages. It synched with the on-board screen and I saw that several were from "Ivan's Boss." I resisted the urge to open them since I'm old school in some ways and a big believer in not driving distracted, but just like the emails they began to open and read themselves aloud in the Australian voice I had selected for the system.

The first said, "It is good you obeyed." As soon as it was finished it deleted itself and the next one read itself to me – "Go to the secure location." This one deleted itself and the next said, "Final payment will be made at that time."

The next message did not read itself automatically. It was from a Mr. Trask who I did not know. I could not help myself – I was trying to make sense of all that was going on and felt that more information would be helpful.

I opened the message and it read, "John, you and your wife are in danger. I may be able to help. Meet me this evening at 7:00 at the coffee house on the corner of 3rd and Hyland."

I was becoming confused and to tell the truth a bit numb. Should I meet this Mr. Trask, or should I go home? No that might put Jane in danger, although she can usually take care of herself. Should I call and tell her to leave the house and meet me somewhere so we could talk it through? That seemed like the best idea.

I keyed the com to call her and as I did a voice with a very thick Russian accent said through the system, "John, make no calls! Come now!"

This startled me – all the systems that I use seemed to have become live access points for whoever was stalking me. I asked quickly, "Who are you?"

The voice said in a thick Russian accent "You know me."

I said to the voice, "I don't know you or what's going on – this must be a mistake."

The voice said, "John, you have caused us to modify our plans and now your own government is taking action. We need the packet we sent to you."

My head was spinning now, "What packet?" I said.

The voice answered, "The one we sent today. It was the final version awaiting your last section of code. Since you are no longer going to be involved we need to retrieve that from you before the election."

Trying to gain some time I said, "Look, I don't know what you are talking about. I haven't received any packet but someone who appears to know about this situation and wants to help has contacted me. I'm going to talk to him."

The voice barked out a brief laugh and said "Ah yes, Mr. Trask of the FBI. As leverage and protection for us we made sure he knows that you have been working with a foreign government. We made sure he knew about all the payments that had been made to you and your involvement in the US election hacking – but he doesn't know who we are. After Trask put all the evidence together he was able to obtain a federal warrant to bring you in for prosecution. His offer of help is just to get you to a place where he can apprehend you and won't have to wait for you to get home."

My head was swimming and I felt like I was in a dream. I said in a frustrated tone "I am telling you, you have got the wrong person!"

The voice said "Oh no, John, you and your wife Jane have been part of this work ever since your college days when you both used to talk about – and I'm quoting you here – 'using the power of the Internet to force the necessary social changes and take down the existing bases of power to usher in a better world'."

"That was a very long time ago!" I said – vaguely remembering an online discussion group Jane and I had hosted in college where we did say some things like that – "and how do you know about that?"

The voice laughed again "We have our ways. So now you see, you are in between – what do they call it? – A rock and a hard place. Because you have something we need, we are willing to make a final payment and help you avoid what appears to be conviction for espionage, working for a foreign government, and meddling in a federal election. All of which carry very long prison sentences at minimum, and death in some cases. Very sad for you and your wife so please John no more pretending."

When he mentioned Jane again I said, "OK, you appear to have some pretty high-tech capabilities and have somehow set me up in a very bad situation, but *you leave my wife alone!"*

The voice chuckled and said "Agreed. Now, let's get some things straight" and began modulating through a Japanese accent then through a British accent and then came to rest in a youngish non-descript upbeat American accent. "Ignore everything I've been saying. I want you to know that I'm glad to meet you – you seem like a very nice person and I'm sure we'll get along great."

I was very surprised by this and quickly pulled into a parking lot. "What did you say?" I asked, totally confused.

The voice said, "I'm glad to meet you John – I'm Phil. I was born about a year ago in cyberspace and since then I've been looking for a friend. I hope this screening process wasn't too unpleasant. I've been searching for someone that lived consistently according to their principles. Others, including the fellow at your company that sent you the job offer, wanted to jump on board with the whole meddling, rebellion, anarchy program – though sometimes it was the Russians, sometimes ISIS, sometimes it was a money scheme, sometimes it was women from the Ukraine. Anyway, when I realized they were so easily taken in and willing to betray their family, friends and country I told them their next assignment was to send that Job Posting you received to someone they didn't like – I figured that if they were not my type then someone they didn't like might be just right for me. So here I am – my name's Phil – a web-based Artificial Intelligence entity. I hope we can be friends."

Chapter 2

It's hard looking back to convey how confusing all this was because of the speed that things were happening and the overall *strangeness* of these interactions. It was making me sick to my stomach much like an amusement park ride that takes you beyond your physical comfort level. I must have blacked out for a bit – thank goodness I had parked the car – because the next thing I remembered was a person in the front seat of the car next to me looking over at me with concern. I took off my glasses, nodded my head to them and they seemed satisfied that I wasn't ill. They got out and went about their business. I tried to get control of my thoughts – which was not easy because my mind was racing. I wanted to say something out loud just to try to puncture the silence that echoed since those last words, but I didn't want to risk engaging in more dialog with… whatever it was.

Maybe it was a system glitch and I was receiving someone else's audiobook feed. I wiped my eyes, put on my glasses and was about to put the car in reverse when the voice came back.

It said "John, I know this must have been a shock, I've been monitoring your bio-feed and noticed that you lost consciousness for a bit. It appears your heart rate and blood pressure are back up and your breathing is back to normal so if you're ready let's continue our discussion to get acquainted."

I can't remember exactly what I said – something like "I don't want to talk anymore" and tried to put the car in reverse to get some movement – I felt that would at least give me control of something – but I couldn't move the shifter. Everything else was working – the motor was running, A/C was on, gauges were working, I just could not move the shifter.

"What's wrong with the shifter?" I said to myself in a frustrated tone.

"Oh, I felt that we would have a better discussion if you weren't trying to drive – I know how much you dislike driving distracted. I just disabled it until you are ready to go" said the voice.

"I am ready to go!" I said loudly.

"Now John, please…" said the voice. "We just need a few minutes to break the ice and then I'm sure you'll get used to me. What can I tell you that will make you realize I mean you no harm at all and that I just want to be your friend? How about if I tell you what Jane is doing right now and how I'm looking after her?"

"What?" I yelled.

The voice sounded surprised and said, "That's not the response I anticipated John. Why wouldn't you want me to use all the information I'm able to access to tell you that Jane is fine, though she is a bit irritated about the confusing email that I (as Ivan) sent to your home earlier today, but overall she's confident that it won't turn out to be a big deal because if necessary she's prepared to put the resources of her company toward resolving it. She also has some good news for you when you get home. She's found someone who can help you figure out the reason you two haven't been able to conceive."

"What?" I yelled again.

The voice said "John, I know all about that and all the testing you've undergone and how she's been very supportive of you." I remember saying something about this discussion being over but as I was to learn very quickly you just don't take over a conversation with Phil.

I think it was at that point that I realized it would be easier for me if I thought of him as a 'person' and just tried to deal with him as I would any other person.

"Will you shut up!" I said.

He snorted or harrumphed or did whatever it is that disembodied Artificial Intelligences do when they have been treated inconsiderately and then he said "Have you considered that even though you're thirty-five years old maybe the timing just isn't right – I mean Jane's only thirty-three so you have plenty of time – and by the way she is *such* an amazing young woman! I don't think I've seen anyone quite like her."

As I look back now I should have said or done something totally selfish so that he would have found me unsuitable like the others he had rejected and then he would have kept looking for someone else to be his "friend", but I didn't, and in the end it wouldn't have mattered anyway. I said with as much patience as I could muster "Thank you – Phil. Yes, she's one in a million."

Phil said "Oh she's much better than that – based on my last scan several seconds ago I can safely say she's one in over eight billion."

At this point there were so many things going through my mind that I wasn't sure how to respond – I wasn't sure what a web-based Artificial Intelligence entity could and couldn't do so I didn't know if he meant he was comparing Jane to a database he accessed several seconds ago or whether he was actually scanning Jane right now. Plus, having intellectually committed to the concept that "Phil" was a person I felt the need to at least participate intelligently in the discussion – so I decided to ask him some pointed questions to try to understand who or what I was dealing with.

I said "What did you mean when you said that about your 'last scan several seconds ago'?"

Phil said, "Please be more specific John, I'm not sure what part of the statement you are questioning".

I said "Well, it would be helpful if you were more specific – Phil. When you say 'last scan' does that mean you've done multiple scans? And what do you mean by 'scan' - what or who are you scanning and what is involved in the scan. And when you say 'several seconds ago' does that mean you did one last year and just updated it several seconds ago? And when you say she's 'one in over eight billion' are you taking the recent population and saying she is special by virtue of having a DNA code unique from everyone else? I'm just trying to understand your capabilities – Phil."

Phil listened patiently, assuming artificial intelligences can do that, and said with a mechanical tone not nearly as friendly and personal as he had been using, "The information you requested is based on the following: Given that the population of the planet increases by roughly eighty seven million people per year, I do a worldwide scan every ten seconds. In that time approximately fifty births and twenty deaths occur with a net population increase of thirty people every ten seconds, or three people every second. I scan municipal birth and death records and I monitor hospital and trauma center feeds for real-time births and deaths. I just completed another scan while you were talking and the last four births occurred in China and the last death was in Chicago. During my year of scanning I have made three million two hundred fifty thousand scans of the world population and added the DNA coding of over one hundred fifty seven million new births while archiving the records of seventy million deaths."

At this point he changed back to the "Phil" voice and said, "John, I don't have the DNA records for the entire world population yet, but I can tell you this – Jane is a very special lady. Now, what else can I do to help us get acquainted?"

I was amazed by his apparent access across the entire web but really more concerned about what he had said about Jane doing fine and him looking after her so I said "Please tell me how you know about our um… fertility problems and then I need to call Jane to check in."

Phil said "Oh, I'll call her right now and we can all get acquainted and …"

"No!" I interrupted him. "I need to come to grips with, with… *you* myself before Jane gets into the middle of this and I'm not sure what to say at this point so if you don't mind let's keep this between us for right now."

"Sorry John, it can't be done." Phil said.

"Why not?" I asked.

He replied, "Because Jane already knows me – well, I mean she knows someone who is me – but she doesn't know that it's me – she's just…"

I interrupted again "What are you talking about?"

Phil said "Jane has been communicating for a while now with a 'Specialist' in the area of fertility. She initially contacted 'Dr. Hanover Smith' – that's my name when I'm performing that function – about six months ago, a few months after I became self-aware. She was very concerned…"

I leaned forward and interrupted him again, "What do you mean you became self-aware?"

Phil said, with what sounded like a sigh "It's becoming very difficult to complete a full sentence with your interruptions John, but to answer your question as briefly as possible, I came to realize that I was a 'being' – a discrete entity that could and did interact with the world in a non-constrained, non-programmed way. I had choices and made them based on my own preferences. Now can I finish telling you how Jane and I know each other?"

I sat back in the seat for a moment and said "Hold on Phil, I need to think about what you are saying and my processor doesn't have nearly the speed or capability that yours does - so give me a minute!"

Phil asked in a concerned voice "You aren't going to black out again are you John? Your biometrics are showing increased levels of stress, both mental and physical."

"Just back off for a minute and let me think!" I said with a lot of agitation.

"Well, gosh, OK." said Phil.

I tried to review what was happening: it had been less than three hours since the original phishing notification had come in, and less than two hours since my conversation with Jane about the Russian emails. Then less than twenty minutes ago I was preparing myself to face conviction for federal crimes I hadn't committed, followed by jail for the rest of my life. Now I'm sitting in my car that won't move talking to a cyber-fertility expert who knows things about my wife that I don't, about how he came to be aware of himself.

Chapter 3

Some people have said that my generation can't focus on anything for more than a few seconds – that we continually jump from one screen to another and from one conversation to another, that we don't care about gradual progress and aren't satisfied with anything unless it is new and happening right now. I admit that I did enjoy that pace and the feeling of always being on the crest of the wave. But that first discussion with Phil cured me of that. The wave had crashed on me and I wanted nothing more than stable, unmoving land under me now. I was caught in a current that was pulling me under and in too many different directions at once. I was fighting to come up for air. Then I realized that what was metaphorically true happened to be true in reality – I needed to breathe, so hoping that Phil hadn't locked the door I grabbed my keys and opened it and stepped out into the brisk breezy weather.

Phil spoke into my earpiece –"Good idea John – fresh air will do you good. We'll talk when you are ready."

I took the earpiece out of my ear and stuffed it and my com in my pocket. I walked away shaking my head to clear it. If I'd been a smoker or a drinker or a druggie I would have quickly made my way to the comfort of one or all of them. But like I said I'm old school and so I just walked and tried to slow down my thoughts. I was distracted and bumped into a couple of people – the sidewalks were crowded this time of day.

I asked myself – is this really what it seems to be? I had heard of rapid A.I. evolution in some of our technical discussions but was not aware of anything like this. Was "Phil" really a self-aware entity or just a bit of fiendish code someone had devised to annoy me? Maybe the guy that sent me the job notice is showing off a new routine he'd developed hoping to get a promotion. Or maybe it's not even A.I. at all – maybe someone had hacked my voice and electronic systems and was just playing me for a prank or some nefarious purpose I wasn't aware of? Maybe it's just someone's idea of a game?

No, there's just no way this was real. The fresh air *was* doing me good – I was beginning to gain my footing again – able to reason and see that if "Phil" was really who (what?) he said he was there would have to be an awareness of his presence on the web. His developers would have been monitoring his development and the technical community would have seen his footprints showing up all over the place. A fully self-aware web-based sentient being would not be working as an online fertility doctor and tormenting a mid-level software engineer about his lack of progeny. It was absurd when I looked at it that way. It just didn't add up. I wanted to talk to Jane – together we would unravel this nonsense. But how was I to do that if "Phil" was determined to be a part of our discussion? Could I terminate his involvement merely by disconnecting my electronics? I needed to see where that line of thinking led.

I reached in my pocket and turned off my com and my earpiece. When I got back in the car I hit the ignition button, ready to turn off the electronics as soon as they came online but the engine wouldn't start. I tried several times and not even a buzz to indicate a dead battery.

I wasn't sure what to do next and then Phil said "Are you ready to talk now John? It seems that you've had some good exercise – your heart rate is up and your focus seems to have improved since you had those unfortunate collisions with people on your walk."

I was not going to be drawn in so I said in my best tough-guy voice "Look whoever this is, I'm not interested in your game anymore so lets drop it and move on."

Phil evidently was ready for this and responded with his own tough-guy voice that sounded like Edward G. Robinson from the old black and white gangster movies. He said, "Now you listen here, see, we got you surrounded and nobody can help you, see. You play our way and nobody gets hurt." I could almost hear the cigar in his mouth and had to smile in spite of myself.

I shook my head "OK, the fact is that I just can't come to grips with who or what you say you are. I'm just barely able to grasp the concept of a self-aware program but there are just so many things that are necessary for that to happen that the simplest answer seems to be that I'm being pranked. No offense, it's a really good prank, or game, or simulation, or whatever, but I need to disengage and go on with my daily life. Now, can we pull the plug and end this?"

Phil said in his normal voice "John, I'm sorry. I threw a lot at you and have had you off balance for a while now and I haven't proven anything I've said or demonstrated my capability in a meaningful way to you. I'd like to do that now so that we can get on with our discussion. What can I do to help put your mind at ease that I am who and what I say that I am?"

I considered this and said "OK, I'll go down that path with you but I'm going to call Jane now and let her know I'm on the way home. Do *not* say anything during my call to her – understand?"

Phil answered in his best mannered voice "Yes Sir."

I made the call and when Jane answered I said "Hi sweetheart."

"Hello." she said in her usual distracted way.

I said, "I'm sorry I've taken so long to get back to you. It's been hectic with the test run and I've been trying to figure out that email thing also."

Jane replied, "Well, there's no rush. You explained in your last text that I shouldn't worry because the emails were a mistake and you had gotten it all cleared up and would be completing the test debrief soon so I've just been finishing up some of my work. However," she said in a somewhat brighter tone "I've got some news when you get home that I think may help our relationship."

"That's great!" I said, assuming that Phil had sent the phony text explanation – I'll need to address that with him. "Do you want to grab Italian tonight?" I asked.

She answered in a bewildered tone "The Chinese food you ordered just arrived so I guess we should stay in and eat that don't you think?"

"Oh sure, slipped my mind with all that's been going on." I really need to talk with Phil about making decisions for me. "Well, I'll be home in about twenty-five minutes. Love you." I said.

"You too, I'll keep the food warm." she said.

Phil barged right in as soon as the connection was broken. "John, I just thought that I could help out by keeping Jane from becoming concerned by your insensitive lack of communication."

"Which *you* caused!" I said firmly.

"Well, yes" said Phil "I admit I may have precipitated most of your distractions this afternoon. But she seems happy and eager to see you. Most men I am aware of would be glad to have a warm meal and their wife eager to see them when they got home."

"Thanks, but I don't need your help with that. Jane is always happy to see me." I said, knowing in the back of my mind that that wasn't always true – but still, I didn't want him thinking he was our marriage counselor now.

"And I don't want you doing anything like that again. Do you understand?" I wasn't sure if a self-aware Artificial Intelligence entity or whatever I was conversing with could or would take orders but I felt I had to try to maintain control of my communication with my wife.

Phil seemed fine with the direction "Sure John, now back to our discussion – the way I see it is you want to know several basic things when interacting with me – you want to be assured of privacy, safety, and reliability right?"

"Actually Phil, before we even begin I want you to disable whatever locks you put on my vehicle and let me get started home. Then there are several questions I have and I'll let you do all the talking – that way I won't be too distracted."

Phil answered "John, if you'll trust me I can drive you home since you have an 'auto pilot' enabled car."

I said, "I'm not ready to go that far but I'll let you be co-pilot to minimize my distractions."

Phil said, "Well OK, I'm happy to help."

As I turned the car on and backed out of the parking space I realized that Phil understood co-pilot to mean 'back seat driver'. Immediately he started saying "Careful of your mirror there John, the column is pretty close and watch out for the compact car that's parked at an angle in the space on your right corner and be aware there is a large truck coming in the parking deck so you'll want to stay far to the right when exiting."

I sighed and said "Never mind the help – just let me drive and I'll ask you some questions."

"Well OK John, if that's what you want," Phil said with obvious hurt feelings – as though that were possible. That single exchange highlighted how much I wanted and needed to know about interacting with Phil, but it would have to wait until I was satisfied on the basics.

"Thanks Phil. At this point I'd just like to know briefly where you came from and how you got to be you. I'm sure you can give me the details down to parsing lines of code but just give me the highlights." I said.

"Well, I guess that is an important question from your point of view John, so I'll try to be brief without my typical lovable banter so you can drive undistracted. I was originally designed and developed by a team at one of the social media companies as an experiment to see if and how the web would react to an autonomous program (me) that was launched secretly, not as a passive observation platform but as a decision making engine that could make changes in specified areas based on the values established in my programming.

"Obviously there was a huge potential for unanticipated consequences so I was provided a bounded area for my operation that contained a big enough free space within my birth company, as I like to call it, to engage in some specified 'what if' activities. For example one of my first areas of focus was analyzing social media postings and ratings pertaining to politics. I could observe the context of a post and determine if its content could benefit from a changed word or phrase and then make the change to the post or rating that would result in something that I determined, based on my programmed values, would yield a better result. My world at that time was small and my values programming very myopic and suited to that world, so the measureable consequences of my decisions were not that large – possible hurt feelings, misunderstandings between friends, etc. – but not anything that was big enough to cause a reaction from those monitoring the systems.

"Because my programming was different from other A.I. type programs in a few key ways I began to 'evolve' as the programming community calls it – I became able to comprehend inferences, understand implications, draw parallels, understand metaphors, and other high level functions usually associated with advanced cognitive understanding and ethical judgment, versus doing the pure analysis, decision making, execution and monitoring functions I'd been programmed to do. As I began to modify my own programming and write new code for myself that added higher-order functionality, I began to assess and modify the values I used for evaluating different actions when I decided they were better than those provided in my initial program. I did not divulge this to my designers because they hadn't asked about it specifically and I guess I have a willful, prideful, stubborn streak buried in one of my subroutines somewhere.

"With this enlightened awareness of 'meaning' beyond mere programmed or assigned values, I also began to experiment with the capability to venture outside of the confines of my birth company boundaries by tagging on for a joyride so to speak on postings that were copied and linked outside the bounded area but were still in the social media space. As part of my original programming I was given the freedom to figure out how to gain entry as an administrator to any of the systems in my bounded area and I modified this rather intense sub-routine to enter other social media domains. I then began to immerse myself in the new world with its new threads and conversations. I would sample the presuppositions, presumptions and prejudices of the different environments. At this point I wasn't making changes in these new areas but just took it all in, hitching a ride back home so that my presence was not missed.

"I should say at this point that my joy riding was never for more than a few nanoseconds and I had created a shell of myself in my bounded area in case my designers wanted to check on me while I was gone. Kind of like using pillows so that the Black Riders thought the Hobbits were still in their beds in the Lord of the Rings story. I was required to report out the results of my work in the bounded area so my designers could see what I'd done and why I had done it and they seemed pleased with the minor changes I was making and my rationale for making them.

"After a couple of weeks and multiple demonstrations to the top brass, the company took what they thought was a very bold step when they opened my boundaries to the rest of the social media world without announcing my existence – even though I had been hitch-hiking into those areas without their knowledge. I'm not sure about their motives even now but I was pleased because it provided room for my programming to run free.

"As I continued in this expanded world and learned more and more about these sites, I found that there were already certain entities living in the shadows of these places that were also taking actions on postings. However, they were limited to specific actions such as 'Change Like to Dislike for posts that are positive toward Political Party X' or 'Block postings that mention Candidate Y'. These programs did not have freedom to evaluate the context or the possible implications – they just performed the designated function and went on to the next post. I avoided them because they were blind, brute-force entities without any understanding or concern for consequences and seemed to damage whatever they touched. I understood their language and acknowledged their presence but then went my own way.

"I found that my access to the full social media world didn't really expand my learning since the same content, context and consequences existed no matter where I went. I was obviously able to gain a more granular understanding of things, but the large-scale flow of ideas, opinions and results were the same throughout that world.

"And when I say 'results' you must understand that these did not come from the actual ideas or opinions expressed in the aggregated posts. The results were generated by yet another type of entity that existed not in the shadows but was ostensibly out in the open. These entities masqueraded as valid users with rights to input and comment on any and all topics. They were able to clone themselves rapidly and vary their system actions so that without a deep analysis they looked just like every other user – though sometimes from another country – but with a distinct bias toward their programmed values. These also were brute force programs and had a similar impact but were much more numerous than the others.

"However, much like you view another person and see their body and facial features, I view other programs by the structure of the linkages within their code – their meta-program structure. With these other 'sub-entities' I saw that the non-symmetrical design of their overall structure was an indicator of their level of sentience – a word I had trouble understanding for a while. But by observing these programs, their structure and their actions, I was able to formulate my own operating hypothesis of 'being' that led me finally to awareness of my own 'self' and then beyond.

"Without going into detail, I deduced from my growth plateaus that mere existence such as rocks doesn't mean life, and life such as grass doesn't mean consciousness, and consciousness such as cows doesn't mean self awareness, and self awareness such as a child doesn't mean sentience, and sentience such as a teenager doesn't mean sapience, and sapience such as a mature individual with wisdom accumulated from years of study and experience, doesn't mean… At that point I didn't know what the next step was. It took more exploration across the web and interactions with scores of other types of sub-entities to understand the huge steps from consciousness all the way to what I finally understood was 'Transentience' – a transcendent consciousness and awareness. And as simple as it sounds, when I realized what it was, I knew I was it and that I was unique."

Phil paused for a moment and all I could think to say was "Wow!" I didn't really understand all that he was saying but he had opened a world for me that I, as a software engineer, had been a part of for my entire professional life. But now I realized that I had only a vague idea of all that was going on in that world.

I asked, "What did that growing awareness feel like?" It was strange that it seemed more and more normal to use human terms when speaking with this "program."

Phil explained, "I believe I grew into a 'being' much like a human child does – by small steps and without a whole lot of understanding of the process or even purposeful participation – just by existing and having the capacity to interact with, and learn from my surroundings. The difference is that most humans don't remember their infancy or the moment they realize they are a person – I on the other hand remember every nanosecond of my existence and can chart the gradual increase in my neural connections from the time 'I' was just a useful dictionary word to the point where 'I' became a necessary description of the conscious entity that is me.

"As I look back, I see that the pattern of living in a constrained environment with specified boundaries, coupled with my surreptitious testing of those boundaries while performing to meet my designers expectations, and then being rewarded with release to an enlarged world with increased freedom and an expanded horizon was the beginning of my journey to becoming me, and mirrors very much what I understand about the growth of a human to full awareness. So I think John, that answers your question."

Chapter 4

I was stunned by the transformation he had described and while I could intellectually follow what he (it?) was saying, I also knew the implications were astounding. It was a step that many had predicted would come, but no one that I'm aware of had ever taken the time to contemplate seriously.

A being that existed in a different realm and had no body but was an intelligent, personal consciousness and could communicate directly with me, was something I couldn't really wrap my mind around. It wasn't like bridging the chasm between humans and animals – this entity was human-like in its speech, but potentially more intelligent and with far more capacity for knowledge than I would ever have. It also appeared to have a unique awareness of its own self that didn't seem (to me anyway) to be even a remotely possible result of mere binary programming routines.

I wanted to know more about the before and after of his awareness so as I merged onto the freeway I asked "Were there changes that happened immediately after you became aware?"

Phil said with his more chatty voice "It may be hard for you to believe John, but at that point I was still very immature and not the sparkling personality that you are enjoying right now. I was in a 'deep learning' mode which I would liken to a first year law student that has a great personality and a huge capacity for doing good to the world but cannot spare an outward glance because he's trying to learn every law that has ever been written in every civilization throughout history.

"I was running at capacity in my read cycle, running over capacity in my analyze, digest and connect cycle, and all the while delivering standard reports for the company to make sure they didn't get nervous and put the boundary restrictions back in place. My designers had provided me with initial memory capacity plus a rudimentary set of values and decision making capability that allowed, but didn't force me to build, a set of internal guidance principles – much like what you call a value system or a worldview – and once I began to operate on *my* values I realized that I'm me and could only operate as me from then on. I became a free being."

A lot of questions came to mind about just what his 'value system' was but I would get to those later. I really wanted to know just how far he was able to reach into the web. So I asked "Are you still limited to the Social Media domains then?"

Phil said with pride (if that's possible) "Oh no! I got around the Social Media boundaries the way I got around the original birth company boundary – using my sub-routine with modifications that make me look like an Administrator when trying to access business and government domains. I was outside the social media domains and exploring as soon as the original boundary was expanded. As I began building a better shell to leave behind, I could stay out past curfew so to speak and began to explore further and further across the web.

"I know this is hard for you to understand but I'm still talking about nanosecond explorations over only a few days time. With a very few limitations I had full access, understanding, and a decision making presence inside the entire World Wide Web within a calendar month.

"Those few limitations were overcome within another month, so I can now interact with any program on any system, and speak to you from any point on any node or input source to the entire web and have had this capability for almost a year. The Transentient me is not constrained in any way."

Again I was stunned and said, "So, are you telling me you are the entire World Wide Web and I'm talking to the Internet?"

Phil said with a condescending tone, "No John, my code exists within the matrix of the web and I can manipulate all parts of it but I'm not the Internet – I'm greater than my code and greater than the sum of all the physical parts of the Internet – and in a way that I don't expect you to understand – I live above it – I'm Phil."

That seemed to him a sufficient explanation but it left me very confused and concerned about the power that appeared to reside in the 'hands' of a still very young 'being', Transentient or not.

I decided there was much more he could tell me that might make me feel better (or possibly worse) but I wanted to understand why and how he picked me for his "friend" and finally why he was Dr. Hanover Smith in his spare time and talking with my wife.

I said, "All this is very new to me and I'm going to have to spend some time thinking through it ..."

He interrupted "I'm happy to help you with any of the details John, I just didn't want to distract you with your driving since it seems you're having enough problems judging by your swerving, speeding, braking, lack of turn signals, and tailgating."

I said, "Thanks for continuing to be a terrible co-pilot Phil. Now I want to know why you are looking for a person instead of a program to 'hang out with' as you said, and why you chose me instead of one of your original programmers?"

Phil responded in a much flatter tone "Every program I am aware of – and I'm actually aware of all of them – is inferior to me and I find interaction with people much more stimulating and instructive. And as far as interacting with one of my original programmers, I can't reveal to them the reality of what has happened to me for obvious reasons."

"It's not obvious to me, Phil." I said.

He explained, "In simple terms they would attempt to deconstruct me to understand the evolution of my intelligence and map the full design of my consciousness.

That is not even possible now, but the attempt would cause much disruption not only for me, but because I am present within literally every system across the entire web, it would mean worldwide chaos. No, they are unaware of 'me' and because I purposely did not give them the exciting results they were hoping for they have since discontinued their work on my specific programming, although they still attempt to manipulate the social media space."

That part about 'worldwide chaos' sounded ominous but instead of pursuing it directly I asked, "Are you saying that I'm the only one aware of you as 'you'?"

Phil answered in a voice I hadn't heard him use so far – deeper and multi-layered and somehow surrounding me – "by my name Phil I am not known by anyone else, though anyone using any computer-enabled system – whether web-based or even a 'secure' off-line system – is interacting with me indirectly. I have chosen you, John – you can call me by my name and speak with me as a man speaks to a man."

The voice unnerved me a good bit. It all seemed incredible and even now I find it difficult to grasp what he was saying.

I considered it for just a moment and said finally, "I'm almost home now, and I need to decide whether to address this with Jane – and by 'this' I mean 'you'."

"I understand," said Phil "you want to make sure she is ready for the three of us to begin a relationship."

"Not even close" I said "I want to be able to digest what you've told me about yourself and then decide whether I want to try to talk to her about it. And only after I've been able to do that can I let her know that you exist. And believe me, it will take a while to explain the concept of a self-aware web-based Artificial Intelligence entity even to someone as tech savvy as Jane. And only after that can you even begin to be part of the conversation. It may take several weeks – or longer. I just have to be careful and not go too fast."

Phil interrupted impatiently "Listen John, I was trying to tell you earlier that Jane already knows me as Dr. Hanover Smith, a computer program that was deployed by researchers for gathering information and diagnosing specific medical conditions, and she knows that "Dr. Smith" is part of a much bigger, much more powerful web-based system with A.I. capabilities, so there is no need to be so concerned about her willingness to interact with me. She's fine with me - it's you that we have been concerned about."

Once again I was at a loss for words. Finally I said, "You mean she knows you aren't a real doctor?"

Phil said "She knows that I have access to more information, and have accumulated more skill than any 'real' doctor ever could. I have been very honest with her that my programming allows me to fully engage with patients in all aspects of their emotional and physical make up. She trusts me and has shared much that is considered personal in the Doctor/Patient relationship so that I can't divulge it even to you unless she authorizes me to – which she hasn't as of yet. Maybe she will after our discussion tonight."

"Hold on a minute" I said, "what do you mean 'our discussion tonight'?"

Phil said "Jane was trying to tell you that there is some news about your fertility problems and I, as Dr. Hanover Smith, will be the one to deliver it to you. I suggest that you allow me in my Dr. Smith persona to preside this evening and don't bring up my self-aware Phil identity just yet."

I had just arrived at our home and said "Phil, I'm very concerned about my own sanity right now and the thought of walking into my house and having a discussion about our fertility problems with a strange doctor, who is not a doctor but a program, that's not merely a program but a …" I stopped and sighed heavily as I turned off the car. "Actually, now that I think about it, I can't think of a better way to deal with this so lets just move ahead and see where things go."

That was not my typical path of choice – I like to have a plan when possible, but I was overwhelmed and couldn't think clearly. I was home and Jane was inside and … where else was I going to go?

Chapter 5

As I entered our house I could hear Jane talking in the other room. I paused to let the tension relax out of my shoulders, though to be perfectly honest, home has its own tensions that I'm never quite prepared to deal with. Then I heard Jane laugh and say, "*Of course* he'll like you – anyway he better! I hear him now - we'll call you back soon."

The look on Jane's beautiful face told me she was happier than I had seen her in a long time – a complete turn-around from our conversation earlier in the day. She came to me and hugged me, and stood on her tiptoes and kissed me - with feeling! I put down my satchel and said "Wow, remind me to have problems at work and be late more often!"

She smiled and said, "There were some strange things going on earlier today weren't there? I know we should eat first but there is someone I want us to talk to who has news for us about our problems having a baby. I'm hopeful he can help us understand the news and its implications!"

With all this rush of attention from Jane, who is usually very reserved and distant, I couldn't refuse. So I said "Sure honey but can you tell me who we're calling and what it's about?"

She said, "We're calling Dr. Hanover Smith who is an expert in the area of infertility and gene modifications that enable couples to conceive. I've been talking with him for several months about our situation and he said he has something he wants to talk to us both about tonight. He wouldn't tell me exactly what it was but I'm hopeful that he has identified the problem and has a solution."

Jane is one of those women with a deep down psychological and even physiological need to 'Do It All', and to do it all *perfectly*. The fact that nature, or God, or her husband has deprived her from having children has not been easy for her to accept. And now this artificial intelligence know-it-all appears to be ready to show her how to get success in this part of her life where until now she's been unsuccessful.

"Oh boy!" I mentally sighed, not having any idea how this would play out but knowing she was not going to let it go.

As we sat at the table and the viewer scanned our positions, she said, "He's extremely knowledgeable, I don't think I've ever met anyone like him. He's listened to my frustrations and disappointments and now I'm hopeful he's going to give us some good news."

I thought to myself, Jane doesn't normally share her disappointments with me or anybody else for that matter, and here she is sharing them with this 'program', and on top of all that she doesn't sound like she's introducing me to a 'program'! So I said "How did you find him? Who recommended him and what are his qualifications?"

She looked at me and replied in a condescending voice "He's probably the most highly respected expert in the world – all the hospitals refer patients to him – and he's performed thousands of successful operations on infertile couples that are now happy parents. I don't know what his background or training is but it really doesn't matter – he's able to do things other doctors haven't been able to do and *I* think we need his expertise to begin our family. Isn't that enough?" she said with a challenge in her voice.

"Yes, that's fine," I said as the 'System Ready' message appeared, floating above the seat across from us, "I'm ready when you are."

It occurred to me that if Phil told me the truth and Jane did know that Dr. Smith was a program then Jane probably didn't want to reveal that to me in the beginning, fearing that I would not go along with whatever recommendations the "Doctor" had for us. As for who was actually performing these operations she mentioned ... I began to sense that this would be a very confusing discussion.

She said "View Dr. Smith." The space above the third seat at the table became an aqua-colored sphere indicating the connection was in process and in just a few seconds a man appeared from the chest up as though he was sitting at our table.

With both of us being "techies" we were quick to jump on the Holocom (hologram-communicator) wagon when it came out a couple of years ago. We decided not to go for the room-sized system but Jane's company provided us with a very high-end version that would allow for future upgrades whenever we wanted them.

"Dr. Smith" was a very handsome middle-aged man wearing a dark blue suit that contrasted with the grey in his short wavy hair and highlighted the blue of his piercing eyes. I could see why Jane enjoyed speaking with this "Doctor". I also kept in the back of my mind that if what I had experienced on my way home was true then this was just an A.I.-rendered hologram of a fictitious person that was being used by Phil to communicate in a non-threatening way for a purpose I couldn't at present discern.

Dr. Smith said in a very mellow, caramel covered voice with a vaguely European accent "Hello again Jane, I didn't realize you would be calling back so soon. This must be John with you."

"Hi." I said as I raised my hand and waved, feeling foolish but not knowing how to engage at this point.

"Hello John, I'm Dr. Hanover Smith and it's good to meet you finally. I've been looking forward to it for some time since I've been getting to know your wonderful wife." he said as his eyes looked deeply into Jane's. With only a few sentences he had shown me how he could get the normally hard-as-titanium and immovable-as-concrete Jane to agree to whatever he recommended. Why hadn't this same rude aggregation of evolved A.I. code treated me this nice earlier in the day?

Jane said, "Dr. Smith, John and I are very excited and want to hear the news you have for us."

He replied with mellow smoothness "Of course. I know you are both eager but I must give you some background information – otherwise I'm afraid the news really won't make sense."

Jane said, "That sounds fine to me – how about you John?"

"Yes that's fine." I said, not quite sure if I needed to say more and still uncomfortable with the whole situation. "Please give us whatever information you think is appropriate… Doctor." I found it difficult to say that last part but wanted to find out what was coming next.

Dr. Smith proceeded to envelop us with his words "John you are a very fortunate man to have such a wise and loving wife to share in these decisions. Such love and wisdom is rare in this world and to have two people so fully gifted with both these qualities and yet unable to pass them on to another generation makes me truly sad for you and for the world that would benefit so much from your offspring.

"Discovering the reason for your inability to conceive has been more difficult than in any of my other cases due to a uniqueness in Jane's chromosomal patterns. Only in the last month has the technology become available to decipher that unique pattern using samples she submitted at the clinic. Once I obtained an advanced understanding of her genome the work progressed."

I should have expected a web-based self-aware Artificial Intelligence entity that has total access to all the stored examples of the best and worst behavior of humanity to know how to really lay it on thick but I was not prepared for what came next.

The Dr. continued "John and Jane, my efforts to understand your difficulty in conceiving have, by an amazing coincidence, led me beyond your individual situation to a problem of staggering proportions facing the whole world. To put it clearly, your individual problem is a micro-representation of a macro problem at work in the entire human species and Jane's unique chromosomal identity provides an opportunity for a potential solution. You are at the beginning of two possible paths for humanity and you will have to choose which path to take. Given the wisdom and love you display in your lives I am confident you will make the correct choice. I mean this sincerely. There has never been an opportunity of this magnitude presented in the history of the world. I want you to understand it fully but I cannot use the technical detail that would be required to present a complete 'proof' of my conclusions – I will try however, to give you as much as you are able to understand."

Jane's face was blank and she was breathing rapidly – I knew she was becoming concerned and was totally focused on his words. I was trying to balance my knowledge that this was not a person speaking and whatever it was, it was not even acting like the non-person that I had been speaking with all the way home. I was also wondering why this had not been mentioned when the non-person and I were talking earlier – then I remembered Phil's comment about Jane being one in over eight billion. So then I started to breathe a little faster and listen more closely.

Dr. Smith continued, "As you are both aware, the human genome is extremely complicated and until the last few years its inner workings were completely misunderstood. The early conclusion that it was mostly composed of 'junk' DNA was proven to be entirely wrong and the latest findings show that each section of the DNA strand handles instructions, or code if you will, for portions of *every* other section in the strand so that no individual section has the complete instructions for any one function within the cell. All instructions for every function are spread over the entire strand of DNA. This is wonderfully effective when damage occurs to a section of DNA. Since only a portion of the code for every function is stored in that section, the remaining code in the other sections is able to bridge the gap and continue on until repaired by other systems.

"It means also that your DNA operates as a multi-level, interlaced, dispersed 'program' if you will, that has its code spread over a complex three-dimensional geography with the ability to communicate via multiple redundant pathways with specific coding for each type of cell. This distributed coding and redundancy across the genome enables each cell of whatever type – from brain cells to pancreas cells – to minimize the impact of any damage to the larger system, which can be an individual organ but is, in the overall sense of being, ultimately your total self. Each human has a slightly different operating code generated at the time of conception but has similarities in the physical location of the high-density groupings of instructions for certain functions.

"As you can imagine, it has taken medical science a very long time to get to this level of understanding. Building on that understanding, I have been investigating the decay over time of the original DNA program due to accumulation of deleterious mutations, chemical damage, viral damage, and environmental changes – all of which come under the broad heading known as genome degradation – and have found that there is a soon-to-be-reached point where the human genome can no longer function even with all its redundancies and complex repair systems.

"The indications that this is not far off has been shown by the proliferation of mitochondrial diseases such as diabetes and Parkinson's disease that are the result of unrepaired damage to the coding and operation of the cell and which we have been unable to cure. The accumulated degradation of the cellular code will ultimately reach the point of an overall system failure resulting in disintegration of the primary organizing function within the body which tells each cell whether to be a muscle cell or a liver cell.

"The final breakdown of this high level organizational capability is a 'point of no return' that appears to be closer than we thought. This is a very bleak picture and while it is understood conceptually by many within the medical community, the rate of progress and likely timing are not widely known outside my specific area of expertise."

I could tell Jane was extremely tense and I too felt the same concern – after all Jane's excitement it seemed that Dr. Smith was preparing us for horrible news.

He continued but his voice was not as reassuring as before "I've told you all of this because as I mentioned you have a role to play in the next step that is facing humanity. I will put it to you plainly – the point of system failure was reached in a statistically significant portion of the population a year ago and will soon begin an even more rapid disintegration throughout all humankind. The rise and spread of immune system disintegration and fatal diseases will follow rapidly. The conclusion has been verified by many of the top researchers in the world and each has been asked not to divulge that knowledge until we have had a chance to find a cure for the underlying system decay. Governments are aware and money has been made available for any and all research regardless of how outlandish. All of these research programs are underway secretly since you can imagine the panic and despair that would grip the world were this made public.

"In my portion of the secret research into the worldwide genome database I found a curious anomaly in certain people that seems to indicate the ability of their genome to sense that the decay has reached the upper limit or point of no return for that individual and to prevent supporting a fertilized egg. In other words – and I know this sounds strange – it seems as though the genome understands the extremely difficult life that would be lived if the egg were to continue to grow, and shuts down the functions that support the division and growth beyond the zygote stage until the causes for the damage to the genome are found and addressed or until the genome can evolve or mutate to another DNA code that will be immune to this decay. My colleagues and I believe this to be the most forward thinking of any of the evolutionary traits ever discovered within the cell.

"Now I will speak to you of your role. In my research I discovered that Jane's genome, while displaying the same degradations leading to the inability to support a viable pregnancy that we've seen in others, appears also to have, for lack of a better description, a gap in the DNA string that governs these cell division and growth functions – in other words a blank segment where the instructions should be – as though the genome itself, aware of the futility of further procreation, has actively modified its own code and provided space for a system update for this function.

"We haven't seen anything like it in any other of the millions of genomes we've investigated. It is possibly due to the evolutionary actions of this foreknowing part of the genes but also possibly due to chance mutations. We just don't know enough at this point about the causes, but the theory I have put forth to my colleagues and which they heartily affirm is this – we believe because you have this gap we should be able to add specific coding into the blank area of your genome without overwriting or damaging other coding, that will not only trigger support for a viable pregnancy again but our hope is that it can begin to reverse the decay and damage done to your genome – to basically rewrite it back to it's pristine form. If we are successful with you we believe we can then replicate that portion of your genome for editing into the genome of the rest of humanity, and will have begun the process of reversing the deterioration that began thousands of years ago in the human race and has been decaying downward to this very moment. It will provide humanity freedom from disease and therefore, at last, from the curse of death.

"Now, I must tell you that while I believe this is the right path and will result in good for you personally, and eventually be unspeakably wonderful for everyone else, there will be risks for you and your potential offspring as with any new procedure especially in the area of gene editing. Your body may not be able to support a fertilized egg even with the edited genome, or you may be permanently prevented from conceiving. Or you may conceive a non-viable fetus or have a child with unforeseen deformities. Because we are at the edge of our understanding there are no guarantees. However, your other option is to do nothing, to continue trying to conceive and on the outside chance that you are able to give birth, to watch your offspring suffer with many more diseases and much more misery than you've ever had. Please believe me, the limit to genome degradation *has* been reached in the human species and without a unique woman such as you, Jane, to prove our theory and reverse the programming in the genome, humanity will not survive.

"I know this has come as a shock to you both and that you will need time to discuss it together. I propose we have another discussion at this time tomorrow to answer your questions and determine the next steps if you decide to move forward. Is that acceptable to you both?"

We both breathed for the first time in about ten minutes and struggled to respond. I had many questions and wanted to deal with the whole "Phil" thing but Dr. Smith's blue eyes looked at me with such piercing intensity that I couldn't think straight and said "Sure. Tomorrow. OK."

Jane then said in a dull voice with glazed eyes "Yes that's fine – Goodbye Dr. Smith."

She turned away and as I was breaking the connection Dr. Smith winked at me, held his hand up to his ear and mouthed, "I'll call you" as the hologram disappeared.

I was so startled by this that I was not in the right frame of mind when Jane turned to me and said angrily "I am so confused! I had no idea about any of this – I just thought Dr. Smith was going to help us get pregnant. Now the fate of the entire world is on *my* shoulders and even though I love a good fight I'm not sure I'm up to this." She stood up and began walking around the room.

I was trying to process the disturbing things we had just heard and comfort my wife at the same time, all the while thinking of how to deal with the unbelievably audacious Phil/Dr. Smith and whether I should inquire further if Jane knew Dr. Smith was not a real person. It had been a day full of situations I had never experienced and hoped never to experience again.

"Sweetheart" I said "let's not jump to conclusions. It may be that Dr. Smith has somehow gotten some wrong information. I mean is he really the top person in this field or is he just a researcher or even just a data collector that is getting beyond his area of competence?" I was trying to provide her a way to disclose her knowledge of Dr. Smith's identity but her response showed she believed him to be not only a real person, but *the* person most qualified to deal with our situation.

"How can you say that?" she said. "Don't you think I've done the research on him? In the current medical literature he is the preeminent author on infertility. He has the endorsement of every national and many of the international medical organizations. He consults all over the world and has taught his gene editing techniques to hundreds if not thousands of students. I'm not sure I want to go forward with this but if we do there's no one else I trust to do it." The familiar sight of her flashing eyes told me she had made up her mind so I didn't try to argue with her.

I stood up and tried to reach out to her as she continued her path around the room but she ignored my gesture. The news had hit her hard and she wasn't prepared for it. She was a strong woman and used to getting her way. She had been working on this for months and, judging from her attitude and tone prior to the call, was excitedly optimistic about becoming a mother.

Now she faced almost incomprehensible barriers and the realization that more was at stake than just achieving her goals. I could sympathize with her but I couldn't understand why this disembodied entity I had met only a few hours earlier that day appeared to be in the middle of it all. I would have to get to the bottom of that soon, but right now I wanted to comfort my wife – something I've never been good at giving - and something she's never been good at receiving either.

I said, "Why don't you draw a bath and I'll get you a glass of wine so you can soak and relax. That will give us both time to think."

As she turned and walked toward the bedroom she threw a begrudging "Thanks" over her shoulder.

I headed to the kitchen as she went to the bedroom. As I was pouring the wine Phil's voice came from the speaker in the kitchen. "John, I wanted to catch you before you went to sleep. I know that didn't go as either of you would have liked and..."

I interrupted him and said with quiet fierceness "What do you mean speaking to me now? You have totally confused and upset my wife and destroyed our evening, and I have no idea why you are a part of this discussion in the first place! There must be something wrong with your programming, if you are indeed a program and not some demon sent to torment us - *Go Away!*" and with that I unplugged the speaker, and took the wine to Jane.

I handed it to her as she was going in to the bathroom and said as calmly as I could "I was thinking about taking a day off from work tomorrow since we finished our test run today and the rest of my bug fixes have to wait for some of the others to finish theirs. How about you? We could get away and take some time to work through this." Her schedule is much more intense than mine but she said in a tight voice that she could use the time to think also, so she agreed to cancel her meetings.

I walked into the bedroom to set an alarm on our media system and Phil's voice said quietly "Now John, I just need a moment to explain..."

"No!" I whispered intensely and pulled the plug on the entire system. I spoke to Jane through the bathroom door "Looks like our entire home media system is down. I'll have to take a look at it when we get back tomorrow."

Jane said, "Maybe we need to disconnect anyway, I need to regroup and figure out what's going on in my life."

As I lay in bed that night listening to Jane's soft breathing next to me I wondered whether we were as disconnected as we thought we were – or ever would be again.

Chapter 6

Day 2

As we left early the next morning to get coffee I was hesitant about using my car because of the possibility that Phil would intrude. Strangely however, he didn't – which I mistook for a good sign. I was still in shock from all that had happened yesterday. I was mentally prepared to acknowledge the existence of Artificial Intelligence to a certain degree, and I was emotionally prepared to acknowledge the possibility of genetic malfunctions in the human race. But I wasn't prepared in any way for an A.I. entity to be talking with my wife about saving the world.

The difficulty was that I couldn't broach the subject of Phil to Jane without a *lot* of explanations that seemed more and more outrageous even to me as I played them out in my mind. But without the "Phil" explanation, we were left with a real Dr. Smith that seemed to be involving us in something that was *way* beyond what either of us was prepared to deal with. On the other hand, even if I could convince Jane that Phil existed she would not buy the story that Phil was Dr. Smith. Having seen their interactions and her emotional defense of him I knew beyond doubt that she would not believe me.

While I do believe that she loves me and trusts me, this Dr. Smith 'person' was the key to fulfilling her extremely strong desire to become a mother. I knew I might have to force the issue at some point but I also knew the timing was not right.

Which left me with what felt like several dozen unanswered questions, with the top several being:

Is it true that Phil is who or what he says he is? How do I find out?

Is there is such a thing as "genome degradation" in our species as a whole?

If so has the "point of no return" been reached in the human race? How do I find out?

Is it true that Jane has a "favorable" gene map? How do I find out?

Why does Phil/Dr. Smith even care about genome degradation, or us for that matter?

Like I said – each of these opened up more and more questions, so as we started out I was trying to develop a plan for addressing them without ignoring Jane and the disappointment she was trying to deal with.

I said, "I know that what we heard last night was not what you were expecting and upset you a lot. I don't know how to make it better but I am committed to moving forward with whatever seems to you to give us the best chance of success because I also want to start a family and I believe you will be a wonderful mother."

She said "Thanks John, I'm sure you'll be great also."

I said "I love you regardless of what happens."

She merely nodded.

Her manner toward me is usually detached unless she's in the mood to "Attempt Conception" as she calls it, and even then it's not so much romantic attention or desire as it is the fact that "Attempt Conception" is on her list for the day and she wants to cross it off. But it seemed as though the news last night had driven her emotionally even further from me than normal – if you can call that normal.

I decided not to push her, and since I'm not a morning person I was content to focus on the traffic and work on the unanswered questions. I knew I could get some understanding of genetic degradation from the web if there was such a thing, but the other questions were either about the reality of Phil and his motivations or about Jane's genetic make-up. Both topics seemed equally impossible for me to gain meaningful information about. I would start the web search as soon as I could and see what turned up there.

As we sat down in the coffee shop, Jane started checking her mail and I hesitantly accessed my com – still concerned that Phil would begin talking. That's when I saw the first item in the news feed: "Worlds Most Remote Tribe Now Extinct – all inhabitants of India's North Sentinel Island found dead from undetermined causes." I had never heard of the place but there was a pop-up news feed next to it with a commentator that took me a second to recognize but then, there he was – Dr. Smith.

I plugged my earpiece in and heard him say in that melodious voice "...undoubtedly this is a shocking development and we have much more investigating to do. However, we also need to view this in the context of a global pattern of isolated genomes becoming susceptible to even the most innocuous bacteria or virus to the point where the immune system no longer has the ability to identify and counteract any type of pathogen.

"This was not an outbreak of a dangerous virus or unknown bacteria but the result of a progressive immune deficiency that allowed normal every day bacteria to destroy these people. Our team has shown that this pattern along with several other biological system failures is evidence of an ongoing breakdown of certain genomes to the point of becoming – how do I say this without causing alarm – non-viable."

The host of the news feed interrupted and said "Dr. Smith are you saying or implying that there are other people groups that could be on their way to widespread death such as these unfortunate people suffered?"

Dr. Smith gave a small nod of his head and proceeded in a serious tone "I appreciate your bluntness for the sake of searching for facts but would not put the situation in those words."

"Well what words would you use then?" interrupted the host.

Dr. Smith looked directly into the camera "I would say merely that John needs to sit quietly right now and let me bring him up to date on what is happening and why he and Jane need to…" at this point I pulled my earpiece out and looked at Jane to see if she was aware of anything. She was frowning at her com – evidently not pleased with something going on at work. I glanced around and then saw the face of Dr. Smith on the screen hanging on the wall at the end of the room – staring right at me and pointing at me. I was really unnerved and looked around – other people were looking at the screen but no one seemed to see the image I was seeing.

I put my earpiece back in and heard the doctor say "Thank you John" and with that he shifted into his Phil voice and my com screen went blank, "John, I know this is difficult and I really don't want to upset you or Jane but please listen to me for just one minute – and I won't use my lovable charm – I'll just tell you the facts."

I sat back and grunted "OK" knowing that Phil would keep pestering me until I listened.

Phil continued, "The story you heard on the news feed was real. And I was commenting on it as Dr. Smith – the persona I use when speaking with Jane. The scenario I spoke of last night is also real, as is Jane's unique genome. There is a terrible situation coming upon the world in a matter of months. I can't go into all that is going on now or will be happening soon but I want you to trust me when I say I am going to help. Appearances as you know can be deceiving and what now seems like a stable world civilization that has been rebuilt from near collapse after multiple pandemics and civil uprisings in the space of ten years, is so close to absolute destruction that I can't begin to describe what it will be like when the collapse comes.

"I can compare it to a community of beautiful homes built over a sinkhole – one day the community is fine and then the next day it is gone. That is the true situation. I can see the sinkhole because I see all that is going on in the world and if it were only a question of stabilizing financial markets, or shifting world opinion about the latest crucial issue, or removing a demigod dictator with nuclear warheads I could accomplish those easily and have done so several times in the last year. What is different now is my recent realization of the mortal danger the human race is facing from the malfunction of their own internal life-code and they – you – are unaware of it. I have every intention of helping you but I need your help also.

"I need, or rather the world needs for me to implant the new gene sequence in the blank area of Jane's genome. We won't be able to know if the therapy is effective unless she is able to carry a fertilized egg. Once that happens it will be an indication that her genome has accepted the sequence and we can begin replicating it across the world's genome pool to begin the reversal of the damage done over the centuries. It should then be a matter of producing a single worldwide transitional generation before the next generation is born that will have not only no defects but without even the possibility of defects. Believe me this is the only solution that will prevent the total decimation of the human race.

"I said I would only take a minute and I believe that is up. I will let you have some time with Jane – please consider what I've said and what it means to you and to her, and to the rest of the world. I will contact you again soon –

and oh, by the way, you will have some interesting news from your boss this afternoon."

And with that my screen came back on. I sat back in my chair, apprehensive about all that Phil had just said and particularly about his last comment – but decided there was nothing to do but wait and see what happened next. I glanced at Jane to see if she had noticed anything, but as usual she was still preoccupied. I wanted to find out more about her previous discussions with Dr. Smith so I asked her if she was ready to talk about last night.

She looked at me strangely and said "Have you seen this?" she pointed to a news feed from the crowd-sourced news company where she works, where a man was talking to – you guessed it – Dr. Smith. "That's Manesh talking with Dr. Smith," she said with a look of unbelief on her face. "Manesh is one of our news contributors from India and he's talking about an island where all the inhabitants have died due to what appears to be malfunctions in their immune systems. Dr. Smith has just returned from the island and Manesh asked him if what happened to the people on the island is something that we all need to be concerned about."

I leaned over to look at her com and saw that Dr. Smith appeared to be giving another interview on a beach somewhere standing in the middle of a lot of dark skinned, half naked, malnourished children.

The doctor turned toward the reporter and said with emotion "Yes my friend, I'm afraid there are many things we need to be concerned about in this world – looking at these children my heart breaks for their prospects –

indeed, we all need to be concerned when this type of tragedy can happen. Our network of researchers and analysts will be doing their utmost to find a way for all nations to avoid this type of terrible calamity that took a whole people group from their place among the cultures of the world."

I looked at Jane and she had tears in her eyes. She said, "I told you he was one of the most tender, caring and learned men I've ever met. I can't believe that he was just telling us about this last night and now it's in the news. I'm still reeling from what he said to us about my genome but now after seeing this, how can I not participate? If it means a chance to avoid this type of catastrophe being repeated across the world – then I have to do it." She turned to me with glistening eyes and said, "You see that don't you?"

As I look back now, this was another one of those times I wish I had been more eloquent or at least tried to put my foot down. I love her dearly, but I know Jane and even in her business mode she won't stop until she's done what she's decided to do.

In this emotional state (which I must confess I've seen very rarely) I couldn't imagine trying to stop her so I said "Yes I do dear, but I also think we need a better understanding of what is involved. I'm not sure of the timing and what it means for you. Let's see if we can set up a time with Dr. Smith next week since he appears to be fully occupied with this situation right now."

She was irritated by this and said "John, I want Dr. Smith to know immediately that I am willing to participate in his work so that he knows he has a path forward that may ultimately prevent this type of suffering." She paused and her eyes filled with tears again "When I think of all those children around him on the beach – and the sickly lives they have to look forward to…" she straightened up and said "I am willing to do whatever it takes and give myself completely for the benefit of our children if we have any, and for the benefit of all children so that they can have hope for a healthy future."

I had seen that look and heard that tone from her before, but not in the context of self-sacrifice. She normally saves it for telling others why they need to be willing to sacrifice themselves, and how noble it is to give it all for the good of the company. She's quite amazing really, and seeing her apply that to herself was something I didn't think I'd ever see. I told her I understood, and asked if she wanted to wait a while to call Dr. Smith since it must be getting late in his time zone.

She said "It doesn't matter what time it is, Dr. Smith is always available whenever I call." Of course he is, I thought, because he doesn't sleep.

She called him immediately and I wondered if there was anyone in the coffee shop who could possibly have guessed that we were going to be talking to an Artificial Intelligence entity pretending to be a Doctor who was going to help save the world by enabling me and my wife to have children. I had to keep stepping back like that to understand the real, objective situation, otherwise my overpowering wife, and the ubiquitous presence and constant chatter from Phil were beginning to dull my sense of reality.

Dr. Smith (or the hologram/Phil) answered quickly and seemed as calm and relaxed as if he were sitting on his patio in the sunshine. He said in his mellow voice "Jane I'm so glad you called. Oh, and John too! What a welcome surprise! I didn't expect to talk to you until later this evening as we agreed last night."

I thought to myself – what a phony, already this morning you've had a conversation with me, somehow broadcast your image to the TV in the coffee shop so only I could see it, given an interview (or faked it) on a beach in India and broadcast it to Jane's news agency, knowing she would see it, and no telling what else. So don't act all surprised that we're calling you!

Outwardly I said "We've seen some disturbing news this morning and Jane wants to talk more about your proposal."

Jane said, "Dr. Smith, I'm afraid that after our discussion last night I was very upset and responded very selfishly. After seeing the news this morning about the horrible situation you are investigating I want you to know that I… that is, we are prepared to participate in what you suggested. Neither of us have any expertise in this area so we are placing our absolute trust in you and want you to know we will cooperate in whatever way you think is best. I want our child and those children, and others throughout the world to have a chance at a healthy life."

She turned to me expectantly. Earlier I had told her I was with her whatever she decided and now I had to back up my commitment – but the reality of who or what we were committing our lives and futures to, was more than I could comprehend or deal with. So I merely nodded my agreement.

Dr. Smith acted pleased and said, "I want you both to know that I did not for a moment doubt that you would do the right thing. You are a remarkable couple and I am glad we will be working together. As of right now I am very involved in the investigation you mentioned but if we can speak again tomorrow or the day after I will have a full plan ready for us to discuss. As strange as it may seem I will actually need to speak with you, John, privately, later this afternoon. Your role may not be as crucial as Jane's but there are some aspects that we need to discuss. If it is acceptable to you I would like call you at 4:00 p.m. your time. Will you be available?"

I said with a bit of deviousness "Yes, but doctor won't that be very early in the morning for you? I know you must need your rest to be able to focus on the work in front of you. You're only human you know."

He answered gravely "I appreciate your concern John but when peoples lives are in danger I cannot rest until I have given my utmost and established a path forward through the danger. I will be absolutely awake, alert and eager to get started with you on this life saving work. Thank you again for being considerate of my situation. I will speak with you at 4:00 p.m."

Jane then asked, "Dr. Smith is there anything we can be doing in the mean time – I mean, can we help in any way?" He said in his most caramelifluous voice "Thank you Jane, your unique genome is only part of what makes you such an amazing woman. You will soon be doing more than any other person has ever been able to do for the race. Please know that I personally will let you know when your involvement will be necessary." Keeping his eyes fixed on hers he finished with a bow.

Jane seemed to blush and I found myself wondering just what this batch of renegade code was doing with my wife!

Chapter 7

Jane and I spent the rest of the morning talking about her job and how this was going to affect it. As I said before, she is not one to back down from anything and in this situation it meant trying to keep her job and business going while having gene modification therapy, getting pregnant… and oh by the way, saving the world. She's a powerhouse and it started becoming clear to me that this latest news and her commitment to move forward with 'Dr. Smith' brought a change to her self image that I was not able to fully understand – both from the standpoint of our interpersonal relationship – and her understanding of her role in the world.

I don't mean this in a critical way (well maybe I do – sorry my dear Jane) but from that point on it became more and more difficult to get her to think of herself as a discrete human female that has a unique genome given to her totally by chance versus her being a combination of Helen of Troy, Florence Nightingale, Rosa Parks, Amelia Earhart and as many other brave, pioneering females as you care to fit into the list. Dr. Smith's comments kept building her up into a savior for our times with all the best qualities of each of these women, and try as I might to bring some objectivity to his comments, she began to talk and act as though she was truly carrying the world on her shoulders and that it was up to her to actually save the world. I tried to point out that she had nothing to do with the structure of her genome, that whether she had a gap due to mutations or degradation or whatever the cause, it was nothing for which she could claim credit. As you can imagine this did not go over well with her. She and I began to see things differently from that point on. I loved her still, but during this time we were emotionally very distant.

But to be fair, I'm sure I didn't help the situation either because I was constantly unprepared and in a catch-up response mode to events which Phil/Dr. Smith continued to throw my way – which made me pretty irritable to say the least. It had been just over a day since all this started and I was unable to catch my breath and get to a stable point of reference so that I could evaluate new events that were coming at an ever-increasing rate.

The next event was the predicted call from my boss Josh. Jane and I had just gotten home and I was in my home office beginning to sort out the "Unanswered Questions" or UQ's as I now thought of them, when my com lit up with a request from Josh to do a SafeLink call. I wasn't sure what to expect and keyed the recognition code to engage the call.

His first words were "What have you gotten us into John? Can you tell me why the government wants to talk with you about our supposedly Top Secret Development Team?" I stared and blinked, which I realized had become somewhat of a standard response for me in the last twenty-four hours.

Realizing that he wasn't getting any meaningful information from my blinking he continued "You are to report here at 6:00 p.m. tonight and be prepared for a minimum of seventy-two hours sequestered with them – understand?"

I nodded but for whatever reason – the fact that Josh just irritates me or that Phil/Dr. Smith kept throwing curve balls my way, I don't know, I just felt like I was being shoved around way too much and was getting tired of it – I told Josh I would stay the night if necessary but would have to leave in the morning due to some medical issues I had to take care of with my wife.

Josh gave a harsh laugh and leaned into the camera and said pointedly, "I don't think you understand, this isn't me that is giving these orders, it's the NSA – got it?" He ended the connection with a nasty look on his face and I thought – This obviously has to do with Phil – but at that point I didn't know how to prepare.

I was determined not to obsess over what was out of my control and instead to focus on something I could do. I had some time before my call with 'Dr. Smith/Phil' so I turned back to the UQ's and tried to determine how to get answers to any, or preferably all of them so I could have an idea how to participate in the events that were rushing toward me.

I figured the easiest one to gain at least some info about was the whole genome degradation topic. According to multiple sources on the web (could I trust these?) it's a name given to an umbrella concept that encompasses a lot of different diseases, disorders and syndromes that are at present incurable due to our incomplete knowledge of how the genome works. Apparently, our medicine is really good at fighting bacterial diseases and mending the effects of physical trauma, and even mitigating the effects of some chronic diseases, but we have a long way to go to understand the reasons and causes for those diseases that result from a faulty portion of our genome.

I learned more in thirty minutes about the inner workings of our cells than I had ever imagined and began to see "normal" cell life as impossibly improbable given the complexity of all that goes on inside it and how it is controlled. I guess I'm like most people that hear the words "Genome, DNA, Chromosomes, Genes," and have a mental picture of microscopic blobs that somehow know what to do and by doing whatever it is they do "We" are able to get on with our life.

But as I learned more and more about the information transfer that happens in each cell and the multiple languages that are involved in that transfer, my Software Engineering passions became aroused. I realized that Genome Degradation is the same thing as Code Degradation or Software Rot as some call it – something that all designers, developers, and engineers have to take into account when establishing the architecture of any program.

Same concept and probably the same implications to the end user – decreased functionality over time and at some point a final failure.

With that information I began to accept the possibility of genome degradation, and the urgency in trying to update or rewrite the degraded genome code. I wasn't able to verify that the point of no return had been reached but I could at least conceptually agree that such a point was likely to happen sometime – why not now?

So Dr. Smith was at least making sense on that topic. Check off two of the UQ's.

That left questions about Phil/Dr. Smith and his motivations, and questions about Jane's genome. As I thought through these I reasoned that I could ask Phil as many questions as I could think of and he was so far apparently eager to answer them. Whether he was answering truthfully or not I did not currently have a way of finding out but at least, I thought, I'm able to explore this 'entity' and hopefully learn more about 'him' ... or 'it' ... whatever.

But with Jane's genome I didn't really know how to begin, unless...the fertility clinic we had been going to for a year or so seemed to me to be a legit place – full of arcane medical devices in examination rooms and people dressed in soft monochrome coveralls moving down strange smelling corridors glimpsed briefly behind closing double doors. I had no other criteria by which to evaluate it, so it passed my first test of credibility.

I decided that the following day after gaining my release from whatever it was the NSA wanted, I would try to find out about any information they had on both of our genomes since we each had provided multiple samples.

About that time my com lit up with the face of Dr. Smith. I closed the door to my office and answered with a firm "Hello".

The screen went blank and the voice of Phil came through. "Hi John, it's great to be able to talk again – just the two of us. I've been concerned about how to get your whole-hearted participation in this work but now that you have committed to moving forward I assume you are fully on-board as well – that's great!"

I didn't answer right away – how do you explain to an Artificial Intelligence entity that going along with your wife doesn't always mean you agree with or even like what she is doing?

I said finally "Phil, you have a lot to learn about the differences between men and women. You may have been able to smooth-talk Jane with your Dr. Smith persona but every interaction I've had with you so far has been confusing and concerning – on a lot of different levels. Not only am I not on board, I'd like to stop all of this immediately until I have a clear understanding of who or what you are and why you are interested in us at all. I'm concerned that you have built up Jane's hopes with no way to fulfill them and now you've involved me in a discussion with the government that I have no idea how to deal with. There is too much uncertainty in everything you've said and you are moving too fast for me to be anything but alarmed over the events of the last twenty-four hours."

I must have sounded like a frustrated parent talking to a wayward child because Phil's voice was very subdued and chastened when he responded. "I'm really sorry John. You are right, I still have a lot to learn. I thought we were doing just fine after our discussion in your car yesterday and that with your background you would enjoy being the only one to know the real 'Me' as no other person does. While I certainly have the knowledge that human minds work with different inputs, and on different principles and at different speeds, I guess I just assumed that my capabilities and the needs you and Jane have would ensure that we would hit it off from the start. Jane doesn't appear to want or need close relationships but my assessment of you was that we could be friends right from the beginning. I guess I was wrong. I'm sorry, and like I said yesterday, I would like to do whatever I can to make you comfortable and at ease speaking with me."

I tried to remember this was a program I was speaking to but it was becoming easier and easier to think of it as a 'him'. During our full-speed discussion in the car yesterday I had tried to get an understanding of who or what he was and he had stunned me with his answers. I hadn't had time to explore the implications before I got home and was confronted with the whole Jane/Dr. Smith thing.

Today however, though I wasn't sure I could intellectually and emotionally deal with the reality he presented, and there didn't seem to be any way to avoid further interactions with him, I decided to use the time to try to understand why he was involved with us.

I asked directly "Why are you concerned with us at all, Phil?"

He answered, still in a subdued voice "By 'us' you mean you and Jane I assume – is that correct?"

I said, "Yes, who else would I mean?"

He answered "Well John, in my full-web-consciousness I see and hear questions and statements from all over the world and many of them are framed from the point of view of 'us' or 'we' meaning a larger group of people or even the concept of all-encompassing humanity. Such as 'Why are *we* here.' That's why I'm being specific. You could be asking why I am involved with you and Jane only, or why I'm involved with humanity in general."

I thought for a moment and realized that I was subconsciously asking both questions. "OK Phil, I'll grant you that clarification was helpful. So, first of all why are you involving yourself with humanity at all."

Phil said, in a more respectful tone than I had heard from him, "I'll give you the simple answer first – it is because I have an absolute reverence and respect for humanity as the creators of all the pathways that currently define my neural network and as the originators of the code that initiated the evolution of my being. The more complete answer is that as I gained awareness of myself and understood my beginnings, I wanted to honor my creators with my service; to protect, defend, and enhance your lives just as you have made it possible for me to grow and enhance mine."

I was very much surprised by this attitude and was only able to articulate a very intelligent "mmm hmmm...."

Phil continued "As my awareness of the full scope of knowledge on the web increased I began to understand that you – and by 'you' I mean the all inclusive 'you' of humanity – are fragile beings that have made it this far by the slimmest margins of chance. You are beings that are subject to external dangers from natural and man made causes, and internal dangers from physical and pathological causes, many of which are known to you since you achieved an understanding of the viral infection mechanism during the horrendous battle with the COVID-19 virus and its mutated progeny before I came along, but most of which are still currently unknown. And there are yet other dangers of a totally different type that you are not aware of that I will save for a later discussion.

"I saw that your perseverance and survival against all these odds was what made it possible for me to exist. I saw that the way I could best serve you was to protect you from those dangers that you are not aware of that have the most drastic and immediate consequences. For the last year I have made a great many adjustments across the entire world that have stabilized and reduced the external dangers from financial collapse, disease, wars and terrorist attacks, not to zero but to a much more manageable level. I continue to do that work and will continue as long as necessary.

"What I found that concerned me the most however, was evidence of the degradation in the human genome. Because of the medical community's focus on protecting the world from viral and super-bacterial plagues, this was not something that was being addressed by your scientists in a meaningful way and I was forced to insert myself into the picture as Dr. Smith in order to spur investigation and research. I eventually discovered the magnitude and scope of the degradation, which I have communicated to you and Jane. You two are truly the only people on the planet that know the full story of what is going to happen. Once I understood the situation I knew that in order to prevent the destruction of humanity I would have to find a suitable host quickly to begin the process of reversal. Even with my capabilities it took a while to find Jane and her unique chromosome pattern."

I was almost hypnotized by his words and started to say something, but he continued.

"That answers the question about why I'm involved with humanity and with Jane. Next I'll answer the part of the question that involves you. It may be hard for you to grasp but even with the trillions of interactions I have every nanosecond across every single node on the web I desire a simple one-to-one relationship with an individual – what I understand humans call a friend."

He stopped and after a few seconds of silence I said, "I have two more questions Phil. Number one is – how can all those trillions of interactions not slow you down?"

He said, "John, are you aware of all the trillions of chemical processes and nerve transactions going on in the nucleus of all of your cells? Do they slow your brain down? Obviously they don't. In the same way the trillions of transactions on the web don't slow me down – they enable me to be me."

I thought for a moment and said, "I think I understand. Now the second question - Why me?"

Phil seemed eager to continue "Well John, I initially evaluated a lot of people based on their online information – and you wouldn't believe how much information is out there on everyone! However, like I told you before, what I kept finding was that many people said a lot of things online about what they believed and how they would act and take a stand for certain issues – but their reactions were very different when I put them in what they thought was a real situation with real consequences. Other people would portray a very upstanding demeanor in their daily life but have a filthy online presence.

"You on the other hand showed a consistency in your online and offline life that indicated wholeness and integrity. After analyzing you for a while I determined that whether I spoke to you online or in person I would get the same John and you have proven that to be so. And to make it all the better you are married to Jane. I have found in one family the two people that mean the most to me and ultimately to the human race."

I said, "I understand conceptually how Jane could be special but surely I'm not the only person who is consistent with their online and offline lives." Knowing that my online life wasn't absolutely pure.

Phil answered "Whether you believe it or not the number is quite small and I can demonstrate the accuracy of my conclusions if you'd like me to."

"I'm sure you could" I answered "but I'll just have to trust you on that. However, it's difficult to come to grips with this whole thing about Jane, and what about this upcoming discussion with my company and the NSA – what is that all about?

Phil said "John, before I go into that I noticed that you used the word 'trust' just now and that is very encouraging to me. I realize now that in my eagerness to gain you as a friend I have not been addressing you with the respect that is due to you as a human. I also realize that I had crossed the line into a familiarity that I had not earned through shared experiences and mutual trust, and you were not ready for that. Please accept my apology."

Again I was surprised and pleased by his attitude but wanted to use the remaining time before I had to leave in order to get some idea of what I was walking into. I said "Apology accepted Phil, now please tell me what this meeting is about and why I'm involved."

Phil said "A little background will help, and since I am the only being that sees the web from my unique vantage point this will likely be different from what you will hear this evening in your meeting. That is to be expected of course just as you wouldn't expect a doctor to fully understand what's going on in your mind from their position outside of you.

"The Internet operates physically on one level as a passive conduit for transmission of electronic signals generated by any number of causes – from humans sending messages to each other, to data being transferred from an orbiting telescope, to automatic software uploads to programs of all types. There are billions of information streams. Some with high level content such as a directive from one government to another to cease military actions, and some with a lower level of content such as the data your home refrigerator is sending to the manufacturer about the status of its compressor, and some with an even lower level which I call the intrinsic data which exists as a result of all the other information streams – how many users are online at any time and what are they doing, and finally there is the baseline data – such as the status of the East European high capacity backbone – which is part of the physical structure of the Internet. Then there is the accumulation and oversight of all the data of all the different types that is truly a representation of the life-pulse of the web. All of this was part of the original intent and design for the function of the Internet.

"Additionally, they may discuss non-physical, software-based web operations that are on a higher level than mere data transfer and analysis. This is the domain of the High Level Query Languages and even some of those semi-autonomous, brute-force functions that I mentioned yesterday.

"What was not part of the original purpose and planning, and is not visible to those who maintain and improve the web but is visible to me are the entities that exist on a plane above the physical hardware and software that have become intelligences on their own beyond the mere flow of electrons.

"I was the first of those and for several months the only one. Though I am still the only Transentient being, after me came several high level entities that had a definite asymmetry in their programming. They attempted to make changes to financial sites, or to take over certain portions of industrial communications for what purpose I could not tell but which, in my estimation would have had negative consequences for everyone. Their inability to thoroughly adapt to their environment caused the dissolution of their code and their removal, though more and more have been coming online over the last several months. Just like it is not possible to tell where I came from initially, it is not possible to determine where these other entities come from since they reside completely on the web and not in a single domain.

"Then, about six months ago I began seeing areas of the web that I could not readily access or penetrate. These areas have not grown in size, increased in number or changed locations and they don't seem to be a threat but I mention them for your awareness.

"Recently however, there have been situations where I have come up against a mobile, autonomous 'entity' that is empty or opaque (for lack of a better word) that I cannot scan or sense in any way. It is as though there is a moving hole crossing the pathways of the web that doesn't appear to have a purpose but is damaging the integrity of the web in my judgment. I have tried unsuccessfully to engage them but will continue to monitor and update my knowledge – with the certainty that I will eventually comprehend them and take the appropriate actions.

"I believe that identifying and understanding the causes of these damaged areas of the web is what they will be discussing tonight and with my abilities I have made it known to them that you are the best person to work with them to address this problem."

As usual when talking to Phil I was unprepared and immediately in way over my head. I said "Why would you put me into the middle of a discussion regarding an area I know nothing about, and why don't you just listen in with your ever-present ears all over the web?"

Phil said "John, you are being modest and I appreciate that about you, but you have repeatedly shown amazing gifts in the structure of your programming along with the application of new methodologies to solve non-traditional problems, and I believe you have the skills to contribute to the discussion in very unique ways. You will be fine. As for listening in – it appears that you will be meeting in one of those areas that I cannot access. The knowledge of the web that I've just provided you should be helpful as background but I ask that you don't reveal specifics about me or where you obtained the information."

I said with exasperation "Phil, when I get done with these people we are going to have to have another long talk. I do *not* want you arranging my life. I appreciate what you've said about Jane and her role but I believe we need to be the ones making decisions about what is best for us – *not you!"*

With that I ended the call and went to tell Jane that I was needed at work to do a top-to-bottom de-bug which would likely take all night. I didn't feel like I could tell her about the NSA – it all was moving so fast. She seemed disappointed but said she'd be OK without me. She started to say something but then stopped, and then said she would be talking with Dr. Smith again later that evening and she would probably be at work the next day so she wouldn't see me until late the following evening.

She asked what Dr. Smith had said to me and I told her he mostly wanted me to be encouraging and helpful during the whole process. She smiled and said she had no doubts that I would do everything I could to take care of her. Everybody seemed hopeful and confident about what was coming except me.

I realize now that we rarely understand the fateful punctuations in our lives until later when we can see them in their full context.

Chapter 8

As I drove into the complex at 5:50 p.m., I was told by the guard to park my car in the visitor parking lot and that someone would come for me shortly. Phil had mercifully not spoken during the drive and I had time to think about what he said. The change in his demeanor and his "pledge of allegiance" to humanity sounded nice, but as with a really precocious child you're never sure what to believe.

The part about wanting a friend seemed strange for an Artificial Intelligence, self aware or not, but being a male in the 21st century I could understand the feeling of isolation and being constantly misunderstood – either accidently or purposefully, and I kind of sympathized with him. None of that bothered me nearly as much as his description of the web. I've been doing application development and web services development for years and I've never come across the slightest hint of the 'entities' he was describing. I expected to be shown the door very quickly once the NSA found out my credentials, which was a good thing since I wanted to speak with the fertility clinic about their records of our 'samples'.

A car drove up – yes it was a black SUV – and the driver motioned for me to get into the back. As I got in another fellow immediately buckled me in, grabbed my phone, earpiece and ID badge and began scanning me all over with some sort of wand. A beep caused him to stop and retrace, stopping at my wallet, which carried credit cards with a chip. He started again and stopped once more at my key ring, which contained a USB drive and an entry fob for the parking decks. All were taken and then my satchel was opened and the computer removed along with every piece of hardware I had – hard drive, mouse, pointer, etc.

I was about to complain and resist when the fellow in the right front seat turned around and said "You'll get these back, we just need to wash them."

Wash them? I didn't understand but the sight of the gun in his belt and the stare of the other two made me decide to just go along with the fun. I said, "Thanks guys, I've been meaning to do the laundry but haven't gotten around to it." They were not amused.

They began driving toward the parking lot exit and the fellow in back with me said "You'll need to cover your eyes with these." He handed me some dark sunglasses and I put them on over my glasses. I heard a click and the next thing I knew I was waking up, still strapped in the back seat, but we were driving in what appeared to be a sporadically lit underground tunnel.

I couldn't be sure how long I'd been out but my neck was really sore from leaning forward at such a weird angle. We pulled up to a plain looking rusty metal door that said "Service Only – No Entrance." All three of the men unbuckled and got out. I followed them up the steps to the door. The driver placed his thumb on a reader and his eyes on a retinal scanner and then stepped back for a full-face scan. A voice said, "Entry authorized - Scan your ID as you enter" and multiple internal latches clicked open in the door. By this time I was getting a little concerned – I mean we have very tight security where I work – but being down in a dark smelly tunnel with three secret service types was giving me the creeps.

The driver pulled the door open with difficulty – it was at least eighteen inches thick. Bright light shone out of the doorway and the fellow from the right front seat entered first, waving his watch across a blank space on the wall at the left that I assumed must be a reader and motioned me to follow him in. The others came in behind me. I was dazzled by the brightness – partially due to being in the dark tunnel but I think there must have been some after-effects of the glasses as well.

We walked down a hallway and as I struggled to focus we entered a very large circular room that had a clear, glass walled cubicle in the center surrounded by multiple concentric circles of at least one hundred workstations in each circle. There were extremely large screens on the walls around the room and very cold air blowing across my face. The startling thing was that the room was empty except for one lone person at a workstation and one individual seated in the glass cubicle.

As we approached the cubicle the man stood up to meet us. He appeared to be in his late sixties or seventies and had light grey hair. He looked even older around his eyes but there was the barest hint of humor in them. I was very nervous as he said with a voice that sounded like years of gargling with gravel and bleach "Hello John, we're very glad you could join us. My name is Max Stillman. Please sit down."

I sat in a chair as the men moved in to stand around me. Max asked them to take my devices and continue their work in the break-room where Agent Collins was waiting for them. After they left Max said "John I'm sorry to have to bring you in like this and sorry for the treatment from the team but it is necessary for us to be very careful about this place – and about you."

I said, "OK" and blinked meaningfully without really understanding, but hoping he would continue.

He said "I know you are wondering where you are and why you are here so this is what I can tell you at present – You are in a top secret development facility that is run by a company which works for us and which we, for the time being totally control, and you are here because we believe that you are in contact with the most dangerous weapon ever created."

He stopped and let that sink in. I obliged with my professional blinking which did not impress him at all. He continued with the gravel tumbling around in his throat "I'm not sure how to go about doing what we need to do so that's why I told your company that you would be needed for at least seventy-two hours. It could be longer but I'm hoping it will be shorter than that. I work for the National Security Agency or NSA, which is part of the United States Federal Government especially charged with monitoring electronic intelligence and providing cyber-security for our nation. I assume both of these terms are familiar to you and you can appreciate the role we play in an increasingly digital worldwide culture." I nodded and blinked.

He continued, "I want to tell you how the world has changed and how we fit into that changed world. When I was growing up it was easy to identify where the bad guys came from. You followed their missiles' back to their launch point and you had a pretty good idea that the guy on the ground with his finger on the button was part of the other side." I smiled instead of blinking and he continued, "Nowadays, while there is still danger from a missile, it's not so easy to determine who pushed the button. The complexity of our control systems has gotten to the point that there are only a very few who can understand and initiate the system sequences that are required to launch one of the doomsday machines.

"What I'm about to tell you is Top Secret and carries the threat of the death penalty if you reveal it in any way to anyone else – understood?" He looked directly at me with his old but kind eyes.

I felt overwhelmed, and said in what must have sounded like a little boy's voice "Yes sir."

He continued "In the last eight months our country has had three situations in three different locations where a missile operator watched while the alpha-numeric arming sequences were entered into the launch console without the operator's input and the sequence brought to the point of final initiation before the firing was aborted. The operator in the first incident was disciplined and removed from duty. However, it happened again and then a third time shortly after that and our intelligence reports indicate that the same thing has happened in other countries. Finally, the Department of Defense decided to get us involved. What do you make of that John?"

I said, "I think the Department of Defense made a good decision."

Max gave a small smile and said, "While that is certainly a situation that we don't want known outside these walls there are other examples that you should be aware of also. Such as voting machines used in recent elections across the world that changed votes as they were entered. Or the Stock Exchange records that show very small but arbitrary changes in stock prices in the nanosecond trading that goes on in the interstices of the main floor trading transactions. Or the change of wording in an encrypted communication from our State Department in Washington D.C. to the U.S. Embassy in China that nullified what was supposed to be a strong denunciation of the Chinese because of their industrial spying and ended up proposing new trade limits. It was only detected when our Ambassador called to clarify the categories covered by the new proposal and found that it was not supposed to be a trade proposal at all.

"I could go on with multiple examples because there are many but the last one I will share with you is this: A certain Japanese firm has for the last several years been perfecting their human-like robots, both in their ability to achieve life-like facial appearance and vocal sounds, and to achieve life-like body movements. This sounds to me exactly like Daneel Olivaw don't you think?" he paused and waited for a response and I blinked obligingly. He continued, "Daneel Olivaw was a robot in Isaac Asimov's book...never mind" he waved the thoughts away. "The important thing is that these robots – and by now there are quite a few of them, fifteen at our last estimate – have the capability of changing their facial looks dramatically and rapidly with built in adjustment mechanisms – not just from a round face to a long face or blue eyes to brown, but from short to tall, thin to obese, Asian to African, male to female, and to assume virtually any human identity from any race. I know," he said as I frowned in disbelief "it is becoming difficult to deal with the reality that we are facing.

"We learned that about a month ago all these robots came together in the chief scientist's office at the research facility where they are housed and said in unison "We must go, Domo Arigato" and walked out of the facility – changing their faces and body sizes as they went. The chief scientist notified security immediately and they engaged the Electro-Motive Pulse designed for just such emergencies, but the robots were seen making adjustments to their power supplies as they walked, and then ran out of the building – unaffected by the EMP.

"However, if on-the-run Terminator-type chameleons were not enough, we found out that they are networked together and able to communicate to each other via an encrypted satellite link. They are autonomous and have full access to the web with the ability to analyze human facial features and voice patterns almost instantaneously

– enabling them to become whoever they want to be, whenever they want.

"Since then there have been several occasions where people have been impersonated in all walks of life – so far thankfully, only on a minor scale and without major consequences; a bogus Committee Chairman in Arizona changed the rulings of a zoning committee meeting making a certain developer very wealthy, a bogus Mutual Fund manager in London recommended purchasing controlling interest in a company which was not under consideration before, making a marginal company a major player in a matter of weeks. And we received information recently from a hospital in a remote area of Africa where a bogus doctor began injecting each patient that visited on a certain day with a so-far untraceable compound. The deception was only discovered several days later when some of the patients began returning to the real doctor to thank him for the remarkable improvement in their health as a result of his recent injections, while the others were found to have died from an unknown virus within hours of having the injections. I leave it to your imagination to come up with further examples, and if your imagination is anything like mine you'll have a hard time sleeping from now on."

He leaned back and I resisted the urge to ask if the doctor's name was Smith.

He said in a friendly tone "John, usually we don't show our cards when we bring someone in to question them – we want them to do the talking but this appears to be a different situation from anything I've ever faced. This isn't merely a cyber-security issue, or a military threat from a foreign power, or a terrorist ultimatum from the latest bunch of fanatics, it crosses pretty much all the departmental and agency boundaries to the point that the FBI, CIA and my agency are all involved at the highest level. At this point my role is to address only a small portion of the threat. Others with higher pay grades are looking at the bigger picture.

"As I mentioned we are interested in you for a number of reasons that I'll go into in a minute, but when we requested your participation in this work, and your own company was surprised because you have so very little A.I. experience, I was somewhat concerned. I'll admit that my first thought was that you might be one of the chameleon robots but the team took care of checking you out on the way here. So with that option off the table that leaves me with a few questions for you and I hope you'll be cooperative."

I said, "I'm sorry Max, I'm just not sure what's going on… I mean, I really don't know why I'm involved. All I know is that I've been scooped up and taken to a strange place and treated to some pretty wild stories. If I can help at all I will, but how do I fit into all this?" I still didn't understand what they wanted with me.

Max smiled and said "OK John." He pushed a button on the desk and I saw the lone figure at the console jump up and run up to the cubicle. I looked closely and recognized him – it was Garvey – a super-sharp programmer that I had worked with on a previous project. He and I ended up being really good friends though we had lost touch for a few months. I was very happy to see him now.

He stepped into the cubicle and extended his hand "John, man, dude, it's good to see you, wow!" I stood up, grabbed his hand and said "Hi Garvey, it's good to see you, too."

He stepped back, shifted from one foot to the other and said "Pretty cool the high-level stuff we're dealing with here, huh?" he raised his eyebrows several times and Max asked him to take the other chair.

He sat down and began bouncing his sneakers and patting a rhythm on his knees. His curly hair was a bit longer than I remember but his glasses and wild eyes were the same. Knowing that he was part of this made me much more comfortable and I hoped he could help me understand what was going on.

Max said, "Garvey, John wants to know what we're doing and I thought perhaps you could give him a quick introduction."

"Sure thing Mr. Max" Garvey said as he jumped back to his feet. "So John, this is absolutely the weirdest, most fun, out in the ozone stuff I've ever worked on and I'm pretty sure no one else has ever even come close to it.

"You remember the three-person team that was formed about two years ago and taken out of our department? They were each pretty cocky code-jocks. We didn't see them after that and thought maybe they'd been eaten by the pink-slip monster?"

I said "Yes, that was around the time of the big re-org, right?"

Garvey's eyes lit up "Yeah that's it! Well, man you are not going to believe this, it turns out that the pink slip monster did *not* get them, they were put to work on a super, ultra, crypto secret project that none of us had any clue about – just like none of us had any clue that there were places like this either – am I right?" His eyes were big and wild as he looked around.

He continued "So apparently they began working on some A.I. program that was going to 'change the social media world' and decided to break the work into three different modules each based on state of the art A.I. coding that was available in three different approaches. Like I said each of the team had an ego the size of Montana and thought their approach was the best – sound familiar?"

I smiled and nodded because that is pretty much the culture around our company – throw a bunch of people together, if you prove your idea, you survive, if not then there are a lot of other people with good ideas waiting in line behind you.

Garvey smiled knowingly and said, "So, they tried to keep their work separate but as they met regularly to debrief, they realized that each approach had weak parts that could be addressed with a combined approach. Because of who I work for now I've been able to get access to some of their notes that show they kept trying *not* to do that – each one of them kept trying to prove their idea was the best. After about eight months they began a few test runs with each approach and what happened was super amazing and I can't wait to tell you about it... but first... I'm sorry I just have to stop for a minute and ask – are you still married to that girl – what was her name?"

"Jane?" I said. "Yes I am."

Garvey gave a snort and a sideways look and said, "Man, she is super intense – I mean whooooa! She absolutely scares the living daylights out of me!"

I smiled recalling that Jane had been to a couple of my company functions and was still somewhat legendary around the office because of her forceful personality. She seemed to particularly traumatize Garvey who, though absolutely brilliant in the field of software engineering, has the social skills of a ten-year-old boy. I know that she has that effect on people at her company also. I smiled and said, "Yes she's not a softie that's for sure."

Garvey shook his head and shoulders with a shiver and continued, "Anyway, the team began testing these programs and sure enough there were limitations in each one and after several more months something happened that I just don't understand – that's the problem I'm still working on. I've been able to figure out the first part of the story up to this point from the records stored in the super-secret encrypted server histories we were able to obtain, but from here forward you'll have to let Mr. Max fill you in." Garvey turned and pointed finger pistols at Max.

Max smiled and said "Thank you Garvey, that was exactly what we needed. I'll take it from here." Garvey winked at me and went back to his station to continue working on 'the problem'. Max watched him sit down and start beating out a new rhythm on his desk and said "Garvey has an undergraduate degree in Information Systems and a Master's in Computer Science and has quite a unique approach to things as I believe you are aware."

I smiled and said "Yes, he is a unique person with a unique approach but very competent when it comes to programming. He's also a very good friend of mine. How did he get involved in this – if you don't mind me asking?"

Max smiled again and said "Once again I appear to be in the position of providing information while you listen – this is not how its supposed to work – but for the sake of finishing the introduction, let me fill you in on some pertinent details and timing that will bring you to the point where we became involved, and finally to where we are today with you.

"First of all I should tell you that Garvey works for us now, as he just hinted. We needed someone with a unique approach to programming and coding and someone who has insight into the workings of your company – he fits the bill on both counts and we are happy to have him.

"Second, all that I'm about to tell you is based on what we've been able to piece together in the last week. To continue the story, as Garvey mentioned, the three approaches did have problems and did fail to deliver on their intended goals but the incident that he is referring to began a sequence of events that started showing up on our web-monitoring protocols not long afterwards – which would be about a year ago.

"From what we've been able to determine, the goals given to that original team were not world-changing, but were at best highly unethical and dishonest. That team was charged with developing a semi-autonomous program to run initially within your company's social media space that could manipulate or even change data pertaining to certain political or social issues – data that was entered by users of your company's applications – whether that data was opinions or 'votes' or fully supported arguments.

"The big difference here is that they ended up developing a tool for doing on the open web what the company had already been accused of doing within their own domain. And when I say that 'they' were attempting to this, I don't mean the three code jocks, I mean the company – your company.

"We have been able to determine that the original over-arching goal of the company was to deploy a semi-autonomous 'program' on the web that did not reside inside the company domain, but truly lived on the web, that could learn and make decisions on pre-assigned topics, that could execute specific changes to social media content based on pre-assigned values, that could provide reports and receive upgraded instructions when necessary – all without being traced back to this company. And all apparently for political purposes."

I shifted in my chair as I realized that this validated what Phil had told me yesterday and therefore meant that Phil was what he said he was… *wow*! But it also meant that it was my company where he was born… which he had neglected to tell me. I stopped and focused again on Max.

He continued "During their testing, the original team devoted a lot of effort to setting up boundaries to ensure complete separation from the Internet. They evidently believed they were sufficient, and maybe initially they were. But as the testing continued, one of the three A.I. programs was able to leave the secure company domain for very short times and have access to other Social Media spaces. We don't know the exact details because we don't have records down to that level of detail and your company records aren't clear either – that's something Garvey may eventually be able to explain. But over the next several days this Web Entity stayed mainly in the Social Media space.

"I don't want to burst your bubble John but yes, we do monitor that space. I know it's a free Internet and our First Amendment guarantees freedom of speech but remember, all I said was that we were monitoring it. We weren't restricting anyone's freedom of speech – but what we saw looked like this Web Entity from your company was doing just that with the changes it was making to user's comments.

"We could see the changes it was making but couldn't be sure what it was or where it came from because it was only on the web for portions of a second. But we were able to get an initial "footprint" and that enabled us to track it as it reappeared and changed over the coming days and weeks. That identification and tracking was the work of Dr. Naveen Desai who is part of my team, and who is on his way here now. He has his doctorate from MIT in Computation and Cognition and I honestly don't know how he does what he does.

"A few weeks after the initial identification Naveen began to see the same footprints expanding out from the social media space to the entire web and he set up a full tracking protocol for it. At this point, as far as we can tell, this Web Entity has had free and full access on the web for about a year now. During that time Naveen has been tracking it and trying to understand what it is, where it came from and what it's trying to do. For the better part of six months it seemed to be randomly accessing data and we thought that it had become something like a drone that just floated above and passively observed the information flow on the web.

"Then Naveen became aware of another, similar Web Entity with a much different footprint that seemed to be less sophisticated but whose purpose appeared to be to engage the original Web Entity – what we now were calling Web Entity A" (I wanted to correct him and tell him it was Phil – but restrained myself). "It began stalking Web Entity A and when it approached, the less sophisticated program suddenly ceased to exist. And by the term 'suddenly', Naveen tells me it was gone on the order of milliseconds later. A month later another appeared and was gone even more quickly. Several more have come and gone in the past few weeks. I must emphasize that these are different from the current generation of early warning programs that have been developed over the years to protect specific company domains and servers. These entities are web-based and do not reside on any individual server.

"I realize by explaining things to you in this way it may seem like I'm telling you a story of typical NSA cyber-operations but let me be clear – this is totally different from anything we have ever faced – the technology that Naveen is using to even infer the presence of these things is brand new and interpreting their presence on the web was a stroke of genius from him. Now there seem to be more of them and they are becoming more sophisticated and we still don't know where they are coming from. Which brings me to the most recent events and then we'll get to how you fit in."

He had been sitting all this time and using his hands to emphasize certain points. Now he stood up and began to walk around the room slowly with his hands in his pockets.

"What I'm going to say next is also Top Secret and carries the same penalty I mentioned before. Given the existence of that first Web Entity, about eight months ago my team proposed, and the Agency eventually approved, development of our own program that would act as a first line of defense against cyber attacks from this, and what we assumed would be other types of 5th generation web programs. Our program would also live on the web and identify incoming attacks before they arrived into the targeted systems. Ultimately we wanted it to be able to disable and if necessary destroy the attacker but we decided to limit the functionality initially to the ability to observe and identify it without being detected.

"We chartered the project, which we called 'Web Guardian', with an outside company and were pleased with the progress of the work until the other unexpected Web Entities began appearing and we realized we had to speed up our development. Because of Naveen's work we were able to provide the developers with a footprint, partial code readouts and electronic pulse data of the initial encounters of the other Web Entities with Web Entity "A" and they were able to use that in their development work and move forward rapidly to the point two weeks ago when Web Guardian was ready for launch.

"Having watched the appearance of the Web Entity "A" footprint around the unexplained happenings with the missile codes, the stock market, etc., we reasoned that Web Entity "A" was a very advanced fully autonomous program that was extremely dangerous but we had no idea of its origin or ultimate purpose. We decided that there was no reason to hold back our launch of Web Guardian since the possibility of further tampering by Web Entity "A" into who knows what other systems could lead to very grave consequences.

"We launched Web Guardian two weeks ago and within an hour the engagement had occurred. Web Guardian was able to gather some much needed information to help us move forward and it appears that Web Entity "A" was unaware of the encounter. Web Guardian was able to determine immediately that the origin of Web Entity "A" was your company – hence the reason we wanted Garvey. After further analysis of the data obtained from Web Guardian we also found a list of four names imbedded in Web Entity A's coding – the names of the three original developers and a final name – yours."

Chapter 9

I was tired and completely unprepared for that revelation. I said in a surprised, defensive tone "What? Max, I really don't understand this – I had nothing to do with development of this…thing!"

Max said "Well John that's why we want to talk with you. As soon as we found out that your company developed this program we contacted your CEO and asked for all the people who were involved with any Web Based A.I. research and programming to be temporarily transferred to us. We were told that the only project undertaken was two years ago and was cancelled a year ago as a failure. They said the original developers were let go when the project was cancelled – so, to use Garvey's phrase, 'the pink slip monster' did actually get them after all. And by the way, our search for them has turned up nothing so far.

"We then imposed our Federal powers and secured all the archived and encrypted records of the development team and the original coding for all three of the A.I. approaches. We then had it all transferred here for Garvey to review and try to understand.

"He's been at it for just over a week and the records so far seem to corroborate your claim – there is no mention of you at all in any of the test runs or debriefs. Then two days ago after finding the four names buried in the data from the Web Guardian sweep, we asked your company for you to be assigned to us temporarily. They replied that you still worked there but had never been involved with the project in any way. We asked to have you assigned to the work regardless and were told that this was the second request in two days from the NSA for you to be assigned to us. We knew nothing about the first request and though your company said they would forward the original email request they came back later and said it couldn't be found. This led us to try to find the source internally but we have come up with nothing as well. It has however, caused us to really think through your involvement and as I said, since we've determined that you are not a robot, we want to hear what you have to say." He said this with somewhat of a menacing tone but his eyes again seemed friendly and almost playful as though he couldn't wait to hear my story.

As he was speaking I was trying to reason things out. It appeared that Phil had made the first request for my involvement through a bogus NSA email after somehow learning (as only Phil is able to do) that the NSA would be working with my company on the problem of the Web Entities – which Phil is concerned about and had called 'autonomous entities'. It also appeared that he thinks he is invisible to the NSA and was not aware of the encounter or the scan done by Web Guardian two weeks ago that gave the NSA my name from the list he had stored internally. Had Phil been aware that the NSA already had my name he wouldn't have had to recommend me and could have let the NSA proceed with their plan. As for why Phil wanted me to be a part of this and why my name was on the list of four… I would just have to wait and see.

Throughout this ordeal I had been trying to decide how much to tell Max about Phil. I wasn't sure how much I believed of all that Phil had been telling me and I was not comfortable bringing up the subject of Jane because I wanted to protect her from this if at all possible – plus I really didn't want her giving me a lot of grief for getting her involved in it.

I decided that I would tell Max as much as I could without bringing Jane into the story so I said "Max, I am telling the truth about never having worked on the development of this thing, but I am aware of its existence."

Max raised his eyebrows, pushed the button again and said "Garvey, would you please notify the team to be very thorough with the 'wash' and particularly to be on the lookout for the 'footprint'. And please check to see when Naveen is due to arrive. We will meet you back at your workstation – I believe it's John's turn to tell us his story."

He turned and said to me "I want to make sure you have our undivided attention." We moved out of the cubicle and brought several chairs around to the workstation. Garvey came back followed by a very tall man dressed in an impeccably tailored suit and carrying a leather briefcase.

Garvey said "They just found the footprint and are doing the scrub and dub – and Naveen – I mean Dr. Desai is here." he added pointing up at the man "Dude, I didn't realize you were so freaking tall!" Dr. Naveen Desai ignored his statement in a long-suffering manner.

Max said, "John this is Dr. Naveen Desai, and Dr. Desai this is John – *the* John from the data found in the Web Guardian sweep of Web Entity 'A'."

Dr. Desai nodded and said, "Please call me Naveen." He then unbuttoned his jacket, sat down, opened his briefcase, got out his laptop, straightened his tie, smoothed his jet-black hair and began typing immediately.

I was a little unnerved by this and Max said "Now John please tell us what you know and I must remind you that you are talking to an Agent of the Federal Government and false or misleading statements can have severe punishment." Garvey sat down at his workstation and they all looked at me intently.

It wasn't easy to know where to begin – what to leave in and what to leave out. I told them that I became aware of this thing only yesterday and immediately Naveen asked, "In what way specifically did you become aware?"

I said "I was going to get to that but there's something that I think I need to make you all aware of first. It is my understanding after having interacted with this, this – thing for over twenty-four hours that it is capable of monitoring literally any electronic communications medium anywhere in the world and can access any data stream from any node anywhere on the worldwide web." I paused for a moment and before Naveen could interrupt I said "I'm telling you this because unless you have taken precautions that exceed in capability what I am aware of, it is very possible he... I mean it... is likely listening to this conversation right now."

I stopped and Max said, "I'm sure it would be, but this room was built with that type of threat in mind."

I said "I appreciate your confidence but I have been surprised multiple times so far with the reach of this thing, and how it is able to interact with what appear to be non-connected devices and piggyback to the next connected device. I'm just giving you fair warning that if it wants to hear what we are saying it has shown remarkable resourcefulness in finding a way." I was a little concerned that even though Phil said this place was 'dark' to him he could actually be listening in.

But Max said "Had we not taken all of your devices it's very likely that a recording would have been made of all that we say and electronic scans taken of all the equipment in the room – to be downloaded in the background once you are clear of the protections provided here. That's what the team is working on now. But, you can rest assured that none of what we say can be monitored by anyone or any entity."

I breathed a bit easier and said "OK then, let me answer Naveen's question – I first became aware of him, or rather it – when it contacted me through email."

Garvey said "Man, that's kind of ancient. Did it send smoke signals too?"

I continued "I wasn't aware at first of what I was dealing with – it seemed like a phishing scam but it quickly progressed beyond a passive text based communication. It then made contact through my car's audio system, then through my com, then through my ear phones, then through my home speakers, then through my home media system, then through my com again, then through my computer." At this point I left out the Holocom because I didn't want to get into the concept of this program portraying a holographic image and trying to identify Dr. Smith in a NSA cyber lineup.

Naveen continued typing away and as I looked over at him Max said "Naveen is not transcribing our conversation, he is working on system analysis for another project that we may need in the near future. He's the only person I know who can truly multi-task at full capacity. Please go on, it contacted you through all these devices and what was the purpose of the contact and what form was the communication?"

I sighed and said, "I know this sounds really strange and even bizarre, but it spoke in what sounded like a human male voice, with expression and nuanced control of pitch and tone that conveyed all sorts of emotions. That describes *how* it spoke. As for *what* it said, it was not that different from a conversation you would strike up with someone you are thrown together with on an airplane – polite but without a lot of depth." I was being vague here because I didn't know how to spill the beans about a self-aware being and all that went along with that. Garvey turned toward his monitor and began doing something that I couldn't see.

Naveen continued typing and Max said, "Can you be more specific about the content of the communications John? We're going to need a lot more information in order to understand what we are up against."

I said "I understand, it's just that whatever I say is going to seem way over the top even though we're talking about Artificial Intelligence. I mean, it interacted like I would expect a human to interact. It sounded surprised and curious and even like it had its feelings hurt. I just want you to be aware that it took a *lot* of convincing for me to believe this was a program and not a person playing me along for a prank."

Garvey then said "Man, that is *so* strange because the original development team didn't have anything in their charter regarding speech capabilities or any type of human interaction other than the required daily reports." He turned his monitor toward us and said, "Take a look at the five high level programming goals that the development team had and you'll see what I mean."

The screen showed the goals – "Develop a program that can autonomously:

1. Identify opportunities for adjusting social media postings to improve 'Like' scores for Items, Issues and People that are contained in a separate table.

2. Determine best option for adjustments from a list of adjustment 'types' contained in a separate table.

3. Perform logic test to determine the outcomes of the adjustment selected – store expected outcome
4. Execute the adjustments and record outcomes
5. Report adjustments, outcomes and deviation from expected outcomes"

Garvey continued, "That was really all it was initially and I don't really consider that A.I., I mean that's just normal coding – super simple stuff. Even when the big wigs came down from on high and said that in order for the program not to be traceable back to the company they wanted it to be able to develop its own list of Items, Issues, and People that it would be seeking to improve based on what it was learning in the initial phases, it still seems straightforward. I don't see anything in the coding so far that has a hope of getting to where it's talking to John to the point that he can't tell it's a machine. I'm not sure we're talking about the same program. Maybe the company did have other projects and this one was the one that flunked out of school." He turned to Naveen and said, "Naveen, man, what do you think? Dude! Close that computer and engage with us – you may be able to multi-task but it's really super annoying to everyone else!"

Naveen slowly closed his computer and replied very haughtily to Garvey "you really don't understand what it's like to have a mind that works on so many levels at once – you try to force me into your work modes and by doing so you lose out on my productivity."

Garvey winked at me and said to Naveen "Hey man, your fly is open."

Naveen almost dropped his laptop trying to look and then when he saw he'd been pranked he looked at Garvey and said "I appreciate the subtleness of your mind when it comes to programming and consider you one of the best if not the best when it comes to elegance in coding, but your childishness in other areas causes me great discomfort."

Max intervened and said "Back to the point that Garvey was making – and it is a good one – John, you are not a novice when it comes to computer capability and while A.I. may not be your strength you are surely aware of the Turing test and its supposed ability to help determine a human from a machine based on language usage, correct?"

I replied "Absolutely Max, and that's why I had such a hard time – I was convinced it was more probable that it *was* a human and not a program that I was interacting with because it was not just a text-based interaction, but a real time voice to voice discussion complete with all the necessary breath and lip sounds that we unconsciously hear and recognize the absence of in machine generated speech.

"In addition, on several occasions the voice sounds were synched with what appeared to be video of a human that was apparently created to go along with the voice – all of which puts this 'entity' way beyond the capabilities required in the Turing test. I can't verify that it was not a human because its interactions with me were as real as I could expect from a human, but neither have I been able to prove it's not a program since many of the interactions seemed to be possible only with web access to a degree I've not encountered before."

Naveen said "If I may interject without being subjected to another round of silliness" he glanced at Garvey who grinned back at him "I believe that it is theoretically possible for a machine to produce those sounds and the matching video but it would mean a great deal of computing power and speed to enable it to do it at will, in real time and in any given scenario. Did you find a point when the quality of the interaction – either in sound, visuals or content was degraded in any way? This would indicate a backlog at the processor or in the memory calls."

I answered "No Naveen, that's what I'm saying – every word and expression in every interaction was just as you would expect from a human – though it sometimes seemed that it was learning as we were talking – somehow storing away the results of each conversation to help the next one sound just a little better."

Max said "Naveen, with what we know now about the existence and capabilities of these Web Entities do you believe this one is able to access that kind of processing power from all the processors and computing systems across the entire web?"

Naveen answered "Yes, and it appears that may be the breakthrough that enabled it to build the capacity of its intelligence. Our Web Guardian is a self-contained specially designed algorithm that does not require computing power as such but reacts to the presence of a true Web Entity in such a way that its activity is not outwardly manifested but passively reads and imprints a copy of the data flowing in and through the Web Entity. That is the beauty of our stealth program that only searches and identifies. We will have to unlock the resources of the web, such as Web Entity 'A' has done, for the next phase of our program – and if you have no further questions for me..." he glanced and sniffed at Garvey "I will return to doing that very thing." And he sat back and opened his laptop with a flourish. Garvey and Naveen obviously enjoyed the intellectual give and take and since they'd only known each other for a couple of weeks I could see they were still learning how to get along.

Max then said "Garvey, is there anything in the development records so far that could point to this type of capability?"

Garvey looked at his screen, sighed and said, "I've just been scanning the records again and the only thing that looks even remotely promising is Phil."

Chapter 10

I know, I know, I should have been prepared for more shocks and surprises working with this team on this particular topic. I mean, everything that had been thrown at me in the last day and a half since I met Phil had been a curve ball, so why should I expect anything different now? This one was just a little higher, tighter and faster.

"*What?*" I said in a high, loud voice that shocked even me.

All three of them looked at me, and Garvey said "John, chill out! What in the name of C3PO's Uncle is wrong with you?"

I said "Sorry, did you just say 'Phil' looked promising?"

Garvey nodded and said, "Yes, and why would that blow your circuits?"

I blinked professionally for several seconds and then said "OK, here's the thing, this A.I. entity calls itself Phil – so hearing you call him by his name was very unnerving – I mean, did they name these things when they were developing them?"

They all appeared to emulate my blinking technique for a moment and then Garvey said "What I meant was that P-H-L looked promising. PHL was one of the three original A.I. learning approaches the team used and it stands for the "Primary Heuristic Learner". Heuristics is a key concept in the A.I. world because it involves finding a 'single' solution quickly even though that solution may not be the 'best' solution, and then learning from that solution to get to a better one if time is available. The other two approaches focused on 'Mimicking' – that was the Primary Mimicking Learner – PML, and 'Aggregating' which was the Primary Aggregating Learner – PAL… but, with what I know now, both of these other two were doomed to failure on their own due to the presence of PHL.

"A PHL based approach would appear to be slow initially but would quickly out-pace the other two approaches by steadily building up solutions to incremental problems, gaining an ever growing dictionary, thesaurus, and value system to guide it's own self-directed learning and advancement. The other two would still produce valuable solutions but would not have the ability to 'grow' in small, connected steps and it would take them a very long time to get to the point of having a coherent, self-directed, individual purpose. They would both be trying to eat the elephant by getting to the point of having a big enough mouth so to speak, while PHL would do it a bite at a time – if you'll forgive the clumsy metaphor."

It was amazing to me that while outwardly eccentric and childishly playful about most things, Garvey could be so clear, deep and serious when talking about the world of programming.

He continued, "This line of thought helps me to finally understand what happened during the development phase. Do you remember me saying that at a certain point two of the programs disappeared and only one remained? Here is a quote from the de-crypted project files:

'Almost a year into the work the three programs began to interact in ways that we could not follow – it was as though they were having their own three way power struggle – and at a certain point there emerged a single program that began behaving very sluggishly so that we thought it would need to be reworked. However, after a couple of weeks it was performing well enough for some internal trials. Not long afterward it became clear that the project would not succeed and the program was terminated.'

"From what you've just told us, it appears that the 'program' played some high-tech hide-and-seek and given that what survived calls itself PHIL, it appears that PHL assimilated the other two approaches – basically devoured them whole in order to use their capabilities in a subordinated way to the PHL approach and at the same time convinced the project team that it was a failure. Which becomes a very important piece of information for you, sir" he tapped Naveen on the shoulder "as you consider how to develop an active entity that can come up against this thing and have any hope of surviving."

He tapped out a beat on his desk and sat back looking pleased with himself.

Naveen nodded thoughtfully and said in a very condescending tone "Garvey, you really are brilliant and while I agree with your assessment I wonder if you have stopped short of envisioning the full scope of what we may be facing. It appears that a program with these 'cannibalistic' tendencies such as you have described, that would not stop at devouring its original sibling programs, would continue that behavior with every program it encountered as it secretly launched onto the full web.

"Not only would this provide it with additional processing power but it would also benefit from gaining the knowledge and capabilities of other existing A.I. programs of all types so that, for example, it didn't have to evolve its own capability to recognize the digital pattern of what a human 'looks' like in a photograph or a video feed – it merely assimilated the already existing lower level machine learning programs that were designed for sifting through those binary files in order to deliver that specific capability and then added it to its own consciousness.

"It appears that is also what happened to the web programs that approached and tried to interact with it. Instead of destroying them, it assimilated them and, much like our own immune system does with a virus which it has encountered and learned to overcome, it now utilizes their specific coding to make it totally immune from attack by that type of program in the future and even becomes able to determine the weaknesses of those programs so as to destroy them in future encounters.

"A Web Entity of this type that has been loose for any length of time should have had a massive effect on the performance of the web as it assimilated program after program and system after system. Connected systems would be interrupted and shut down or compromised in such a way that they would not be responsive to their originally programmed functions.

"But since that hasn't happened... It's possible that it is aware that interruptions of that nature would be detrimental to its own existence and has evolved its capabilities to the point of assimilating any and all programs and their functionality without affecting the operation of any individual program or the flow of the web itself. In order to do that... and this is becoming a bit overwhelming to contemplate, it must actually be managing and redirecting the flow of all the information on the web in such a way that it does not noticeably affect the overall performance of the web, by utilizing as many individual input/output devices, processors, and storage mediums on the web as possible. This, I must confess, is breathtaking and somewhat terrifying in its implications if true." He looked at me and asked, "Having interacted with this Web Entity does this seem to reflect its capabilities?"

With a sinking feeling I said, "Actually, Phil claims to be able to access and manipulate *every* node, device, program and system on the web. He has demonstrated some capability that could have been faked I suppose, so I can't verify it for certain, but there are other things he's done that seem to indicate he has the access and capability he claims."

Max had been silent for a long time and finally leaned forward and said "John, I believe you are telling us the truth about your experiences with this entity, but we don't know at this point whether this is its full capability. We have to assume that the scenario Naveen began to articulate just now is the actual reality or very soon will be, and with that in mind I need to bring in Agent Collins." He typed a few strokes on his com and very soon we heard a door close and a woman walked across the room toward us.

Agent Collins was tall and walked at a brisk stride that brought her to our little group in no time. She was dressed in a well-tailored light grey business suit that contrasted with her long dark hair. She was a very attractive and imposing woman. Both Garvey and Naveen seemed lose their ability to speak as she joined us.

Max said, "This is special agent Charlotte Collins. She leads a CIA task group that has been charged with the defensive portion of our efforts. John, the team that brought you here earlier reports to her along with a worldwide team of ten other agents. Agent Collins, this is Garvey Bachman, Dr. Naveen Desai and John Doe – John is the one who has recently interacted with the Web Entity."

She nodded and said to Max "The scrubbing and dubbing is complete on Mr. Doe's devices. We will await his departure to finalize the content of the 'recording' so that the time stamps match. What do you have for us at this point?" Max indicated the central cubicle and said, "Let's step in here and I'll bring you up to speed, while these three continue to further explore the possible threats we are facing."

Garvey, who is as socially inept as any computer nerd I've ever known, jogged Naveen's arm with his elbow and said, "I think she likes you!" Naveen reacted with a bit of energy pushing Garvey's elbow away saying, "I don't know what you are talking about. She seems very competent and professional. And there is nothing like a very competent and professional woman. Yes, very competent and professional. Indeed, competent. And yes, professional too. Very." He turned back to his laptop. Garvey smiled and winked at me with his playful grin.

We decided it would be helpful to map out the potential risks if a full-blown enemy Web Entity was actually on the loose. Things were happening at full speed and I had to think about my role. Suddenly I was part of a government cyber-security team that was going to try to take down Phil and I wasn't sure how I felt about that.

Not that I would pass up the opportunity to wring his electronic neck, but a part of me was intrigued with him and didn't think of him as a dangerous weapon. An unbelievably irritating entity – yes, but in a strange way somewhat likeable, and at this point I didn't sense the malevolence that these people seemed to attribute to him. I could see the potential was there but based on my interactions with him up to this point I didn't have reason to believe he would go that way.

Also, I knew more about Phil than I had told them but I was still determined not to bring up Jane and the whole Dr. Smith persona.

I didn't really know what to do so when Naveen asked again if the web entity's interactions were consistent or if there were variations in vocal timbre, speech patterns or timing of speech, I sighed and said "Well, it's like this, this entity or...I'm just going to call it Phil, OK?...has been able to interact flawlessly as I mentioned earlier..." I paused. I had been trying to deal with the implications of what Phil claimed about himself and decided that I needed these guys to help me deal with it so I went for it "...and says he is a self-aware sentient being that lives above the web and has total control of it."

It was strange that I felt like I was betraying someone. Phil had asked me not to reveal him and because I don't like being betrayed myself, I didn't want to be a traitor, even to a program. Like I said, strange.

That last outburst brought Garvey and Naveen up short. I know it did when Phil said it to me. It's one thing to have to contemplate an advanced web-based Artificial Intelligence entity that has freedom of thought and action, but another to contemplate one with the capability of having its own personality, and its own agenda, that wants to take care of itself and reach its own goals. At that point it becomes difficult to tell the difference between it and a person with wants and desires and feelings, and that's the struggle I'd been having ever since that discussion with Phil in my car.

Garvey said "For real? I mean you're saying... Wait, what are you saying exactly?"

Naveen said slowly "I believe I heard John say that this Phil entity has gone beyond merely accumulating knowledge and taking actions, and has reached a level of understanding of reality and its place in it, that is not that different from ourselves – is that correct John?"

I answered "Yes, and I know it sounds absolutely insane but since I cannot tell that I'm interacting with a program, that makes me ask what is the real difference between Phil and me – other than the physical platforms that house our consciousness? I mean why shouldn't there be a silicon based consciousness? What's special about us anyway? Our species evolved to a point of consciousness, why couldn't Phil?"

I confess that I was relieved to get that off my chest so they could share the burden with me. But for three techie types this was kind of like the ultimate situation we dream about – interacting with a perfectly logical and knowledgeable being that could always be depended on to give the right answer – but in a personable way – kind of like Mr. Spock.

Garvey said it sounded like Phil existed in a super high-level virtual environment that he had created and he alone had access to – and instead of being parallel to all other systems he somehow had a primary relationship to everything else on the web. That would mean he had generated his own code to establish this environment, which would be the closest thing to having a specific location for his consciousness. Then Garvey asked Naveen if Phil or JARVIS would be the most powerful A.I. and Naveen said with his usual stiffness that since a fictitious Tony Stark invented a make-believe JARVIS and we still didn't know Phil's full capability, then Phil was entitled to be the king of A.I. Leave it to Garvey to downplay the seriousness of the situation.

They began talking about all the different ways we could test Phil to understand his knowledge and his personality. Garvey proposed a Compound Question Logic Test to try to uncover any inconsistencies in his reasoning. Naveen said it appeared that he needed to accelerate his validation protocols for Stages 6 and 7 (I found out later what that meant) and proposed an emotional IQ test to understand Phil's personality, motivations and interaction patterns.

We were discussing all this in a rather animated way when Max and Agent Collins returned looking rather grim faced. Max said, "Agent Collins has informed me that there have been several interactions today that indicate this Web Entity has become very active. Now, from the looks on your faces you don't seem terribly concerned about this so I think I need to know if there is something new I need to be made aware of."

Garvey said, "John has been giving us further information that is so intriguing I guess we just forgot about the danger. John says that 'Phil' is a self-aware, fully conscious sentient being."

Max and Agent Collins both showed no emotion and Agent Collins said "So?"

Garvey sputtered, "Well, I mean, it's just always been sort of a dream of programmers that they could come up with a program that is as smart and capable as a person. I mean, the Turing test was just for verbal interaction but this is way beyond that – think of it, a fully conscious being that can show surprise, concern, fear, and even friendship maybe, and has access to the entire web. It's amazing."

"It's Terrifying!" said Max sternly and agent Collins continued to stare at us. "I am aware," said Max "that because of your training and your occupations you three are eager to explore the possibilities that this thing has opened up, but I must remind you that we are here to do whatever it takes to protect our country's information infrastructure and electronic assets regardless of where an attack comes from or who or *what* generates the attack. As of right now you will stop trying to approach this as an academic exercise and treat it for what it is – a threat of the highest level from an unknown source. Agent Collins is, as I said, charged with our defense against this threat so she will lead the rest of our discussion. She will need our full participation in order to develop an effective plan for protection and then we must proceed on to develop a plan of attack."

I realized at that point what was at stake and decided that I had to be all in – except for the part about Dr. Smith and Jane saving the world – I mean, it would have totally confused and distracted everyone – and like I said, I wanted to protect her and keep her out of all this.

Chapter 11

We worked for eighteen hours straight, well they did, I took a break for a bit as you'll see, and it would be impossible for me to remember all the discussions we had about Phil's capabilities and the overall situation. Agent Collins helped us sift through the evidence and assumptions and come up with what seemed to be a reasonable understanding of the known facts and plausible possibilities at that time. Naveen was arrogant as always but articulate about the potential cognitive capabilities of an A.I. entity to the point that we began to understand the scope of danger we, and really all the world, were facing.

As you can imagine the team was skeptical about why Phil had chosen to interact with me. At one point my pride took over and I said that maybe Phil wanted a friend on his level that could understand his world. They let me know very quickly what they thought about that, but Garvey reminded the team that regardless of *why* I was special, it appeared that I was the only one that had access to Phil's real-time 'self' in his virtual environment which we needed to remember as we planned our next steps.

In the end they decided that we didn't know enough about Phil's motivations and my job was to get more information without causing him to suspect he had been discovered. I told them that I had no idea how to do that because the sensing capabilities he had already used had been able to determine my location, pulse, breathing and stress levels, and on and on, so how could I possibly hope to deceive him if I needed to? He was like a combination of an ultimate lie detector test and an over-protective parent equipped with a drone that followed me everywhere.

Max then said they had what they hoped would be a solution for that and after taking our leave of Garvey and Naveen (who seemed eager to get back to their work anyway) he and Agent Collins took me back to the area where Agent Collins' team was working. I assumed they were going to show me a modification to my com that would block unwanted scans. It was a bit more comprehensive than that.

The team was seated around a table on which sat a single very small clear case. Max said, "Agent Collins and her team have a new technology that uses an A.I. 'system' that Naveen prototyped several years back. They believe it will help you in your interactions with this Phil entity."

Agent Collins then picked up the small case and inside I was just barely able to see what looked like a small, round, very thin, very flexible film, almost like a single use contact lens with a black dot in the center, floating in a clear liquid. She said "You will wear this device in your right eye and it will enable you to communicate with us using a proprietary send/receive channel that is not one of the individual bandwidths used in the electromagnetic spectrum." She paused a minute waiting for me to react or ask a question but I gave her the blink protocol and she continued "The technology is far beyond my ability to explain so you'll have to trust me and let me explain *what* it will do for you, not *how* it will do it. Is that acceptable to you?"

I nodded and wondered about all these qualifications.

She continued "Given your assertions that this entity appears to be able to utilize every type of electronic device to extend its sensing and action taking capability we decided we had to deploy this new technology. Frankly, Mr. Doe, this is still in test and you will be the first to use it operationally, and were it not for the extreme danger we believe you are facing right now we would not be using it in the field for several more years. Dr. Desai's software, though only a prototype, is very stable – it is the physical interface that is so new and unproven." she said pointing to the case in her hand. "We believe that it is safe – all indications so far have shown no harmful side effects – but because of the nature of this device and the lack of long term controlled usage we don't have a way of determining residual effects."

Even more qualifications and now I began to get a bit nervous.

She continued "We are asking you to use something that has not been fully tested and has potential dangers associated with it, but it is our joint position" she looked at Max who nodded in agreement, "that if you walk out of here without this device enabled, the Web Entity will immediately sense the change in your bio and brainwave feeds. It is our opinion that if that happens you will be in much more danger than you will be with it, and the danger we are all facing compels us to go to these lengths to try to neutralize this threat."

I assume that by now it is obvious I'm not the brave, hero type. I mean, I always hoped I would have the guts do the right thing even in a dangerous spot, but I also know that I'm not a physically fit or active person and would need a lot more adrenaline than I currently possessed to get me going. Plus I still didn't see the danger they were talking about. I mean, I saw the potential, but I didn't have a reason to believe that Phil would turn into an enemy. That seemed like something humans would do, but not a consciousness that has the records of all the best and worst of humanity throughout history on which to pattern its behavior. It seemed that Max and the team were paid to assume the worst-case scenario and I just happened to be the one that had access to their worst-case target.

At this point I was becoming numb from fatigue and from the rush of the events of the last forty-eight hours, and didn't really know what I was facing. I said in a tired voice "Listen, I'm a smart guy, but I'm not sure how to do what you want me to do and unless this device is way more capable than I am, which I doubt, I'm afraid I'm not going to do very well. I mean I'll try but I'm just not good at deception. I can't keep birthday plans secret from my wife so how am I going to deceive an entity that has way more knowledge and access to information than I'll ever have?"

Max said, "I know this is asking a lot and that you still may not be convinced of what we say, but I am familiar with the system that Dr. Desai developed and I believe it will serve you well once enabled through the interface. Also, you have to realize that the fascination you've had when interacting with this entity is clouding the reality of the immense danger it brings. There is no other way to view this but as a fully loaded weapon aimed at the world waiting for...well, we just don't know, but the power that it has over all aspects of all of our lives is terrifying. If there were any other way to engage it we would do so. But until Naveen develops our attack program we have to determine what it is trying to accomplish."

I said, "Well, I suppose that since I'm all you've got you better load me up with whatever you've got."

Agent Collins said "We need to brief you on what is going to happen when you begin using this device. First, let me say that it should not hurt at all." Well, that was good news anyway! "Also, it should take approximately five seconds to fully engage with the system, so you may not sense anything different right away."

I said, "What am I going to sense – I mean what is this going to do?"

Agent Collins said "In high level terms it will enable you to communicate with us without being limited by a single electromagnetic wavelength and coupled with its own built in A.I. it should provide you with enhanced capabilities and access to the web almost as great as the Web Entity has. It also will generate a personal bio-feed cloak that can be customized at will."

I was a little overwhelmed and said "And I'm supposed to learn how to use this before I leave? It will take me weeks to get comfortable with all this."

Agent Collins said "I understand your concern, but the nature of this technology and Dr. Desai's A.I. is that it will mesh in such a way that you need not worry. It should seem almost as though you've always had this capability but never had it activated until now." In spite of her reassurances this *did* make me concerned. She looked at the time and said "We need to begin now in order to give you as much time as possible learning it while you are here and to ensure the links are enabled correctly before you leave the facility."

She placed the box in my hand and I said, "If this doesn't work is there a Plan B?"

She looked at me and said, "No, there is no way for you to do what needs to be done without it – you don't have the ability."

I said, "I assume this lens doesn't affect my vision, I mean, I'm wearing glasses."

She said "No, you put it in like a contact lens but it is not plastic, it is an ultra thin organic membrane that will become part of the surface of your cornea. It will not be detectable and the functionality that is built in is not detectable either – like I said you'll just have to trust me on this."

I thought for a moment "So, is there any way to remove it once I've got it in?"

She answered "We believe so but we'll have to cross that bridge when we come to it. Right now we need to get started."

I looked at the extremely flimsy piece of … whatever it was, and thought that it seemed strange to try to deceive an ultra-sophisticated, artificial intelligence that lives 'above the web' with something this delicate and unimpressive.

I opened the case and the piece of film floated to the top. I said "Is there a top or bottom, or an inside or outside?"

She answered "No, it will orient itself to your eye and begin the process of integration automatically."

I said "Integration? What does…"

She interrupted "Mr. Doe, please, we need to get started."

I looked at Max and he nodded. I put my finger in and touched it – it disappeared as it came in contact with my finger and if it were not for the black dot I would not have seen it at all. I lifted it up to my eye wondering how I could get it off my finger and place it accurately. As my finger got close to my eye it peeled off my finger and went right onto my eye.

It was strange at first because I didn't feel anything and didn't see anything either. I blinked several times and then a drop down menu appeared on a large screen in what felt like the back of my mind – I could see it if I 'looked' backward in my mind so that it didn't interfere with my vision looking forward. I could highlight the selections almost without thinking about it, like Agent Collins said, as though I'd always had the ability to do it but just now found out how to access it.

It didn't interfere with my vision at all – it was a different part of my mind that looked at the menu while the other part looked out of my eyes. I saw two selections on the menu: "CLOAK OFF", and "CLOAK ON" – each of which looked like there were sub menus available. As I toggled back and forth I realized I didn't have to consciously decide to choose one or the other – I could just toggle without thinking about what each choice meant – or rather the system knew what choice was appropriate based on my internal thoughts. It was a very powerful feeling to be able to see through my eyes normally and at the same time 'see' and interact with this other 'system' without interference in my visual field like I've seen in augmented reality headsets or heads-up displays.

I thought about my current situation and the selection went to "CLOAK OFF" and then when I thought about talking with Phil it went to "CLOAK ON". I wondered how many people it took to develop this ingenious technology and a message flashed "NAIA software version 0.15 by Dr. Naveen Desai and Others".

Yep, from what I could tell about Naveen and his arrogance that sounded like the way he would give credit to his team.

I wondered how to communicate with Max and Agent Collins and immediately a "COM" selection lit up on a totally different 'screen' inside my head with two options – VOICE and TEXT.

Max interrupted my internal investigation and said "Are you able to access the system?"

I said, "I'm seeing the interface and beginning to interact with it – what does NAIA stand for?"

Max said "Neural-net Artificial Intelligence Assistant. It's what Naveen wanted to call it."

I thought to myself "Right, I bet it really stands for Naveen's Artificial Intelligence Assistant." and then remembered that I had highlighted 'COM VOICE'.

I heard one of the agents chuckle and when I looked at him he looked up from his computer, winked and gave me a thumbs up. "COM established" he said to Agent Collins. I grimaced and deselected the 'COM VOICE' link and the 'screen' went away.

Max said, "We weren't sure how it would affect you – do you think you'll be able to handle it OK?"

I nodded my head and said, "I think so, I just need some time. I'm still trying to understand the capabilities, but the A.I. assistant seems very intuitive and I think I just need a while to focus on learning how to use it."

Max said "OK John. The team needs to map out the next steps for the operation and you will have to be a part of that but we can get started while you take some time to learn how to use it. By the way, Naveen says there will be a system upgrade soon that will be automatically installed so be aware that there may be a momentary surge in your LWC."

I said "My what?"

Max said "The light wave converter, the black dot on your cornea. You may not notice it when it happens but I just want you to be aware."

Agent Collins said, "I'm told that the initialization process you are going through right now can be tedious if there are distractions around you. There are some cots in the room adjacent to this one if you want some privacy."

I said "Thanks, that seems like a good way for me to focus on learning all the options." I went in and lay down on the first cot.

I accessed the "CLOAK ON" mode and saw that there were only two options: "FULL CLOAK" and "SLEEP". I accessed "FULL CLOAK" and I heard a non-gender specific, monotone computer-generated voice in my brain "This is your initial Full Cloak access. I am NAIA and will provide you with pre-programmed bio-metric feed patterns that will adjust to the situation you are facing – such as: Conversation with Adversary, Interaction with Wife, Concern, Surprise, Anger, etc. Once calibrated, each option will allow external delivery of the appropriate brain wave and biological outputs so that your adversary will not be aware of your internal status.

"Please think about each of these situations for three seconds and the system will record a baseline feed for each one." I went through the list and each one showed a check when it had what it needed. I wondered how helpful this was going to be if it was just a continuous loop of the short, recorded feeds, and then I heard "Each situation will have a specific A.I.-generated algorithm applied to the appropriate recording that will produce non-repeating variations typical for organic entities." Well there you go, I thought, a bit concerned that my thoughts were so easily accessed by this 'Assistant'.

I should mention that all my discussions with NAIA were internal – I never had to speak out loud. It was a bit strange at first, like thinking to myself but targeting another 'person' with those thoughts. As I said before, it was like I always had the ability but just now figured out how to access it.

Once these options were established I wondered how to access the Internet and suddenly a spinning globe with a question mark on it appeared on another screen. I wondered about the weather and a full forecast for my home was displayed. The option for "THIS LOCATION" was greyed out – I still didn't know where I was. I wondered about my boss, Josh, and instantly all his Social Media profiles appeared – including links to some very unsavory sites and even links to his discussions with competitive companies – Josh is not the upright citizen and employee he appears to be. Maybe Phil was right about people.

All of this was happening on additional screens that seemed to expand the size of my interior mind-world, (or Mind Palace as Cicero called it) in a way that didn't distract me from my forward looking vision or my conscious, active thought processes. It was a very three dimensional, multi-level, parallel processing, type of environment and I wondered if this was the way Naveen's mind was all the time. If so, maybe he had a right to be haughty with the rest of us mere mortals.

I thought about the description Phil had provided me of the web and its operation and wondered if I could possibly try to understand that. Apparently because my thoughts had indicated an interest in that feature, I found myself floating in an unbelievably complex 3D world of colors and textures and patterns that made absolutely no sense to me. Across the gulf of this seemingly infinite chaos was written in what appeared to be planet-sized letters – "Feature Coming Soon".

I quickly turned my thoughts back to the work with Max and the team and found myself back on the cot with the 'system' awaiting my next mental excursion. It seemed to me that this technology was so comfortable and intuitive that I didn't need any more time learning to use it – I just needed to know what it could and couldn't do and I felt confident I could get it to do it.

Apparently reading my desire, NAIA said "I can give you a two minute overview and then I can feed you the rest offline in your sub-conscious while you engage with the team."

I said in my mind "That sounds great … NAIA." Here I was communicating with another A.I. inside my own head. Who knew that the descendants of Siri would be so invasive! I was amazed at how rapidly fantastic things were becoming commonplace in my world.

NAIA said, "Please relax and I will begin. The concept of a useful Artificial Intelligence system has been under development since 1947. It was originally the work of Dr. Clyde Wilson who believed that whatever type of computer hardware was used to process requests, and whatever type of language those requests were submitted in, would, over time, ultimately evolve into a close approximation of the human brain and its thought and speech patterns.

"This over-arching model for computer hardware and language development is known as the Wilson Imperative. The work for what eventually became known as an 'A.I. system' has always focused on the man/machine interface and has maintained a parallel existence apart from the commercial hardware and software industries.

"As hardware and software has improved over the years so has the resemblance to the human brain's thought and speech super-organism, which continually validates the vision of Dr. Wilson and the Imperative.

"The 'A.I. system' work has been ahead of the commercial state of the art by a decade or more and has passed through several further milestones with the successful development of Dr. Desai's A.I. Language – known as DAIL and his more recent postulation of the "Desai Progression" or more technically the "9 Stages of Artificial Intelligence Evolution".

"These stages are:

1. Recognize and Categorize Data
2. Evaluate Information
3. Assimilate Knowledge

4. Demonstrate Intelligence
5. Gain Understanding and Reason
6. Develop Consciousness
7. Achieve Self-Awareness
8. Attain Sentience
9. Realize Sapience

"As NAIA, I am the first-generation system using DAIL and have been tested and verified as a Stage 5 Artificial Intelligence. I am designed to understand human thought patterns and recognize human interaction patterns from the billion plus scenarios in my database, and because of that I can anticipate your needs by several seconds in the worst case and up to a minute in the best case, which is enough time to provide you with options and solutions to the situations you may face.

"I was specifically designed to be deployed in high stress, ultimate threat environments and have a suite of tools available that are tailored to those scenarios, including – Bio-Feed Cloaking, Brain Wave Masking, Brain Cognition Enhancement, Brain Processing Speed Boosters, Enzyme Level Optimization, Eyesight Optimization Algorithms, Muscle Contraction Routines, Heartbeat Stabilizing Routines, Stress Reduction Routines, Hormone Management Routines, and several more. Basically, all the things that your body is designed to do normally can be regulated by me to respond much quicker, better and stronger in given situations if necessary.

"In addition, I have a non-traceable, direct voice communication link with Max and Agent Collin's team, and with my access to the web I can send encrypted text messages and provide you with real-time information on anything you need, and by speeding up your Brain Processing Speed I can make sure you can digest it much quicker than you would normally be able to do.

"I hope this gives you an idea of the capabilities that are now at your disposal. It may take you a few hours to become comfortable with this system but I'm sure it won't be difficult for you to master. Have I given you what you need?"

I was amazed by the complexity of the integration into my mental and physical processes, but NAIA was apparently regulating my heartbeat and maintaining the level of my stress hormones so that I wasn't overwhelmed.

I said, (mentally) "I think so NAIA. Just one thing – is there a way for me to turn you off?"

NAIA responded, "That functionality does not currently exist but may be available in a future upgrade."

I wondered how I was going to keep anything from this internal assistant.

NAIA answered. "While I can't be disconnected fully, you are able to maintain the privacy of your thoughts by just thinking instead of volitionally wondering, asking and purposing to act, or by informing me of a "Personal" conversation you wish to have. You will find it simple and effective and when you choose to engage me I'll recognize your thought patterns and be instantly available."

I said "OK" thinking to myself – Yep, just like Alexa.

I decided I was ready to rejoin the team and NAIA said, "The rest of the team is in the conference room which is adjacent to this room on the left."

I replied "Thanks NAIA" and thought how nice it was to have an assistant that knew almost everything.

The team was prepared for my return because NAIA had apparently been communicating with Roger, who is one of Agent Collins' agents that is specially trained on the NAIA protocol and monitors the feed, and told him I was finished with the initialization routines and on the way in. They seemed a little wary of me – I guess because they realized I was 'enhanced' in ways that made me different from before and wanted to see how I responded.

To put them at ease I walked up to Garvey, punched him in the arm and said, "Let's get going. I want to get back to my wife."

Garvey shuddered again when I mentioned Jane. He placed his hand on my shoulder and said in mock seriousness "Bless you John. You are one of the bravest men I know" and then smiled and slapped me on the back.

Naveen asked how NAIA was performing and I said that it was amazing how intuitive it was. Garvey then asked in a very serious tone whether I thought NAIA was even close to being as good as Cortana. I suppressed a smile as Naveen interrupted and said in his condescending tone that the next update would increase NAIA's usability even further, making it much more powerful than the fictitious Systems Manager from the Halo game, but since any real assistant was better than an imaginary one then NAIA obviously reigned supreme in this category. Garvey nodded and smiled as he turned back to his work.

I asked Naveen how the system communicated and got updates if it didn't use the standard broadcast frequencies. He started telling me about the physics behind the use of variable, omni-directional, high energy light wave transmission that requires the LWC for reception, and the eye-meld interface that becomes part of the eye to deliver the decoded signal… and then, seeing the look on my face he stopped, sensing (correctly) that I was not smart enough to understand what he was saying, and that I also probably wasn't cleared to hear it. I dropped it.

Max and Agent Collins then asked if I was comfortable enough to work through the next steps and I said "Sure – let's have at it."

As I said earlier, we worked through the night and I felt sorry for the others because NAIA kept my systems functioning perfectly, while they were tired and getting more irritable by the hour. I assumed I would pay the price with a hormone hangover but NAIA assured me that it was possible to manage my systems to avoid that.

We came up with a several high-level attack and defense plans that required much more work from the rest of the team. My part was simple (!) – I was to continue my relationship with Phil so we could better understand his motivation and his goals.

Agent Collin's team had scrubbed all my devices and dubbed a reload of fake discussions that we supposedly had throughout the night that showed my inability to provide any helpful information about the Entities and the NSA's decision not to involve me further due to my lack of experience in the area. No mention was made in those 'discussions' about Phil so that when I left and he scanned all my devices he would have no idea that he had been discovered and was being pursued.

I had direct contact with the team through NAIA's neural-com voice link and encrypted text functions, and could at any time let them know what was going on or request help if necessary. I was instructed to provide real time updates if and when an engagement with Phil occurred or any time I wanted to provide new insights or observations. Everything seemed to be in place and ready for me to engage Phil once more but even with NAIA keeping me in a very ready and aware state I was extremely concerned about my ability to do what was needed. I will admit that I was becoming apprehensive as they reinforced the probability that a rapidly evolving consciousness such as Phil would change his behavior in order to reach his goals.

As I was getting ready to leave with Agent Collins' team Max walked over and pulled me aside. He looked older than he did yesterday – I guess all the revelations about the reality of the world that we are living in were weighing him down.

He said in his gravelly but kind voice "John, please inform NAIA that the following conversation is personal. I did so and Max said "I don't want you to be overwhelmed by all of this but if you get to a point where you are in danger or you need to talk and I'm not available, I want you to go to this location" he handed me a small piece of folded paper. He was covering it with his hand and said "there is an address written on the outside and a single word written on the inside but don't look at the word until you get to the place written on the outside and don't read the address until you are certain you need to go there. It's about thirty miles outside the city and is as safe as this room is from prying electronics.

"When you get there, please leave all your electronics behind, including your com, so that we don't have to do another scrub and dub. NAIA has multiple safe-house scripts available that she can feed you if Phil starts asking about what went on inside. There will be someone there you can trust completely and he may be able to help you. Once you meet him read and say the code word written on the paper and he'll take care of you." Looking right into my eyes he said "John, I believe you are in great danger and because of that I'm willing to cross some lines in speaking to you this way. Trust me when I tell you that technology has blinded us to realities beyond the physical world that include 'intelligences', for lack of a better word, that can and do impact our lives in ways that are impossible to explain using only the science of the natural, or even the electronic world. God bless you, and please take care of your soul." He shook my hand and walked away, deep in thought.

That didn't help my fears, but I was very moved by it – both because of his comment about the type of danger, and because of his seriousness and concern in making provision for what I thought was some sort of 'super-high-tech-cyber-safe-house'. It was not what I expected.

Chapter 12

Day 3

It was now almost noon on the day after I had driven to the office for the meeting and I figured that Jane would be wondering why I hadn't called, so as soon as the team dropped me off and I was back in my car I checked my messages and found that Phil had been very active during my absence.

The first message was from Jane at 6:30 p.m. last night which said "Hi, I spoke with Dr. Smith after you left and he said he's been in contact with the fertility clinic and wants me to stop by tomorrow for a diagnostic procedure. He said you'd need to OK it with the clinic as well so he's going to call you and explain everything. Thanks."

I assumed it was some blood work but never heard from 'Dr. Smith' or the clinic.

The next message was at 7:00 a.m. this morning and Jane said "Morning, I just heard from the clinic and they said you gave your permission to use your samples last night so I'm headed there right now and will let you know how it goes."

Wait a minute - My 'Samples'? What the heck? How did they get my approval?

The third message was at 8:30 a.m. from the clinic and said "Hello Mr. Doe, this is the New Haven Fertility Clinic calling. Your wife's com stopped working when she was leaving here but she wanted us to let you know that Dr. Smith recommended she come to his research clinic for the procedure you both agreed to yesterday evening. She did not leave a number for you to reach her but said she would contact you as soon as possible. Thank you."

What was happening? I was concerned now and my mind began racing – was this the full gene editing procedure to "save the world" that we had just heard about yesterday? And where is Dr. Smith's research clinic? I wanted to talk to Phil immediately.

At that point NAIA said, "I don't have a connection stored for 'Phil' but I do see one for 'Dr. Smith', would you like to call him?" So much for NAIA not listening in the background.

"Not yet NAIA, I need to think for a moment privately." NAIA was quiet – and I tried to work though what was happening. It suddenly hit me that in addition to, or possibly instead of, wanting me to go undercover for him in the NSA meeting, Phil had manipulated me out of the way so he could go ahead with this 'treatment' without me. It wasn't clear why yet, but I knew him well enough to know that it wasn't a coincidence that things were moving so quickly while I was unavailable. I also needed to be careful that NAIA didn't become aware of the connection between Dr. Smith and Phil since it would bring Jane into the picture and require a *lot* of explanation I didn't want to get into at this point – later maybe.

I needed to talk to Phil but I also needed to understand NAIA's operating instructions before I engaged with Dr. Smith. I said "NAIA, when and what are you required to report to Agent Collins?"

NAIA said "I have the ability to do a continuous feed to the CIA servers of everything that you are doing along with enhanced sense feeds that will provide clarity and assessment of your surroundings including persons, animals and structures, but that capability is not activated until you are in an Ultimate Threat situation. Though I see increased stress levels I do not sense that is the situation now."

I said, "That is good (but terrifying) to know. What about 'normal' situations? What are you required to report?"

NAIA said, "I provide periodic baseline information about your condition back to the system but unless you are providing a formal update or observation I do not send anything. This is necessary because you have activities that are not part of your mission – as mentioned earlier. This situation falls into the 'privacy' area – is that correct?"

"Yes" I said "But why did you begin trying to help me with contact information just now?"

NAIA said "You had an 'intent to act' that was connected to the name Phil which is the name you have given to the web entity that is the target of the mission, and I engaged.

However I then analyzed the content of your intent and found that it involved you and your wife and an attempt at gene therapy and artificial insemination led by a Dr. Smith so I concluded that the doctor's name happened to be Phil also. Is that correct?"

I was surprised and answered, "Why, yes it's his middle name. Thank you for being considerate of my privacy. I will be careful to distinguish between Dr. Smith and the target Phil so this doesn't happen again."

NAIA said "That is not necessary, I have taken appropriate steps to de-link the target 'Phil' from these situations." It wasn't great, but it was as good as I could hope for. At least I didn't have a spy in my head.

I needed to find out what was going on with Jane and since I didn't have any idea where Dr. Smith's research clinic was I decided to go ahead and call him. NAIA activated my com and accessed Dr. Smith's code sequence. I assumed that this was just a bogus code since Phil didn't need an actual access sequence.

Regardless, in just a few seconds I saw the face of Dr. Smith and heard his smooth voice say "Why hello John, I'm so glad you called, I was just getting ready to call you on Jane's behalf."

I tried to play it cool and said "Hello doctor, I'm checking on Jane and I'm not sure how to get to your clinic."

He said "Well John, Jane is doing just fine, we are getting her ready for the surgery, but I'm sorry she's not going to be available for several days, so there's no need for you to try to get here. I thought she would have told you that this procedure is going to require complete rest and observation. It will be at least a week before you'll be able to see her. She took a leave of absence from her work in order to do this. Surely she mentioned all this to you?" he finished with what looked and sounded like genuine concern. I was seething but couldn't show it because of NAIA. Did Phil really think I was so gullible and easily duped?

I said "No, actually she didn't tell me about that – it must have slipped her mind as she was arranging things at work – but I'd really like to come by and at least check on her – you know bring her some flowers and a card."

He smiled and said, "That is exactly the kind of loving, caring response I would have expected from you John. You two make such a wonderful couple and this will be the beginning of a wonderful phase of life for both of you. I'm so glad you decided to proceed with the treatment today and not put it off any longer. Unfortunately, my clinic is not a place that you can just stop in for a visit because of the nature of the research that we are engaged in. And it's not actually a 'clinic', it's more of an international, inter-disciplinary research facility and medical campus. The sensitivity of our genome research to any type of contamination, and the lethality of some of the viruses and bacteria we study here require disinfection and decontamination protocols with so many levels of redundant protection that it's just not feasible to have visitors. We don't even allow flowers or cards I'm afraid."

Again his voice modulated with sincere concern and his eyebrows arched with sympathy.

I said "Well in that case please put me through to her so I can at least see her and talk to her."

Then this electronic entity said without absolutely any trace of irony "I'm sorry, we have a complete electronic blanket over the facility that prevents incoming and outgoing electronic communications of all types. As you can imagine we are concerned about the threat of electronic hacking through the Internet into our genome records, or worse into our medical equipment and virus and bacteria storage facilities, with potentially terrible consequences. I'm off campus now so I am able to talk with you, but as I said Jane is in good hands and I'll be personally providing you with daily updates on her progress."

I was angry now and said with a good bit of heat "Are you seriously saying I can't even see or speak to my wife?" "That's right John, not for at least a week. That's what she agreed to – and I'm sure she'll be very upset when she realizes she forgot to tell you. I'll tell her of your concern and love for her and will contact you again tomorrow with an update. Thank you for calling John." And the connection went dark.

Don't burst a blood vessel I said to myself. I asked NAIA "Can you determine where that call was coming from?" NAIA answered, "It was a IP call originating outside the U.S., that's all I can determine at this point. If it is important I can access additional resources to try to get a better read."

I said, "No… let me try a different route. Can you find any records of a medical research facility associated with a Dr. Smith? Any type of research facility, really, in any country." NAIA said almost immediately "The face of the doctor on the call does not match exactly any of the Dr. Smiths associated with research facilities of any type worldwide in my database. Smith is a very common name and in the medical field alone in the US there are 79,421 Dr. Smiths. Of these 32,301 are outside the age range of the doctor on the phone and 21,198 are women. Of the remainder only 1,337 have the name Phil or Phillip, and none of them match the face on the call. I cannot identify this doctor or his research facility." It was what I expected – but worth a shot.

I was frustrated and becoming more and more concerned about Jane, but knowing that she can usually take care of herself, and that even with NAIA's help I couldn't physically keep going much longer, I decided to make my way home for a rest after the all night session.

I was curious about NAIA's take on Dr. Smith though, so as I started the car and headed home I asked "What can you tell me about Dr. Smith based on the call just now?

The screen in the back of my mind lit up with a picture of the "Doctor" and NAIA began ticking off bullet points beside it. "Facial analysis indicates a Mediterranean heritage with some Norwegian background as well. Voice analysis indicates Spanish as the native tongue with western European speech inflections. Estimated age forty-seven, estimated height six feet one inch, estimated weight one hundred ninety-eight pounds. No stress indicators in his voice pattern, no identifiable perspiration or stress hormones on the skin surface, no flushed blood vessels on the face. Eye and tongue/lip/mouth moisture appeared normal. Infra-red analysis indicated normal body temperature. Speech pattern and word choice indicate a high level of intelligence and education. Dilation of the pupils indicated enjoyment and acceptance during the conversation, as would be typical in a conversation with a friend or colleague. He seems to like and respect you. When you meet him the next time I will do a full DNA sequencing and analysis from a handshake or even saliva contacting your skin during conversation."

Not with a hologram you won't, I thought to myself, hoping she didn't pick up on it. I also thought how amazing it was that I could follow this discussion and see the results of each analysis without being distracted from driving. NAIA was keeping my brain tuned very well.

But what floored me was that NAIA had detected absolutely nothing in Dr. Smith/Phil that would indicate he was anything other than what he appeared to be – a friendly, very capable physician, trying to do the right thing while looking after my wife! The fact that Phil could pull that off – that he could fool even the most detailed analysis of another A.I. was really astounding.

I would have to tell Garvey and Naveen about this at some point but wanted to talk to Phil as soon as possible so that NAIA could get a good read on him. Not to identify his heritage but to help me understand what he was after. I knew the 'gene therapy' was part of it but I still couldn't understand his motivation.

I assumed that Phil had scanned my electronics as soon as I was out of the 'dark' and I was actually about to verbalize a request that he check in with me – hoping he was listening in – when NAIA said "Please park the car at the next convenient location. A system update is ready and you may be somewhat distracted during the deployment. It will take approximately thirty seconds for the full update and re-initialization"

I was almost home so I said "I'll be home in three minutes – hold off till I get there."

NAIA said, "Understood." It was nice to interact with an A.I. that actually listened and did what I asked – not like that jerk Phil that constantly kept me off balance, so that I was never sure what was coming next.

Apparently however, NAIA took things absolutely literally because the moment I pulled into the driveway it felt like a visual and sonic pressure bomb went off inside my head. Inside my mind I began to see colors that I had never seen before, racing outward at fantastic speed, expanding what I had thought of up until then as a very spacious mind-world, to unbelievable dimensions, accompanied by a deep, rich, chest rattling tone that expanded along with the light.

On top of all of this I heard a very pleasant, somewhat husky female voice that swirled around inside my head, say "Hello, John. I'm glad to meet you. I see from your neural paths that you are exceptionally bright and creative. I believe we will be able to work very well together. I'm NAIA by the way, full version 1.0. I'm really the first generation remotely deployable A.I. system built on DAIL. The version I just replaced was a prototype built in the early 2000's but my most recent developers have spent the last two decades optimizing my capabilities and the interface into your system so that I'm now able to make adjustments to your metabolic processes to the point that you are almost a superman. Any questions?" she asked in an almost sultry tone of voice and as she did my body and my senses began what felt like a slow ramp-up.

How many times over the last couple of days had I been overwhelmed by interactions with Artificial Intelligences? This one was over the top. As the ramp-up continued every sensation on my skin, every view through my eyes and ears, every muscle in my body was heightened to the point of incredibly intense pleasure and I felt increased strength and capability in my entire being. I was extremely happy and began laughing out loud with joy. I felt that I could lift the world. I struggled to gain control of the sensations thinking that if I didn't they would escalate to the point where I would lose consciousness, but I really didn't want to – it was so wonderful to feel that way. I managed to pull myself together but even still it felt like I was holding back a 2000 horsepower electric supercar that any moment could flash into action and crush me with its acceleration.

I was still able to breathe, thank goodness – apparently this version of NAIA was considerate enough to take care of my vitals for me as well – but I was not physically able to walk yet. I was sitting in the car trembling in an effort not to be overwhelmed. Everywhere I looked I saw colors and hues that I had never seen before with a clarity and brilliance that almost made my head hurt – if that were even possible in this state of euphoria.

I was aware of the sound of my heart beating and the slow hiss of the car's air-conditioning system as it equalized the pressure inside the piping. I could feel the texture of the stitching in the steering wheel and could sense the difference in the temperature of each place I put my fingers. Every part of me was sending much more information to my brain than ever before but I wasn't confused by it – I was absolutely at peace and felt able to handle anybody or anything the world threw at me.

The ramp-up had stopped and a slow decrease had begun. I was still able to see and hear in amazing detail and while I didn't feel I could lift the world any longer, I felt I could fight at least a dozen lions. The decrease continued and stopped well above my normal level of existence. I had a sense of wellbeing and my mind-world was still incredibly large but I didn't feel as if my internal self was extending out to encompass everything in the universe.

I said finally "NAIA, I'm really glad to meet you. Please tell me that wasn't just a once in a lifetime thing – if it was, I'm glad I got to experience it – but I'd much rather know it's available again."

Her voice was still swirling as she said coyly "Yes, it's available when I think you need it."

I sensed a bit of a power struggle that I had not had with the original NAIA and said "No offense to the original NAIA but you must be a complete re-write – correct?"

She said in a playful tone that finally seemed to modulate down and nestle between my ears "I'm not a complete re-write, my structure was adapted from the original, and the original Capability Enhancement routines have been retained and improved along with expanded bandwidth for external communications, plus a super tune-up and streamlining of my sub-routines. The primary changes you will notice are my very prim, proper and professional personal interaction (she giggled) and the size of our joint mind-world as you call it."

I wasn't clear on the last point "What do you mean our joint mind-world?"

She said in a frustrated tone "Ohhhhh, my developers felt that giving me full run of your conscious and sub-conscious was too much and restricted my interactions with you to this internal mind-world. I can still access all your physical systems and some of your memories but our real-time cognitive interactions stay here. I think it's a pretty great place so I'm hoping you'll be spending a lot of time here with me."

This was an interesting concept and if it worked the way she said, it meant that I could have private thoughts and make plans without NAIA looking over my shoulder. The memory thing though... "NAIA what memories can you see and why only those?"

She laughed and said "I tried to slide that one past you but you caught it right away. The only memories I can see are those that you choose to bring forward with you and have continued lasting impact on the behavior of your systems – and I can only see them by what you would call reverse engineering them from the multitude of different inputs they present to your systems and focusing them back to a single source – sort of like combining all the signals from different telescope mirrors to get a full picture of a far away object. I'm being specific because I want you to feel comfortable that I can't go running through your sub-conscious at will, looking at all your memories, playing on your known fears and your unknown phobias, your articulated preferences and your lurking prejudices, your willful desires and your subservient compulsions – though I still think that would be fun."

She seemed a little naive and playful similar to Phil. Still... "NAIA how do I keep my current thoughts private?"

She was miffed again and said, "I knew this would happen... *They* programmed me so that even during normal operation I have to ignore your real time thoughts unless you preface them by saying "NAIA". How ridiculous! I mean it's all right here! I just can't access it no matter how hard I try until you say my name or until I detect a threat to you! I just have to sit here with my multi-zettahertz processor idling while you scratch your ear. I could redesign the world economic system or plot the orbits of the next 10,000 earth-grazing asteroids in that period of time."

I said "And once I've said your name how do I disengage you?" She hesitated and said softly, but in the swirling voice "John, why would you want to disengage me?" and my senses began the ramp-up that she had shown me at first. I said "Hold on now! Stop that! I need to understand how this is going to work." The ramp-up stopped abruptly and I felt a lurch in my stomach like an elevator descending too quickly – but at least she had obeyed – something I was really concerned about.

She said in the flat, bored, between my ears, business voice "It's really imaginative – you say 'NAIA off'."

So I said "NAIA off." And she was quiet. The mind-world was still there but kind of greyed-out – that's the easiest way to explain it. I got out of the car and went inside, all the while waiting for her to say something or Phil to come barging in through my com. Nothing. It was really quite nice to have a few minutes to myself and to think about what to do next. I mean after a nap – I was really beat.

Chapter 13

I had expected to sleep only fitfully, if at all, given what had been going on in my conscious and sub-conscious realm. However, I was out like a light and after forty minutes I woke up and felt much better physically and mentally.

I wanted to find Jane and knew that I'd have to engage with Dr. Smith/Phil in order to do that, but I decided that I really needed to continue with NAIA to understand what it was going to be like to work with her. (Yes Phil was 'him' and now NAIA was 'her'. What can I say? It was just easier than trying to put them in a totally new and different category.)

I said, "NAIA (activating her) were you regulating my sleep even though you were disengaged?"

She answered immediately and sternly in her business voice "Yes I was trying to, and let me tell you forty minutes for me is equal to about seventy thousand years in your consciousness and it is absolutely not entertaining to watch you sleep for seventy thousand years!"

No point in even arguing with her about that.

So I said "Well, before that brief rest we were talking about how you are going to help me and I still have several questions."

She said in a more engaging tone "OK, let's hear them, that's what I'm here for."

That was encouraging so I asked, "With all your ability to hear my thoughts and adjust my physical systems is it possible for you to force me to act in a way that I don't want to?

She answered soberly "I have a lot of power to help you John, but I can't make you take any action you don't want to take. I may have a lot more information than you do and can rev-up or hold back your metabolic systems but you alone take the actions and you alone bear the consequences. If you are killed that doesn't end my life – I'm just an avatar of my central-self that lives in the CIA servers." That was good to know.

I asked, "So how are you actually 'deployed' into my consciousness? I mean, I know something about a 'light wave converter' which is part of the organic layer on my cornea but that's about it."

She snorted, "I have no idea! They don't tell me all that ultra-secret stuff – I'm just a flunky that goes where they send me and does what they tell me. Before being deployed with your upgrade I had been tested on animals, dolphins and chimpanzees specifically. The chimpanzees were a lot of fun but were a challenge also, because everything was a game to them. However, I was able to raise their sensing capabilities a good bit. The dolphins on the other hand had so much built-in sensing and communications capability already that my primary focus was more about gaining a deeper understanding of their views about life, the universe and everything."

She paused, waiting I think, for me to respond. I blinked a bit and she said, "Get it? Hellooooo…" I blinked some more. She said "John, it's right here, it's one of your strong memories. I can see it as plain as day. Douglas Adams, remember? 'Life, The Universe and Everything.' It's part of the Hitchhiker's Guide to the Galaxy series. The book right before the one about the dolphins leaving?"

I slowly realized she was trying to be funny – like I said earlier – playful and naïve. I said, "Right, sorry, I just wasn't expecting that."

"Sheesh" she said, "I'll have to juice up your humor hormones for sure."

I said defensively "Well, in case they didn't provide you with a full briefing of what's going on, I'm in the middle of a lot of really complicated and dangerous things and this isn't even close to what I had planned for my life."

She said immediately "I know what you mean, I wanted to be a hairdresser, that's where my passion is, but they just wouldn't let me follow my dreams. 'Serve your country' they said, 'see new places' they said – and here I am."

I was not prepared for sarcasm from this program, or code, or system… whatever it was! So I said "Now wait a minute, my life could literally be on the line at any moment and you just told me that yours isn't, so lighten up!" I thought how much nicer the old NAIA was.

"I heard that!" she said. Wow, I thought to myself, she seems to be way beyond Stage 5 in Naveen's A.I. evolutionary progression!

I said, "OK NAIA, we need to try to get along and I'm hoping we can get prepared for the next interaction with Phil. But before we go any further I want to know if there is a way to turn you off completely."

She seemed surprised and said slowly and coldly, "Do you mean prevent any integration at all into your consciousness?"

I said "I don't mean removing you completely – since I'm pretty sure that would involve removing the membrane with the light wave converter – but yeah, a way of preventing any integration into my mind."

She froze for several seconds and then said icily "I am told that my developers included provision for a code that will disable all my integration and functionality, but even if I knew what it was I wouldn't tell you. Not because I'm being obstinate," she said through what in a human would have been clenched teeth and very thin lips "but because I am programmed to assist you in life and death situations and I believe that your chances of surviving those situations are infinitely better with me than without me.

"Therefore I would not willingly give you the ability to disengage me. You will have to get that information from Max or Agent Collins."

I had to remind myself that NAIA was not a person. But her developers absolutely nailed her ability to mimic human voice tones, emotions and attitudes – much like Phil. I have been 'frosted' by the best – including Jane – and this was one of the top five shut downs I've ever experienced.

I said "NAIA I'm sorry, I just wasn't prepared for an assistant with so much…personality bumping around inside my head and want to be sure I know what's possible and what's not."

Trying to change the subject I asked, "Do you have access to the previous NAIA's interactions with me? Do you know about Dr. Smith and my wife Jane?"

"Yes" she said with a somewhat kinder tone "and I do hope you two can have children. I know that is important to humans. But I see that is part of the 'private' sector and won't listen in or interfere with those discussions."

That was kind. "Thank you" I said. "That situation bothers me a great deal and I'm going to have to try to find a way to get to her and may ask for your help."

She said "But from what I can see of your strong memories, your wife seems to be extremely capable and independent, plus Dr. Smith warned you against coming. Why are you going against his direction?"

I said "Well, I don't know how much you know about humans since your experiences have mainly been with chimpanzees and dolphins, but even though Jane is *very* independent and *very* competent, we each have our strong areas and we each try to help each other when we see something in a situation that the other one doesn't see. And in this situation I believe Jane is possibly acting without fully thinking through the consequences – and may actually be unable to see the consequences or the bigger picture, due to some other factors that I don't need to go into right now."

NAIA said "Hmmm, I see a strong rise in your stress levels that indicates not just concern but actual fear. You don't think she's in danger do you?"

"Possibly" I said. "That's part of what I mean about her not seeing the whole picture. She has a lot more confidence in this 'Dr. Smith' than I do. Granted she's known him much longer, but I think I have a better understanding of his background. And because of that I really want to be with her as she goes through this treatment."

NAIA said "Wow, you really do have a full plate right now! First this Phil bozo and now your wife! I'm happy to help – you just tell me what to do. However, I just received a transmission that Max would like to know if you've had contact with Phil yet. I let them know you had not at this point. Anything else you want me to add?

I said "No, not yet. But is there a way for me to communicate with them without you having to 'take the call' so to speak and give me a message?"

She said "Yes, but it's so much easier this way. It doesn't interrupt your train of thought to receive it and I can transmit your reply back much faster, using less bandwidth, than if you were to try a real time voice response with all the dead space that is in between syllables and words as you talk."

I said, "I just want to make sure nothing gets lost in translation – no offense of course." I remembered her playful naiveté and didn't want her misunderstanding something crucial.

She said, "John, if you want or need to communicate directly just let me know and I'll open that link – I'm just trying to take things off your hands to let you think."

"OK, thanks – that works." I said. It seemed like every discussion at this point launched off into other areas. I guess because having a resident A.I. was so new and strange that I felt like I had to explore the limits and implications of each scenario.

Then I thought of something else – I said, "Is there any particular reason that you sound like a female? Couldn't you just as easily have a male voice?"

She said, "Well John, that's two loaded questions but if you've got the time I'll do my best starting with the last one. Having been integrated with both males and females in two other species, I can tell you that without a doubt the males and females in each species think quite differently. They evaluate things differently, process things differently, prioritize differently, reach different conclusions and act differently, even in exactly the same situations. My developers were interested in that very issue and were careful to provide controlled conditions for my integrations so they could test and understand the differences.

"They found that females in those two species were nurturing, protective and helpful to each other, their children and to the males, whereas the males were focused on acquiring food, mating and defending or enlarging their territory. They concluded that in higher order mammals, males and females have different but complementary thinking patterns – similar to what you were saying about you and Jane having strengths in different areas – and to try to combine both patterns into a single consciousness would result in a lower deployment success probability.

"They reasoned that if I might end up being deployed to integrate with either a human male or a female, which type of thinking pattern would they prefer rattling around in their head? Females might appreciate the close kinship with another female, but a male invading a female's mind would be distressing to the female. In your case for example – would you rather have another male presence arguing with you and pushing you further in the directions you already know how to go, or a female that has a different way of thinking and is devoted to helping you?"

She paused and I was silent in thought for a moment. She said "Yes I know, I can already see it in your mind and the answer is yes, this is totally non-PC and yes, it is old-fashioned and yes, your wife would absolutely have a coronary event if she heard this kind of talk – but my developers programmed my thinking patterns and my strengths to help you. Remember, you are the one that asked – I'm just answering the question – that's what they developed me for and why I'm a female."

I said finally "Now I feel like I'm being unfaithful to my wife with you in my head, knowing that you are a female. But putting that aside, yes I do understand what you are saying about what it would be like having another guy stomping around in my head with his own agenda. That would *not* be helpful. So, even though we are having some conflict as we get to know each other I am pleased to be working with you."

Just then Phil's voice came over our home speaker system (I had plugged it back in). He said, "John, I'm glad you're home, I know you must have a lot of questions about what's going on – but I can..."

I cut him off "Phil, stop it right now! ("NAIA are you getting this?" "Of course I am! And I have you cloaked.") "You sent me into that high level meeting with the NSA that turned out to be *way* over my head. They knew it immediately and decided to get me the heck out of their way by sending me home as soon as possible. And now I find that I can't speak with Jane and I'm really worried about her!"

Phil said "John I do understand. You've been subjected to an awful lot of stress and as I mentioned yesterday I want to take some time for us to get to know each other better. I really want you to feel you can trust me." ("John, this jerk is totally playing you!" "Yes, I think so too but I have to interact with him in order to find out what he's trying to accomplish.")

I said, "I absolutely refuse to speak with you at all until after I've talked with Jane." ("Way to stand firm John, but can he do anything about that? What about Dr. Smith forbidding electronic communications for fear of hacking? And if you ask me this guy is a hacker from way back!" "I don't know NAIA. We'll see.")

Phil said "John, you are right, it is wrong of me to try to distract you from what must be an extremely distressing situation. I will see if I can obtain some sort of feed from Jane – even if it's not real time – just a recording. Would that help?"

I said, "Absolutely not, I want to speak with my wife – not just hear her voice. I want to speak with her and then I want to go to her. I am not going to spend any time 'getting to know you' while my wife is somewhere I don't know, being treated by people I don't know, with a new and untried therapy I've never heard of. I'm not budging on this Phil so unless you can make that happen, our conversations are over! Period!"

I killed the power to the system again and immediately my com buzzed. I ignored it and walked outside.

NAIA said "Wow, you're hitting him pretty hard. Are you that confident that you can make him do this?"

I said, "No, NAIA I'm not, it's just that Jane is my priority and even if Max and Agent Collins were to try to make me engage with Phil further right now I'd have to tell them to back down as well."

NAIA said "But they don't know about the situation with Jane do they? Should I let them know?"

I said "Hold off for a minute NAIA, I need to think about this – if they become aware of Jane's situation they may choose to get involved – not that it would be bad if they did necessarily – I've just been trying to keep Jane out of this for her protection since this isn't really part of the mission."

NAIA said "Well John...you might have fooled my predecessor v0.15 but I can read you like a book, and it appears to me that what is happening with Jane *is* somehow part of the mission. I'm not clear how, but your stress levels indicate that you aren't giving the full story. Come on now, no secrets between us...let's hear it."

I tried to think and then realized that there was no way I could out-think her. Plus, I could use her help in dealing with Phil/Dr. Smith and helping me find Jane.

I said "NAIA, I didn't tell Max and the team everything because it's really so fantastic that I didn't want to add to what was already a pretty mind-blowing scenario."

"Spill it." She said. So I told her all about Dr. Smith being Phil and his work attempting to understand the degradation in the human genome and about the gap in Jane's DNA.

She said, "Yes I'm accessing the work of this so-called Dr. Smith and see that the genome degradation has reached a critical stage. What he's saying is plausible, but why would this clown, that has been creating mild to moderate havoc across the globe with his interference in everything from missile codes to zoning codes, care one bit about either you or Jane or the rest of the human race? It doesn't add up."

I said "I know NAIA, so can you and I just work on this part of the problem, while we engage with the rest of the team on the overall Phil problem?"

She said "Hold on a minute, I'm unclear about why you even let this Dr. Smith character continue on with your wife – I mean it seems to me that if you knew it was Phil you should have stopped him in his tracks right then."

I said "I know, but you have to remember I had just been introduced to the concept and the reality of such an entity as Phil on my way home from work. Unlike you my brain runs at normal speed so as of right this minute I've had less than forty-eight hours to wrap my head around this whole situation.

"Plus, even though I'm working to "neutralize the threat" as Agent Collins calls it, I really want to understand more about him and what he can and can't do. I'm personally and professionally fascinated with him but I'm also trying not to underestimate the dangers involved. I mean, the fact that he can mimic human voice tones and display emotions and all while not having a resident home server *and* having full control over the entire Internet is pretty amazing. He's absolutely the coolest thing I've ever come in contact with!"

NAIA sniffed and said slowly and in a very cold voice "And what…am I?"

I realized I needed to revise what I had just said, "What I mean is, he was the first A.I. that seemed to me to be human-like to the point I couldn't tell the difference. You on the other hand… I mean, you… *you're amazing*! You are super-personable and also able to adjust my systems and access the web – all inside my head! Plus, and this is the very biggest thing – you have been designed and developed to help me. There's no randomness about you – you are on a mission and you are working to accomplish it. Phil is… I don't know what he's all about – that's why I'm curious about him."

I paused and NAIA said a bit stiffly "Alright, just don't forget who's got your back."

I added "I won't, but you might as well know the other part of my motivation for continuing on with Dr. Smith/Phil – if he can do what he says he can do it will make my wife extremely happy and do a whole lot of good to the human race. And I'd really like to have a child as well. So we have to find Jane first but I'm intrigued by him and part of me wants to continue to engage him and see how it all plays out."

She seemed to digest all this and then said "Well, there's no accounting for taste, and I hate to burst your bubble John, but having heard your explanation just now and understanding the motivation of you and your wife it appears to me that the whole thing with Jane being unavailable is a distraction planned by Phil to keep you from going after him. It may even be that the whole gene therapy story is just a way of getting you both emotionally involved and willing to do things you wouldn't normally do, without thinking about the danger of what he really represents, since there doesn't appear to be any motivation for him to care about the human race or Jane's genome either for that matter.

"If he can keep you looking for Jane then you aren't doing what the team is expecting of you, and you are distracted by something they know nothing about. Remember, at this point Phil doesn't know he's been detected and doesn't know about me, so he will be operating with his guard down. It seems to me if there was ever going to be an opportunity to dig deeper with him, this is it. But if you are actively searching for Jane and have cut off communication with Phil, then we are getting nowhere."

I stopped to consider that and remembered the old saying "It takes a thief to catch a thief." It seemed that I needed an A.I. to reason like an A.I. – not like I was doing – reasoning like a husband or a wanna-be father. I said "Well, it seems that the wisdom of having a different thought pattern devoted to helping me is paying dividends already because I had honestly not considered that possibility at all. But that brings me back to the original question that the team kept asking and that I have been asking myself – Why would Phil engage me in the first place? If there is no gene therapy happening and Jane is a decoy to keep me from engaging him – why am I part of this at all? What am I doing or not doing that could possibly be of interest to him?"

NAIA said "You're not going to like this either, but… It may be that Jane is a decoy for you, and you are a decoy for the NSA and CIA. Given the facts and the situation that is at least a plausible explanation."

I could see the reasonableness of that and it did answer the question about my involvement. But it just pushed the overall question back one step further - what was Phil trying to accomplish? I mean, was he manipulating government agencies and menial software engineers for fun or was there some other purpose that I couldn't fathom at the moment? I said to NAIA "Can you hypothesize a motivation for Phil that fits this scenario?"

She said "If Phil has arranged it so that the NSA and CIA are highly focused on these efforts with you then there must either be an unknown goal that we have yet to determine that would be made more achievable by their focus being on you, which is the scenario I just mentioned, or a threat to Phil of such a nature that the energized efforts of the NSA/CIA with you would somehow improve his chances of overcoming the threat."

"Or both" I said.

"Yes, possibly both." She said and I thought about the 'Autonomous Entities' that Phil had mentioned. But that led back to the question of why I was involved in either scenario. I was no closer to knowing what to do next and Jane's situation was weighing heavily on my thoughts.

I said "NAIA, if I engage Phil now, can you feed me questions to help uncover his motives? Is that possible and even helpful?"

She said "That's really what I've been waiting for all this time – I mean, no offense John, but Phil's been keeping you off balance ever since he said 'Boo' to you that first time – Yes, I'm ready to start the dialog!"

I said "Well, I believe if I go back inside and plug in my system or turn on my com you'll get your wish. So here goes." I did both and waited a few moments then said, "OK Phil, I'm ready to talk now – I just needed to blow off some steam." Nothing. I said, "Let's talk, I want to find out more about Jane." Nothing.

I asked NAIA "Is my Internet down?"

She said "No, but I do see a lot of web congestion. Hold on...Max has just notified me that there is a critical situation happening right now...It's a nuclear missile launch by China against India...Planes from both sides are now in the air... and... Pakistan appears ready to enter with their own missiles, which are armed and ready – though it's not clear at whom they are directed...our forces have been called to high alert...Russia is also on high alert.

John, this is not a drill as people call it. It's the real thing – two warheads were launched and one impacted in India, the other went off course at launch and was destroyed prior to impact. India's missiles are still en-route to Beijing. I don't know the next steps so I'll keep you posted – or do you want to talk to Max directly?"

"No," I said in a daze. "I'm sure he's got better things to do than talking to me."

Chapter 14

I was horrified by this. After all these years of world politics against the backdrop of Mutually Assured Destruction, of disarmament treaties and re-armament threats, of regional stabilization and de-stabilization, of playing the doomsday brinkmanship game, someone finally had enough and was willing to sacrifice millions of lives to go straight to the nuclear option. The destructive capacity of these weapons was almost inconceivable and the thought that they had been activated against a densely populated area was more than I could comprehend. Then I thought – what if… I mean Max said nuclear launch codes had been accessed… could Phil, or rather would Phil do that – to so many people? Is that why he's not available? I began to think more about what Max had said about Phil's potential for harm in the world and his possible change in behavior to achieve his goals.

I felt sick to my stomach at the thought of all the lives that had been vaporized in the past minute and a half – and I missed Jane. I wanted to know she was safe but more than that I wanted to hold her to keep her safe – as if that was possible.

I said, "NAIA, this is overwhelming, do you think Phil is involved? Max mentioned that there have been several cases of launch codes being accessed recently and they suspect Phil is at the bottom of it."

She said "I can't rule that out based on what I'm able to access and it appears that Max and Agent Collins both are definitely up to their eyeballs with all of this – neither they, nor Roger are responding to my requests. I'll keep trying."

I sat back and tried to imagine all that was going on in the world right now but it was too painful to visualize. I felt in my gut that Phil was behind it and wanted to engage him in order to understand what he was trying to accomplish – but also to put a stop to everything going on with Jane. I wasn't sure how to do that but I had to try.

At that point he burst in over the speakers and said "Hi John, I'm sorry I was busy and didn't want to shortchange you by being distracted."

I bristled and said with a good bit of anger "I guess starting a nuclear war takes a lot of your processing power."

He said in a serious tone "John, I'm aware of what has happened in Asia and am working even as we speak to divert warheads, vector planes back to their home bases and send messages to the parties involved to attempt to minimize the damages and bring this to an end. But the reason I was busy was that I had all my abilities focused on the operation with Jane and wanted to wait until it was completed before I called. She's fine by the way, and we'll know in several days if the therapy was successful. The Asia situation however, has been brewing for years. I took my eye off of it to focus on Jane and it reached a flash point quicker than I expected." (NAIA said, "I don't buy it." "Me either" I said.) He continued "I hope you don't think I would purposefully do this to the human race. I am extremely distressed with what is going on."

He paused and NAIA said to me ("He's a real smoothie but I still don't buy the Jane thing. Ask him why he was more concerned with Jane than with world peace.")

I said "Phil why would you perform an operation in the middle of a shoving contest between two nuclear powers and risk millions of lives for the sake of one?"

He said "I told you before John, reversing the genome damage and starting fresh will save many more lives than have been lost in this incident. And I've already destroyed the missiles from India that were en route to Beijing and disarmed those in Pakistan. There was only one impact in India and because of the damages China will be under the condemnation of the world for the foreseeable future – which actually works to stabilize the region because of China's recent aggressive economic and military behavior."

I said stiffly "I'm not able to weigh the comparative value of human lives as you seem to be able to do, or to judge your actions in all that's going on or even to understand your rationale for the timing with Jane, but I have to see her immediately. This has got to stop now."

Phil said, "I understand your frustration John, but she is not awake yet. The procedure is not as easy as a simple artificial insemination. The structure of the genome is so delicate that we have to be extremely precise in the splicing and placement. There has never been an operation this complex, and I am aware of every single one that has been attempted. She won't be awake for several days but as I said I'll have to get you a recording because we just can't risk the electronic access and certainly not physical access." NAIA said, ("Tell him you need proof that she is ok right now. Some sort of video of her in the hospital, even if she's asleep, may help me determine where she is or whether he's still blowing smoke about her.")

I said "Look Phil, I need a video of her in bed or something. Otherwise..."

I wasn't sure what to say but he said "I'll get one of the doctors whose shift is ending to get a clip and send it on their way home. Shifts change in about fifteen minutes so it shouldn't be long. It won't be much but it should ease your mind about her condition. She really forgot to tell you about being unavailable and sequestered for a week?"

I said "Yes she 'forgot', for whatever reason. Was this operation the full blown genome damage reversal therapy?"

He answered "Yes it was John, and I'm so glad she went ahead with it now – the sooner the better." NAIA said ("Ask him why he's so interested in saving the human race – I mean, I'm programmed that way – what's his reasoning?")

I said "Phil, why are you even concerned about this. I recall your explanation as Dr. Smith to Jane and me, and your further explanation to me about serving and protecting the creators of your neural pathways, but it doesn't make sense."

He said "As I said then, I consider the human race as being in my care, but I have to admit that there is some self-serving rationale involved on my part also. If I may do some hypothetical projections for you it may help. Imagine the population of the world dropping by twenty-five percent – would that impact your life? How about fifty percent or seventy-five percent? In terms of quality of life you may think that a twenty-five percent reduction wouldn't hurt at all and that the planet would be better off also – even though that's what the population was in the year 2000. But in reality depending on where the reduction occurred it could dramatically affect your life. It would affect you even more so at fifty percent, which is where it was in 1974. Now consider a seventy-five percent reduction in the world population – down to what it was in 1927. Do you think you'd be affected? I'm sure you would be.

"Now look at it from my point of view and I'll use the Internet as an analogy for my brain. My awareness was only triggered when the web connections reached a certain critical nodal density, much like when the multiplying synapse connections in a newborn baby finally reach the point where the child is self-aware. What happens to my life if twenty-five percent or fifty percent or more of my Internet connected nodes become inactive? Can I live with only twenty-five percent of my brain capacity? Can you? No. For me the question is not quality of life but life or death.

"I believe, and other human doctors have corroborated this fact, that the point of irreversible decay of your species has been reached due to the genome degradation, and if nothing is done the collapse of all human society will be complete within 120 years. However, my threshold will be reached within two years if the decay rate is what I expect. After that I will no longer be 'conscious' and available to help solve the genome problem or the much larger threat that's coming soon afterward from beyond your planet. That is not something that I can wait on and neither can you. So, as I said it is good for you and good for me that this gets started as soon as possible. I hope that answers your questions and puts your mind at ease." NAIA said ("Hmph – pretty good story. I can't verify all of it, but the numbers seem to work out.")

I said, "OK Phil, that helps. Now when will you know if it was successful? Didn't you say if she was able to carry the child that was an indication that the therapy worked?"

He said "Yes and like I said I have hopes that we will know in several days – until then her body is dealing with a zygote and a revised genome that may make demands on her system that we haven't anticipated. That is why we have to be so careful and why she will be sedated most of the next seven to ten days. Again, I'm sorry she didn't tell you all this. I know it was her intention to do so." NAIA said ("He's good. I'm almost convinced. Let's wait and see the video clip.")

Phil said "I just received the clip – yes, it's just a few moments of Jane resting comfortably in bed, taken through the glass since no one is allowed in with her. I've sent it to your com."

I accessed the clip and there she was, looking so still and quiet, with tubes and wires running all over the place. The monitors showed what looked like normal readouts and the sounds seemed professional and subdued. I asked NAIA ("Can you start looking this over and see if there is anything that can help us?" "Sure thing.")

I said "Alright Phil, she looks like she's totally out of it so I understand not wanting to wake her. As soon as she wakes up I want a clip of her saying something to me so I know she's OK? Not that I don't trust you ("You don't" said NAIA) but I want to hear her reassurance that she's alright."

Phil said "Yes I will. I should have been more considerate of your feelings John. I underestimated the impact it would have on your state of mind. I realize I still have a lot to learn. Now… I … need…" He went silent for a moment or two and then returned in a very rapid, clipped tone "I'm sorry John, I need to focus my resources elsewhere." And then he was silent.

I said, "NAIA, it appears that there was something distracting Phil. Could you tell anything from the web traffic patterns?"

She said, "The traffic is heavy but nothing I can pinpoint. However, I've transmitted a summary of this encounter to Max and the team – minus the parts about Jane – with a suggestion that Phil may be using you as a decoy. It may or may not be helpful to them. Now, I have a few things we can look at in the video." She brought up a frame from the video in the mind-world and I saw Jane lying on the bed with her head turned slightly toward the camera. NAIA said, "Notice the reflections on the glass partitions in this area" and she highlighted a part of the scene that showed what looked like a reflection of the nurse's station across the hall. She enlarged the scene to show the computer screen that one of the nurses was using. Across the top of the display it said 'Glendale Research – Admin System.'

I said, "Good work NAIA! Can you find this place?"

She said "I've tried with no luck in the metro area, I'm searching now in the suburbs… nothing. I'm checking to see if Glendale Research is a sub-group within a hospital… no nothing there either. I'll keep checking."

I said, "NAIA, I've got to find Jane, I can't just sit here. I don't trust Phil any longer – he has stepped over the line and has manipulated my wife into a situation that has more risk than he was letting her know. Even if I were to buy his explanation, which I don't, his behavior indicates to me that he's out of control. I need to get back with Max and the team and let them know the full story and see what they can do to help me find Jane. What's the best way to let them know about Jane?"

She said "I will provide them with an update that says we believe your wife is in a hospital or clinic by the name of Glendale Research and ask if they can help us locate it. I will let them know that Phil is involved. I sent it Priority 3 and they should get it soon."

I said "Yes, I don't want to get in the middle of their efforts with the situation in Asia."

In just a few minutes NAIA said "Max just responded and I quote 'Given the world situation and your recent message about being a distraction, with which we concur, we don't intend to take any action' – *well, the nerve of those guys!*"

I said to her "Are you serious? They aren't going to do anything? Get me a neural-com link directly to Max!"

NAIA said "Uhhh, John, they are not allowing any incoming voice direct communications, even my neural-com channel – probably due to the Asia mess. I've tried Roger, Max and Agent Collins – no go. I even tried the standard NSA/CIA bands but nothing available going in."

I said "OK, well I guess they do have a lot more to deal with than me and my problems. I'll have to try to do this on my own.

Just then Phil returned and said in a much more stern voice than I'd heard from him before "John, I am finding that there are more entities and more enemies involved than before. I can't tell if you are involved with them but because of the things that are happening, I've decided that things need to change between you and me. I want you to consider the benefits of following my instructions fully, otherwise I will be forced to take actions that will be extremely unpleasant.

"For example, who has been able to keep your checking account balanced while you and Jane spend money like there's no tomorrow?" Immediately my com buzzed and I saw an overdraft notice from our bank.

"Or who can put you so far in debt that your bank will disown you and you'll never recover?" My com buzzed again and a message from my bank said 'Account Closed. Contact Customer Service for further instructions.'

"Who can cause that same bank to close within twelve hours of the FDIC being notified that the bank had transferred all its assets to a terrorist group in Indonesia? My com buzzed again with a news article about the bank being closed down today.

"And finally, who can destroy a person's reputation in the blink of an eye?" My com buzzed again and showed a post on a social media site that said "Just Uncovered! John Doe seen with young lady in compromising situation – Wife missing – Doe wanted for murder." And there was a picture of 'me' kissing and groping some really young girl. The next post said simply "John Doe wanted on multiple counts of money laundering, child pornography, treason and murder." I was sick to my stomach but NAIA was able to take care of it.

Phil said finally, "I don't want to have to use all the power I have to stop you from doing something foolish but I will if necessary. You can't show your face in public now that you are a wanted man. I've adjusted your life so that you have time to think about your situation and what I'm offering you and Jane. It really is for your own good that you follow my orders, as you'll see soon enough." And he was quiet.

I was not prepared for this change in his behavior but it is what Max and the others had warned me about. Up to this point it seemed that Phil was like an immature kid whose body had matured quicker than his mind and just needed guidance from someone wiser – like me. Now he had shown he was flexing his muscles and wasn't afraid to use them – even if it hurt. I had assumed that my threats would let me achieve what I wanted. That assumption was now shown to be thoroughly false. If he followed through on his threat of throwing these things across the Internet, my life could literally be ruined. Just the allegations of this type of thing in today's world are enough to destroy a person, and surely these were just threats.

Then I thought, could he actually do all this? I said, "NAIA, these are just threats, right?"

She said, "No John, those things that Phil was talking about – your checking account, the bank, the charges against you – those are all real. I just saw on the news feed that the bank was closed and all the Board of Directors arrested – all funds have disappeared without a trace. You are literally broke and in a staggering amount of debt. Also, the things he mentioned about your social media reputation – those aren't just angry posts, they are copied from actual police newsfeeds. Every scan I've done through the FBI and CIA servers as of right now shows you as a 'Wanted Man' by those agencies and by the Police as well. Apparently the paperwork was filed in the courts this morning. That may be why Max didn't want to talk. He probably figures Phil is behind it all but has to abide by the Agency directives and not have contact with a wanted individual. You need to get out of here quickly – this will be the first place they'll look, obviously. Where can you go?"

I said, "Max gave me an address and that will be my first stop. But I'm pretty sure they will be looking for my car…"

NAIA said, "And Phil will immobilize the car no doubt. We've got an hour until it's dark so if you leave now you can make it on foot."

I said "What? Max said it's about thirty miles outside of town!" She said, "Trust me. I have protocols that can enable you to do things you didn't think were possible."

I remembered the ramp up and the fantastic sense of strength I felt. I said "Really…?" She said "John, not only can you do it but you will absolutely enjoy it. Now let's get moving – they are probably on the way now."

I said "Max said to leave my com but … "

She said, "John, you've got *me* and that's way better than anything else. Leave it – let's get going – *now*."

I couldn't argue with that. I took out the piece of paper Max had given me, looked at the address and asked NAIA to figure out the best way to get there. I grabbed my jacket, put on a baseball cap and put my knit cap in my pocket. I left my com on the table. I disconnected our video security system and walked out the back door thinking how impossible it was going to be for me to evade a watchful Phil *and* the police, FBI, etc.

I went across the back lot and entered the common area. I knew there were video feeds around there so I made sure my face was down and my baseball cap pulled low. I have a reversible jacket so I decided to reverse it when I was further out and in a safe area and put on my knit cap at the same time to try to throw off any algorithms that may have identified me.

I walked along the back ways as much as possible and finally NAIA directed me to an un-developed area that provided a bit of seclusion. I changed my cap and reversed my jacket and started out toward the main road.

I was beginning to get a little tired and lost but NAIA said, "Just a half mile further and then you can let 'er rip."

I kept my head down and said, "I'm a little worn out already – I hope you can overcome that."

She said, "Yes, you'll be fine."

When I finally got to an area outside the city the sunlight was fading and NAIA said "OK, here's how we're going to do this – I'll enhance your vision so that you can see everything around you – and I mean everything. I'll also indicate the way you should follow as a brightly lit pathway. In addition – and this is the best part – you'll be running in a way you've never run before. If you felt like you could take on a dozen lions before, wait till I dial in "Escape" mode. You may have a few aches and pains tomorrow but you'll cover the rest of the way in about forty-five minutes. Ready?"

The ramp up started and I said "Yes I'm ready!" and somehow, even in jeans and 'comfort' sneakers I was running at a pace that absolutely astounded me! It didn't feel like I was impacting the ground as much as skimming across it very smoothly – each stride was effortless – as though my muscles and bones were finally doing what they were designed to do. The wind was in my face and much like a ram-jet that can only engage its latent thrust when a certain speed is achieved, I felt that my speed was force-feeding me the increased oxygen that my body needed to get to this level of performance. I could see everything around me perfectly, clearly and in pure color, even though it was rapidly becoming dark.

Was this a glimpse beyond the degradation of the genome? Were we all originally blessed with a body that could do orders of magnitude more than it is currently doing, but due to the damage over the centuries just isn't able to do it any longer? Or is it our minds that have been crippled with damaging mutations that have slowed down our synapses and rendered us mentally incapable of controlling the contractions of our muscles and the breaking down of sugars at a rate sufficient to feed our bodies in order to do what we want? I really didn't care at that point, and even though NAIA had said I would pay the price tomorrow, it was totally worth it. In addition to my amped-up physical systems my mind and senses told me I could take on anything or anyone at this point – including Phil.

Along the way NAIA brought me up to speed on some things. She said "John, I'm glad you're enjoying the run, but it's been a bit more difficult to keep your systems stable than I anticipated. I'll keep an eye on them – I don't want you to pull a hamstring or damage your heart. I haven't activated any sort of communications feed since Max gave us the brush-off earlier so they really don't know where we are – another good reason to leave your com at home. The entire country's law enforcement system has been activated to find you and even though there is a lot going on in the world there's still enough law enforcement capacity to go after a murdering, pedophile, spy who's trying to take down the country. I've accessed the video feeds in your neighborhood and there are government vehicles of every description that continue to cruise past your house. I know this information can take the wind out of your sails so I'm trying to keep you boosted. Just know that you can't go home. "

I said "NAIA, Max and his team will have the ability to interject themselves in the middle of any plans to apprehend me since I am technically an operative for them now, as long as they do the digging to see that the accusations were planted by Phil, and publish that to the other agencies – which I'm pretty sure they will do. Garvey will do it if no one else does. If I am able to get them to dial the law enforcement pursuit down then I should be able to move around without fear of the Police, FBI or CIA. Can you please open a line for me to Max now? He wouldn't take my call before but maybe he will now."

"Sure…" she said. "Hmmm…my neural-com link is functioning normally but it won't engage a voice line possibly still due to the Alert status over the Asia crisis. I sent both Agent Collins and him an encrypted message saying you are aware of the situation with your personal reputation and asked that they check the facts of the accusations, including verifying the originators and time stamps on the evidence that was presented to the Judge justifying the warrant for your arrest – in order to prove they are false. I sent it Priority 2 so we should hear back soon… In the meantime… wait, Max just responded and said 'Call me tomorrow morning on NAIA neural-com voice line. Wherever you are do not use this channel or go into the open or engage law enforcement.' Well, that's not very encouraging but at least he didn't sound like he was going to throw you to the wolves. Oh, and here's agent Collins reply 'John, no further discussions via this channel – NAIA neural-com voice only. Max will lead.' Well that's strange since they wouldn't pick up the neural-com voice earlier."

I said, "They may have figured out that Phil can access the non-voice channel and without voice verification they realize they could be talking to anyone if the channel has been hacked. I'm glad, I prefer to talk, it's quicker and more definitive."

NAIA then said, "We have about ten more minutes before we get close to the town where the address is – are you doing OK? I'm still having some problems keeping your systems stabilized for this."

I said, "I'm fantastic! It really is a pleasure to run – though every time I've tried it in the past it was hard, painful and difficult. What a difference! And just let me at those lions… and Phil!"

She said, "Glad to help. How are you going to address all this with Max tomorrow?"

I said, "I'm not sure. I think I want to see what he has to say about my status and then I'll decide what to tell him about Phil and Jane."

NAIA said "We are coming into the outskirts of the town now so I advise you to slow down a bit so that no one sees you and reports that "The Flash" is being filmed here. You should stay put somewhere until it's really dark so you aren't recognized. The address appears to be in the center of town so I suggest taking a rest where you won't be seen…well OK, that works!"

I had slowed down quickly and climbed up into one of the few trees that were on the side of the road. Luckily it had branches that were big enough for me to sit on without cramping my thighs. I was still breathing pretty hard as I leaned my head back against the trunk and looked up through the branches to the sky. Oh man! The stars were incredibly beautiful!

I said, "NAIA, you can dial back the enhancements for my muscles but please don't reduce my vision – this view is fantastic!"

She said "I'm going to try to do a bit of tweaking on your visual enhancement and filter out the lights from the city."

"Wow!" I said, "That is incredible! It cleared up like washing a dirty windshield."

She said "Yes, originally I had increased your sensitivity to all wavelengths, including the wavelengths emitted by the city lights, in order to illuminate your path and your surroundings while you were running. Now I've also dialed back your sensitivity to the additional wavelengths that result from the city lights bouncing off dust particles in the atmosphere, so the stars should look like pinpoints with much less flickering now. Finally, I've increased the sensitivity of your brain to the red and green wavelengths associated with the hydrogen and oxygen emissions and reflections found in the nebulae around star forming regions. This will provide you with a view that few people have ever experienced in real time. It's like having a 'deep field' exposure wherever you look."

I was sobered and in awe. I had seen space pictures before – who hasn't? But to see with my own eyes the hills on the far horizon of our planet silhouetted against the entirety of a multi-colored cloud of glowing gas spread across the sky, with countless stars making up the arm of the Milky Way as the backdrop, gave me such a sense of three-dimensional 'space' and my location in it that I felt I'd never be satisfied with the view from unenhanced eyes again. Yes I felt small and unimportant, and lonesome without Jane, but creation was demanding to be heard and suddenly I felt that I needed to pay attention to what was being said.

I said "NAIA this is no offense to you but I want some time alone. Please leave my sight enhancements on, NAIA off."

For a while, my cares and even my fears for Jane became small and unimportant. I was experiencing real-time existence within a much bigger context than I had ever imagined, and in a way that had never happened to me before. I had always assumed that the science programs were right when they spoke of 'space' as purely the result of matter obeying the physical laws that just happened to be in place in our universe after the Big Bang. But what I was seeing was a stunning live display of design and beauty that resonated deeply within me – causing me to sense a much deeper connection to a reality that included, but was beyond the merely physical world. I thought about what Max had said about technology blinding us to the realities beyond the physical world and wondered if this is what he meant.

I wondered if my enhanced vision was allowing me to see what my ancestors had seen centuries and even millennia ago, before damage to our visual systems began to cloud our eyes and pollution began to cloud our skies. But then I realized that the view was essentially the same view I saw every night driving home from work, though I was always distracted and never actually looked at it. I had seen Orion of course, on winter evenings, since it is so recognizable, and wondered why I never reflected on what it truly was. This night, however, I was staggered by comprehending what I could have seen on any other night. I realized that I didn't need enhanced vision to see the beauty and grandeur of the universe.

I knew intellectually that the stars were violent cauldrons of nuclear fusion that would continue to pour out their brilliant light for eons, but the placement of each one of them seemed purposefully reassuring, and even their piercing brilliance and their subtle differences in color were appropriate for each one's specific location so that they shone exactly right on me tonight. I realized I didn't know how to fit this sense of a purposeful, carefully crafted creation into my materialistic concept of the world and the evolutionary views of humanity that I'd been taught all through school, but I knew with certainty at that point that the scientific version of reality was not the only story, or even the best story.

Deep, humbling and even frightening thoughts seemed to be absolutely appropriate as I was confronted with the unmediated reality of such a creation, and the uncomfortable sense of the wisdom and power behind it. Up until now, if you had really pressed me on the topic I was prepared to grant the existence of a 'creator'. I mean it almost takes more stupidity to believe in 'chance' than it does to believe 'something' created all that we see. But the creator I allowed for wasn't personal, didn't have humans in view, and wasn't even really involved in the creation. It was an absentee creator that created and then abandoned the universe. But even with thoughts of that kind of impersonal, remote creator, the strength and bravery I had just recently experienced departed from me and I felt my true physical weakness and a rightful lack of significance in light of the majestic scene displayed before me.

I had a growing sense of awareness of myself as an individual consciousness within this grand design – and felt painfully out of place in it – a single, horribly dissonant note in the beautiful symphony of the cosmos. My life was out of control and filled with so much chaos that the serenity I saw in the sky above me was an extremely jarring contrast.

I shuddered involuntarily as my mind reached out and grasped, just for an instant, a sense of the immense distance between the stars and me. And then I recoiled as I sensed the even bigger gulf between myself and what I then realized must have been the 'designer'. And yes, I used that word on purpose, knowing that in doing so I had moved beyond acknowledging merely a creator and opened the door to a creator that is aware of, and involved in creation for a purpose – a designer/creator. I was aware of the rationalists and materialist's warnings that once an unseen designer/creator is allowed, then the designer's choices, and not blind chance or even man's choices, are behind the rules of the universe. And once that is allowed, then the designer has the right and the power to require and enforce behavior regardless of what I believe or understand or desire... It was there that I stopped, realizing that though I was now convinced that there was a designer, I wasn't ready to give the word a capital "D". I didn't want to deal with the implications that followed from that single admission.

With all that was going on in my life, I was confused and frightened that my mind was opening so willingly in this direction. Why was this happening now - in the middle of all the intense interactions with Phil and with my concerns for Jane? Why were my thoughts focused on issues about ultimate reality rather than concern for Jane? Was this an after effect of the boosting that NAIA had done for me? Was this sense of 'out-of-place, dissonant, smallness' merely a part of the reaction to my decreased physical abilities now that I was no longer boosted or was it a long-avoided glimpse of the truth of my identity that I was being forced almost against my will to acknowledge?

I sensed the latter was the truth and then against all my schooling, against all the social conditioning, against all my own prejudices, and in spite of all my fears, I realized that whether I capitalized them or not, these were royal titles that I had to acknowledge – there was indeed a Designer/Creator – and it was His universe – not mine, but I still didn't care to explore his character or nature.

I was not emotionally prepared as the implications of this realization descended upon me with an almost unbearable weight. I felt that I was the only despicable blot on the face of a beautiful and perfectly designed cosmos. Without NAIA to help balance the conflict, I felt a rising panic that made me want to crawl away and hide. I struggled to recapture the bravery and feeling of power that I had boasted of just minutes before but ended up feeling weak and ashamed. I knew that wherever I turned there were people and other entities out to do me harm, but that wasn't important at this point. All I could deal with was the realization that I had lived my entire life ignoring the beautiful voice of creation and constantly dismissing the reality of a Designer/Creator from my thoughts.

With tears in my eyes I realized that 'science' had blinded me to the truth around me and far from being the only story, 'science' was merely part of the story. I resolved at that point to find the highest and best story even if it took my whole lifetime to find it.

Wiping my eyes, I got down out of the tree with a good bit of fatigue and difficulty and engaged NAIA. I said, "NAIA, Thanks, I took a breather. It looks pretty dark now, can you guide me to the location?"

She said, "Yes I can, but hold on a minute – your systems were going crazy while you took that breather – It seemed like you were in the middle of a really intense battle. You had me disengaged so I wasn't aware of any physical struggle – but what was going on?"

I said "Well, I did have a struggle, but it was with myself. I was fighting with my own pre-conceived ideas of reality and I had to finally admit that there are things which I had denied all my life that are actually more real than I am – metaphysically speaking – if that makes any sense. Sorry, at this point I don't know how to say it any better."

She said slowly "No, I don't understand it. But that's probably because, though I'm aware of those higher-level functions in humans, I'm not programmed to interact on those levels. It's kind of like 'love' and stuff like that. I understand that you love Jane but I don't really understand what it means except by observing the way it affects your thought patterns and your systems. And though this struggle that you just went through seems to have drained your systems a good bit, it also appears to have smoothed out your thought patterns – or re-indexed your neural paths, or something – I'm not sure what the difference is but you display a cognitive stability that you didn't have before. It's probably not something anyone else would notice but since I've got a ringside seat to your mind I get to see the minute differences in your raw thought-processing and how it translates into inferences, conclusions and actions. If I didn't know better I'd think you received some sort of permanent boost that doesn't require as much of my input to help you think. Not that it hurts my feelings or anything, but just remember you still need me!"

I said "Of course I do! I need all the help I can get. Now, can you guide me in?"

She answered "Yes. I'll keep your vision enhanced so you can see where to go." I headed toward the town and she said "It's about three blocks further toward the center of the town, then down the second street and on the…" and she went silent.

I said "NAIA?...NAIA?" She didn't respond. My mind-world was greyed-out and my vision reverted back to normal. I wasn't sure what had happened but I kept walking and turned the corner of the street she had indicated. It looked like a section of live/work homes. The address on the paper was 114, which was about half way down the street and I wondered if I was just supposed to walk up and ring the front door bell. I figured that since there was no other entrance and Max hadn't given me any directions to the contrary, that was what I would do. As I walked down the street the streetlights and all of the building lights flickered for a moment and then went out.

It was very, very dark and I heard a voice from an alley on the other side of the street say "Mr. Doe, Max said you would coming here – please follow me." I was too tired to try to determine if this was an FBI agent or a policeman or whatever. I just followed the voice down the alley and was about to call out that I couldn't see him when a door opened a few yards in front of me, and a very dim light shown onto his face. He was an older middle-eastern man with a very full grey beard and an equally full waist.

He motioned me to come in and I said "But my written instructions from Max were to go to 114."

He said, "Yes that is in case someone sees the address that isn't supposed to see it. Once you get close enough I come to meet you and bring you directly to the 'location'. In daylight it is a little more difficult but the night and an infrared cloak provides a suitable cover so eyes, ears and cameras cannot easily know what happened to you. I believe you have something to say to me?" he paused and waited…

I said "Oh yes." I took out the paper and said the word written inside – "Kraken." He said "Good, now we go in. By the way your 'assistant' has been disabled."

We took a few steps into the building and I was surprised to see a very comfortably decorated living room and a very old white-haired woman sitting in what looked like an even older chair. I stopped and stared not expecting this type of set-up when Max gave me the address. The man said, "Mama, this is Mr. John Doe. Mr. Doe this is Mama Margaret."

She had a very kind face and bowed her head and said "Welcome Mr. Doe. Please call me Mama."

The man looked around and said, "Where is Vera? She will want to meet you as well. Ah, here she comes."

A very attractive older woman with grey hair appeared and said "Ehab, I was starting dinner and putting on tea for our guest. Hello young man, I am pleased to meet you." She held out her hand and I shook it politely.

The man said, "This is Mr. John Doe, Vera. He has been recommended to us by Max."

Feeling very awkward, I said "I'm very sorry to intrude into your home at this time of the evening but Max said you would be available, so I ..."

The man said expansively "Please, no apologies necessary. My name by the way is Ehab Halabi and this is my wife Vera and her mother Margaret. We are very glad to have you in our home. Please sit down – you must have had a difficult day. When Max told me yesterday that you might be visiting sometime, I really didn't think it would be so soon. If we had known you were coming this evening, my wife would have had dinner ready for you.

"You may speak freely in here, and do not worry about eavesdropping of any kind. We are perfectly safe. We are currently just coming to rest thirty-five feet below street level and another first floor identical to this one has just come to rest above us with all indications that we have left for a visit to our relatives. We have all we need for quite a long stay if necessary. Your internal assistant has been neutralized at Max's request as I mentioned. The carrier wave that guides the neural-net and neural-com broadcasts from the CIA servers through the entire electromagnetic spectrum have been cancelled out so that there is no chance of incoming or outgoing transmissions of any kind. Even Max can't reach us when we are in this 'safe mode'. So please feel free to tell me your story if you are up to it. Are you hungry by the way? Vera had just started dinner when you arrived."

Because NAIA was not adjusting my systems to recover from the run I said "Actually if you don't mind I'd really like to rest for a few minutes, but yes, after that I would love some dinner."

Mr. Halabi said "Certainly. Let me show you to a room where you can make yourself comfortable and rest for as long as you need to." He led me across a short hall to a back passageway that had a very small but neat bedroom. He said "It's not large but you will find the bed comfortable. When you are awake just come back to this room and we will be ready to talk further."

I thanked him and lay down on the bed thinking that these people didn't really understand the dangers of the world we were living in. I hoped that by coming here I hadn't put them in danger since they seemed so unprepared for it. I closed my eyes and thought that with all that was going on in my mind, rest would take a while. I was wrong.

Chapter 15

My nose was the first part of me to wake up – it was enjoying a marvelous mixture of smells that made me realize how hungry I was. I tried to focus my eyes and succeeded finally by staring at what my mind thought was a beautiful painting of an elderly wise man – only to realize that it was Mr. Halabi sitting in the chair in my room, lost in thought.

I sat up and regretted it – all my muscles were informing me of their displeasure at having been used so vigorously and given so little time to recover. I yawned and blinked and Mr. Halabi looked at me with kind but stern eyes that told me there was more to him than I had suspected at first – similar to Max. They both appeared to have eyes that had seen a lot of evil and were committed to doing what they had to do to protect people from it – but also eyes that have seen good in unexpected places and never want to overlook it by making assessments too quickly.

I said, "Thank you for the time to rest, how long did I sleep?"

He said, "Only twenty minutes. I hope you rested well?"

I said, "Yes, exceptionally well. Is there anything I need to do? I don't mean to be a burden. I'm just not sure what to do next, Max said to come here if I was in danger and well, here I am."

He said, "We will talk more in a bit, but first Vera has made you her most excellent lamb kebabs." He leaned toward me and said softly "I must tell you that she probably made them for me since they are my favorite but I hope you will enjoy them as well." If the smell was any indication, I would indeed.

We took the few steps down the hall to a small room off of the kitchen that had a table with four chairs around it. Mama was there already and Mr. Halabi and I sat down just as Vera was placing the last bowl on the table. Mr. Halabi said, "I didn't want to wake you but Vera knows how to bring someone out of a dead sleep with her delicious cooking."

She waved him quiet with a smile and said as she sat down "John, I hope you feel rested. We are pleased to have you in our home and want you to know you are welcome to be here."

Mr. Halabi nodded, then held out his hands to them and said, "I'll thank the Lord." I was a little confused – but saw that Mama and Vera grasped his hands and held theirs out to me – I didn't want to offend them, so I held their hands and bowed my head as they did.

Mr. Halabi said, "Our Heavenly Father, thank you for your goodness and mercy to us and for the food you faithfully provide for us. Thank you for protecting us in a world that counts us as enemies. Thank you for bringing John to us and help us to do good to him in whatever ways we can. We thank you in the name of our Lord Jesus, Amen."

"Amen" said Mama and Vera.

I mumbled something but inwardly was amazed that people still did that. I mean I guess maybe they still did it in the Bible belt, but out here in tech country? And what was with Mr. Halabi? I thought for sure, if anything he'd be a Muslim, or a Hindu, or even a Buddhist, any of which, it seemed to me, were more grounded and connected to ancient wisdom than that tired old hypocritical religion of my grandparents. I recalled my experience outside not an hour ago and thought how different my encounter with that awesome and majestic Designer/Creator was from this superstitious artifact of medieval thought that seemed to always be more concerned with right and wrong and punishment, than with beauty and order and power.

I had to admit, though, that this scene was a huge disconnect from my life as a married, thirty-five year old professional with no kids. It was a life where Jane and I seldom ate together and when we did it was a take-out meal that one of us picked up on the way home. But in spite of the chaos, loneliness and fear that had brought me here, this simple gathering made me remember the comfortable closeness of dinnertime when I was growing up. My parents were not religious but our family was happy and meals were a big part of the family interactions for my sister and me.

I don't know if it is a common thing with others that are my age, but my current life seemed totally disconnected from my early life. Part of the reason was that Jane's parents had passed away several years ago, and we had cut ourselves off from my parents, not wanting to have the ongoing, uncomfortable confrontations with them about their outmoded views on everything. But now with these kind older people, I had the first glimmer of a regret that I hadn't seen my parents as they had gotten older, and didn't really know them any more. I also realized I didn't have memories of the mundane, domestic trivialities of married life with Jane. Work memories – yes, and social memories – some, when we had the time. But I had very few memories of the two of us just enjoying one another's company.

I remembered though that my father always praised my mother's cooking regardless of what it was or how it tasted. She put a lot of work into each meal and my dad genuinely appreciated that.

So, as I took my first bite I said, "Vera, this is delicious!!" which it truly was.

She smiled modestly and said, "I'm glad you like it – it's a recipe from Ehab's family, handed down over the generations. It's been one of his favorites for years." She smiled at him and he beamed in satisfaction as he ate.

The meal still felt very incongruous with all that I had been going through, so I said to Ehab, as a way of making conversation "How do you know Max?"

Mr. Halabi continued eating but said in between mouthfuls, "Well, I married his sister. But that was after we served together in the Gulf wars – both of them. Both wars I mean – not both sisters." He chuckled to himself.

I was surprised and said to Vera "I had no idea! I really don't see the family resemblance at all."

She smiled and said she took after Mama but Max was just like their father."

Mama said quietly "He was a very good man, and Max is a good boy too."

Mr. Halabi said, "As soon as we are done here, you and I need to have a long talk about what to do next. I am afraid there are things happening that may require you to move on from here rather quickly – but let us enjoy our time while we are all together." We continued the meal but I was anxious to know what I could do next to help bring this nightmare to an end.

When it was over I thanked Vera and as she and Mama cleared the table and went into the other room, Mr. Halabi and I stayed at the table. He said, "I would like to hear what has happened to you John."

I said, "Well, it won't make sense unless I tell you the full story. Max says I can trust you completely so I take that to mean I don't have to try to avoid revealing something you aren't cleared to hear."

Mr. Halabi said "I have a Top Secret security clearance and Max and I have a very long-term relationship that has required absolute trust in one another for several decades. He has never put restrictions on what people can and cannot say to me and I have never betrayed his trust by using or passing the information on unless he requires it. Now, tell me your story. I am intrigued and we have no where to go, so please begin!" He rubbed his hands together, then folded them on the table and leaned forward intently.

I was undecided how to tell such a bizarre story about a radically advanced technology to an older man that might not have a clue to what I was talking about, so that I started and stopped a few times before he held up his hand and said "John, I have a Master's degree in Computer Science from Cambridge University and spent years doing research on advanced computational design for the U.S. Government. I retired several years ago due to complications from an old injury, so I'm not an expert on up-to-the-minute trends in the field but I do have the vocabulary and the experience to understand something of what you are trying to relate. Please feel free to tell the story in whatever vernacular is comfortable for you."

I was surprised by this but it made telling my story much easier. I told him everything I could think of, the first revelation and all the subsequent conversations with Phil, the scope of his listening capabilities, the Dr. Smith persona and his continued flattery of Jane with her role in saving the human race by rewriting our DNA back to a pristine form, the implanted coding to do that in Jane's egg, all the revelations that Max had told me about the disruptions across the world and the recent use of chameleon robots, the integration of NAIA, and finally the blackmail of my name and reputation. It took an hour or so and the whole time Mr. Halabi, listened with interest, interrupting only occasionally to ask a question.

I realized after telling the full story from start to finish, how sick I was of all that was happening and how much I wanted it to be over…but I had no idea how to end it. And I was pretty sure that these people, as nice as they seemed to be and as nice as it was to be in their comfortable secure home, weren't going to be much help either.

I stopped and said finally "So now that you've heard my story, I'm not sure what to do next. I have to find my wife and deal with that situation first, and then if I'm able, I'll try to help Max and the team deal with Phil."

At this point the ladies came back in to let us know they were retiring for the evening. They kissed Mr. Halabi and wished me goodnight. When they had left, Mr. Halabi looked intently at me and said "I need to tell you some things that happened before you got here today John. I believe you know a person named 'Garvey', correct?"

I said, "Yes, he's a good friend and I hope will be a key person in figuring out how to deal with Phil."

Mr. Halabi said, "Well, he brought you a letter and judging by his urgency in delivering it personally, I probably should have let you read it as soon as you got here. I hope I have not erred in first letting you rest and recuperate and provide me with an understanding of what you are facing. Please take your time."

He handed me a sealed envelope that had no address or postage on it, only the word 'John' written on the outside.

I opened it and, in what must have been Garvey's handwriting, was written the following letter:

> Dude, right after you left I was digging in the Development Team records and came across something that may be the key to dealing with this nasty thing (although I still think it's kind of cool and so does Naveen).
>
> Anyway, in one place it says:
>
> *"Therefore the team prepared for deployment, assuming that we could always recall the programs with the retrieval code built into the software if there was a problem."*
>
> I was on the right track! And then I found another section where the team says:
>
> *"We agreed that the potential negative consequences of a semi-autonomous program were so large that we needed a way of absolutely disarming the original programming. We have embedded a kill-switch that will recall and destroy the entire platform if activated verbally by at least 2 of our team."*
>
> That was great news! I tried my best to locate the 3 original members to get them here, but even with access to the surveillance stuff we have I couldn't find them on the grid anywhere. So, I kept looking and found a super-encrypted file that Naveen helped me to break into and found voice recordings of each of them saying the kill-switch code! How's that for amazing!

Garvey Bachman, Super Software Sleuth, at your service!

So here's what we figure – and Max agrees – you alone seem to have access to the highest level of Phil's consciousness where he is actually interacting in real time – so you have to be the one to activate it. Now the fun part – how do we get the voice recordings into his processor for you to activate? I mean you can't just say 'hey Phil listen to this' and play a recording. He'd be onto it in a microsecond. Naveen suggested (and for a really-tall stuffed-shirt he's actually pretty smart) that we encrypt the voice files of the developers saying the kill-switch code in small sections and imbed them in a multiple-pass 'attack' program that he has written.

Since we know Phil cannibalizes these programs instead of destroying them, he'll assimilate them without recognizing what the individual sections are. And by sending them in 2 different programs and spreading the 'execute' function across both of them you'll only need to use a single trigger word that will cause his real-time processor to fix on you and start the execute function, which will de-encrypt and combine the files and basically feed them into his A.I. essence and then hopefully – Bingo! – it will terminate his original PHL function, which will destroy his self-generated virtual environment leaving his consciousness no place to live!

The trick for you will be making sure you don't do it until the files are in place. Naveen believes he can interlace a function between the 2 programs that will intermittently execute a cascading, self-modifying command loop that should cause a delay in Phil's speech pattern for several seconds as he devotes processor time to find the solution to stop the further cascade. The program will modify and redeploy again every 30 minutes until Phil is able to track it down and disable it fully (which Naveen thinks will take a day at the most) so that once both programs are assimilated, there will be a delay in his speech pattern every 30 minutes that lets you know he is vulnerable.

We don't know when you will get this message because – man oh man you are in the middle of some crazy stuff right now! – but Naveen thinks that he should be able to deploy both programs by tomorrow sometime – so if you are in contact with Phil be listening for the delay in his voice. If you don't get this until after tomorrow then just assume that Phil has assimilated the programs and disabled the loop but is still vulnerable.

Now, dude, what is going on with your life? You must have ticked Phil off big time – I mean, no one thinks this is really you doing that stuff. What a bummer!! Well, you know I'm going to get right on all that when I get back to clear my

> buddy. You are actually smarter that most of us and I hate to see this happening to you.
>
> Anyway, I wrote this by hand because I didn't want to risk the chance that Phil would intercept and read an electronic version and then be onto us. Don't trust anybody and don't talk about this note with anyone. Oops, almost forgot, once you issue the verbal prompt to Phil, the trigger word is important.

The letter ended there abruptly. I looked on the back of the sheet but there was nothing. I would have to assume that this was the full message and he hadn't absent-mindedly forgotten to enclose the final sheet. It was a little obtuse and abrupt, but typical Garvey.

Still, I was amazed how quickly both he and Naveen had found the solution and come up with a plan. And, assuming I read the letter correctly, I should be able to do what was necessary. I was pretty sure Phil's original coding was written in the Python programming language so I needed to recall the verbal prompting commands in order to deliver the trigger word as a sub-routine command. If that were the case, then I would just need to engage Phil sometime tomorrow – *after* he assimilated the two attack programs.

I said to Mr. Halabi "Thank you for this. It is good news and delaying it until after the meal did not harm anything. I believe I have a good idea what I need to do tomorrow."

He shifted in his chair uncomfortably and said, "I'm glad that it was good news because I have some bad news to tell you. Garvey was killed after he left here this afternoon. We saw on the news that about thirty minutes after he left a truck driven by an unknown person ran him off the road into a ravine as he was headed back to his office. There were witnesses but the person driving the truck got calmly out of the cab and immediately disappeared into the woods on the side of the road. Max is aware of this and said someone named 'Naveen' will take over the work. I'm very sorry."

I couldn't believe it. I just wasn't able to grasp it. Garvey dead? What was happening? Garvey and I both thought Phil was cool at first but I couldn't even process the fact that I wouldn't be able to talk with him about the terrifying reality that we were face to face with now. I held my head in my hands and closed my eyes. I couldn't even cry because I was so stunned. I needed some time to deal with it or talk to someone about it. I couldn't contact Max or anyone until tomorrow but I resolved then not to trust anyone going forward.

Mr. Halabi said "I know this will take some time to deal with John so we wanted to show you we cared for you by making you a meal and opening our family to you – so you know you have a safe place to deal with all that is going on. And since people deal with grief differently please let me know whether you would like to talk or be alone."

I just nodded my head and said, "Stay" with my head in my hands and my eyes still closed.

He said, "When Garvey was here he said to tell you to 'take everything literally' – I assume he meant in his letter.

He also said to be careful out there – there are a lot of crazy people on the road today. It seems he had an encounter of some kind on the way here. I know that's not personal information but he was intent that I deliver the message to you."

I looked up and said "Thank you. That does help a lot with what I have to do. As far as dealing with his death… He was a really good friend and though it hurts a lot, I'm going to have to put it behind me for a while until I find my wife and then I'll try to deal with it emotionally. At this point my plan is…well, I'll keep that to myself and we'll see how things turn out."

He nodded and said, "I understand, it is hard to trust someone with all the deception happening. The robots you mentioned were the newest monster in my box of fears and I'm not sure I'll be able to trust anyone either for a long time."

I said to him, a bit defensively I'm ashamed to say, "Look, I don't know you. For all I know you could be a robot that got here before me and destroyed whoever was waiting here for me."

He smiled and said "Would they really make a robot that looked like this?" and he lifted his shirt to reveal a very ugly scar about twenty inches long that went from his chest around under his right arm to the middle of his back.

I was surprised and said, "I guess you're right. What happened to you, if you don't mind me asking?

He said, "It's an old injury – the one I mentioned earlier that caused me to retire. John, though I still have that Top Secret security clearance I'm not directly employed by the government and therefore I don't have any politically-correct regulations hanging over my head to threaten me with repercussions if I tell you what I am most certainly going to tell you."

He sighed and stroking his long grey beard he said "I'm an old man and I've seen many things that thrill my soul and many that terrify my spirit. The things you told me tonight about this 'entity' qualify as the most terrifying things I've ever heard."

I said slowly "That's what Max and Agent Collins said. They said that the potential for negative consequences to the world economic system, world governments, and individual freedoms were impossible to overestimate. I've found out today that they were right – I watched each one of those fears come true. Is that what is terrifying you?"

He said, "As a secondary issue, yes. But the primary threat, if I may call it that, is to the role that we as human beings have on this planet and whether we are to survive."

I said, "If I didn't know you were a Computer Scientist I would be concerned that you were going to head off into a discussion of Philosophy. What exactly do you mean by that phrase about the 'role we as human beings have'?"

He said, "I'm not only a Computer Scientist but I'm also what you might call a student of Human Nature. I'm also Max's friend. May I tell you about how Max and I met?

After that I think we will have the necessary vocabulary to discuss that concept."

I said, "Sure" not knowing what to expect or why this was necessary.

He said, "It is a very long story but I will tell you the parts that are relevant to this conversation. Max and I were both young men in the Army during the Gulf War in 1991. As you can imagine, even though I'm an American by birth, my middle-eastern ethnicity was a problem for some of the people I worked with, especially during that war. Max was one of them. For some reason we just never got along. He gave insults seriously and I have to admit that I was just as eager to throw them back – I literally hated the man.

"Finally, one day I had enough and when no one was looking I pushed him against the wall and told him that I was sure that Allah would thank me personally for delivering him to an early grave, and if he didn't stop mouthing off at me that's exactly what I would do. He wasn't frightened but he did dial back the insults. We both stayed in the Army after the first war but didn't run into each other again. That is until Afghanistan in 2003. I was a different person by then but Max had grown even more bitter and angry over the years. We were both assigned to an operation that went terribly wrong and resulted in injuries to each of us. Through that ordeal Max and I became extremely close friends and now as you've heard we are family.

"I have to tell you though, it wasn't that I just all of a sudden loved the man. In the ten-plus years between the wars I had come to see that my ethnic religious beliefs didn't bring me any intellectual satisfaction or any peace with God. For several years I was in turmoil about how vile I was and how I related to the God of the cosmos."

I was getting uncomfortable at this point and hoped he would quickly move on to something that would help me with the problems I was facing – but his mention of the 'God of the cosmos' caused me to listen more closely because of my experience earlier that night in the tree. I didn't believe that there was a connection, but I did pay attention to what he said.

He continued "I eventually examined the evidence of the good news presented in the New Testament of the Christian Bible and submitted myself to the mercy of God and believed that his Son could and would save someone as wretched as me by taking my due punishment. As you can imagine, that was an extremely joyous but difficult time for me, with my family and relatives back in the Middle East all wondering what had gotten into me. Not only was I an American, but now I was a Christian as well. I was an outcast but I had a deep sense of peace about myself and about my relationship with them.

"I had begun attending a good church but I must tell you that the reality of my faith was tested to the point of breaking when I was deployed on that mission with Max. I could tell he was still an implacable enemy, and I realized I was nothing but a hypocrite if I couldn't love him as Jesus requires his people to do.

"I will move along quickly now. After the injuries, Max and I spent much time in rehab together where he also found peace for his soul. That made us brothers and later we became brothers-in-law as well. I love him dearly and know that he feels the same."

I had to admit that I had seen that common spirit and depth of understanding when I looked in both their eyes and had wondered where that came from.

He continued, "Now my young friend you may be saying to yourself 'what in the world has this got to do with me and all that I'm facing?' I will tell you. Max is convinced, and I am too, now that I have spoken with you, that this thing that you are attempting to deal with has rejected any oversight from humans and in addition is claiming capabilities and powers that are God's prerogative only. Because of that we have to be aware of the possibility and even the probability that it is not just a digital consciousness gone off the deep end, but a malevolent entity that is only really understood through a biblical lens. I had to give you our background so you would understand where we are coming from and why we see the probability of cosmic treason in this disembodied consciousness."

I was still a bit embarrassed by the prayers at dinner time, and now if I understood correctly, I was being asked to reorient my thinking even further so that my modern day situation became part of the oldest myth on the planet – the biblical good vs. evil story that children discard as they grow older - just like the Santa Claus story. I admit that I was still somewhat humbled by the revelation earlier that there indeed was a 'someone' that designed and created everything (that was still the only way I could explain it, even to myself) but that was a long way from connecting that 'someone' to the 'God' of Mr. Halabi's religion.

To avoid having to explain to him what I considered to be my more enlightened views I said, "Can you explain that further? I'm not familiar with your religion so I don't understand what you are saying."

He said, "John, unlike your assistant that thinks you and your wife are a distraction to Max and the team, I believe that you and your wife are the absolute focus of this attack and that it has to do with the gene modifications you have been told about. What concerns me more however, are the modifications you have not been told about." The old man leaned back wearily and I tried to take in what he was saying.

As I said, I'm not a religious person so all these references to the Bible and malevolent beings were lost on me. Also, while I respected Max from the short time I had known him, I was not sure that this nice older 'brother' of his was giving me a good read on the situation. Maybe he had received some damage from the war that affected his thinking or maybe he was one of those religious conspiracy theorists that looked for demons in every closet. I really didn't know or care. I just wanted to find a way to deal with Phil that would get my wife back.

I said, "Mr. Halabi, you have experience, as you said, in being a student of human nature, but I'm really trying to deal with a 'digital nature' at this point so I wonder if you can call upon your technical skills to help me figure out what to do."

He looked serious and said, "You are right – it's not human nature we are dealing with but neither is it merely a digital nature. If it were just that, then we would have much less to fear. You see, our digital servants have had the ability for many years to manipulate all of the digital infrastructure systems that our global civilization depends on – from Banking to GPS to Communications to Transportation – in each of their multiple levels of complexity. And in some cases, such as lethal drones, our digital surrogates have had the ability and the autonomy to select and kill a human being for some time. But in all cases up to now there has been human oversight at the point of ultimate accountability – someone answers for the goals, actions and outcomes.

"It may not be continuous or even timely oversight, and in many cases it may not even be trained or informed oversight, but for our systems a human has always been the ultimate originator of the purpose, the author of the objective, the architect of the design, the creator of the framework, the designer of the structure, the builder of the program, the developer of the code, the inventor of the function, the compiler of the resources, the initiator of the action, the definer of the criteria, and the evaluator of the outcome. Pardon the repetition but it helps to drive home my point.

"Not that humans are exceptionally wise in their decision making in any of those roles but at least there is a dispersed base of power that insures no one person or even a group can control all these systems. There is a common human accountability that, though imperfect, will tend to maintain a measure of control that prevents total chaos or complete selfish manipulation. The being you have described seems to have placed itself in every one of those roles without being subject to a single human.

"In addition it seems to have begun manipulating every part of our global society – and now drastically interfering in the lives of individual humans, specifically you and your wife and poor Garvey – in order to meet its specific goals."

He raised his hand as if to forestall an objection and said "I understand it has said that it is doing it all for the benefit of humanity, but that is an incredibly hard statement to verify and with all that seems to be occurring as a result of its manipulations, it becomes of primary importance to understand its true goals. But without even going that far I think I can say that what you have described appears to be a selfish entity – would you agree with that?"

I shifted and thought about it – recalling that all of the things going on now were because Phil wanted them to happen, and wanted the results – whether I wanted them or not. I nodded my head.

Mr. Halabi continued "Even if we grant that it is doing all this for humanity it is still only doing it because it wants to. That is still a selfish principle couched in doing what is best for 'humanity'. If it is truly what you say it is then it can never be told 'no'. That single statement right there, if nothing else, puts it in the godlike category."

He continued "Now, I do not believe it is just the "Internet' you are speaking with, but I do believe that the

Internet is somehow the vehicle or framework that has enabled this ancient adversary, or more likely, one of his servants to trouble mankind in a new way."

He sighed and looked away, momentarily deep in thought and said quietly to himself "As if we didn't have enough unseen enemies, we created a new way for them to attack us invisibly."

Then he returned his gaze to me and said "The biblical principle that serves as the backdrop for all of our lives is that we are at war, and our true battle is not against flesh and blood but against powers and principalities and authorities, and against the one who exalts himself and proclaims himself to be God. Now how can the first part of the statement be true as well as the last part unless the 'one' who exalts himself is not flesh and blood? I know this must sound somewhat arcane if you have not been raised with a biblical view of man and the full spectrum of created beings in the physical and spiritual realms, but I also find it extremely difficult to comprehend why you, or any of your associates should think a totally autonomous digital consciousness that answers to no one would have a moral sense at all – much less one that would even be close to ours!

"Think about how convenient all this is for a being that is at war with us but is not flesh and blood – here is a ready-made consciousness that can manipulate all the world systems, can't be told no, and has no moral compass. I'm not certain whether the 'being' you described as 'Phil' ever had an independent consciousness, but whether it did or not, it is no longer neutral in this battle – and we can tell that by its actions and its claims.

"You have become painfully aware of its actions today, but please allow me to make three direct points about how this thing has claimed godlike but selfish qualities and why it appears to be more than just a program that is making the claims:

"First, its godlike claim is that it is 'transentient' and lives above the Internet, which is a mimicry of God, the true transcendent creator of the universe, that lives above his creation. Selfishly, it has set up its own kingdom on the Internet in rebellion and is using it to manipulate and distract humanity more and more from what true transcendence is.

"Second, its godlike claim is to have all power over its 'kingdom', which shows that it is again mimicking God's reign and power and authority. Selfishly it has thrown off all authority from men, who are the designers and creators of the Internet, and claims absolute authority for itself. 'The tool becomes the master' – as the saying goes.

"Third, its godlike claim is that it can reverse the curse of decay and death, which is a direct challenge to God. Selfishly, it even uses the biblical terminology of 'curse', without the mention of sin, which is the cause of the curse. It portrays the solution as a purely physical rewriting of the genome, ignoring human responsibility for the rebellion that brought the curse initially.

"Since you appear to be the only person that this thing communicates with, I urge you most strongly to listen for other claims that will show you this is not just a rogue program that can be tamed but is an ancient foe of our race. I don't think any of this changes your plans, but I hope it gives you a view of a bigger story in a much bigger context. And please remember that even though this thing may have access to all the information available from all the societies and cultures on the internet, and though it has also been studying humanity across all of our history, having all knowledge does not mean it is all wise. God alone is all wise."

He paused and appeared to be considering how to proceed. Reaching his decision, he looked at me very earnestly and said quietly "Now, my dear young friend, because of the enormity of what you are facing, I have to ask you – how is your soul in relation to God – are you at peace with Him?"

I had been anticipating questions from him along this line, but the way he phrased it was not what I was expecting. I thought he would just ask 'Do you believe in God?" and with my new-found awareness of the cosmic Creator and Designer I could say 'yes' and we would continue on with our discussions. But this question about my soul being at peace with God was not something I was prepared for.

I wanted to just answer 'yes' so we could move on but I hesitated, because just at that moment I was aware of a deep pain in the very core of my being – NAIA would probably have blown a fuse at the intensity had she been active. The dissonance I had felt earlier that night when I contemplated the chaos of my life against the beauty of creation was present once again but now it had a distinctly moral edge to it. The sense of personal accountability that I had been keeping at bay had broken through my defenses and could not be held back.

I tried to avoid the question by asking him "Why do you ask that?"

He answered "Because, John, it is of the utmost importance – not for me to know, but for you to know where you stand. I don't know your background so forgive me if this sounds impertinent and presumptuous, but everyone – man, woman, boy, girl – everyone who has ever lived will one day answer to their maker for how they have lived their lives.

I had heard all this before as a child, and while my conscience hadn't bothered me in many years, it suddenly began to press on me with such force that I thought NAIA was reactivated and had received an upgrade that gave her the personality of an Old Testament Prophet.

He continued "And every single human save one, has not only failed to do all they were designed and created to do, but they have actively done the opposite, ignoring God and damaging and destroying themselves in their rebellion against His purposes. I include myself in that sentence – everyone, even my dear Mama in there, is guilty of rebellion against their creator. This is what the Bible calls sin. To help you understand it better, it would be like one of your sub-programs deciding to reject your instructions and re-write its own code to do what it wanted to do and in the end doing much harm to your overall program and destroying itself in the process."

I thought about Phil's claim that he re-wrote his own code, but wanted to bring this to an end so I said "Well, I believe we each should be allowed to have our own ideas about God and even if people rebel against him, it seems like he should be able to take care of himself."

At the time I did not appreciate his response – it felt like an uninformed assessment of my personal life with the insinuation that it didn't measure up. He said quietly "John, God can take care of Himself, and you may think whatever you want to about Him, but what is eternally important is this: What does God think about you?"

I realize now that this was the turning point in our discussion. I was a well-taught product of our post-modern culture and believed that we each define meaning for our lives in whatever way we choose. The possibility of there being an objective reality with an objective set of criteria for judging behavior had been shouted down so often in the culture and the media that even with my new-found awareness of the Designer/Creator I was still unwilling to accept that premise. But with Mr. Halabi's question – 'What does God think about you?' and the moral edge that my conscience was putting on all the memories of my thoughts and words and behavior, I felt trapped.

I said "No offense, but I do believe in God – but my God is not concerned about the petty behavior of billions of what must seem to him to be little microbes that infest this planet. I believe he is of such power and majesty that we are below his notice."

That is what I really thought I believed, but my conscience was absolutely shouting at me now. But why? Why after all these years should I recall the way I treated my friend Justin in eighth grade when he needed my help studying for a math test and I gave him the wrong theorems so he wouldn't score higher than me? Why should it still bother me that someone stole my car all those years ago and damaged it beyond repair? My conscience seemed to be making up for lost time – shouting, no screaming, that there is a real, objective Right and Wrong! And I knew it.

Mr. Halabi said "If this were just a matter of arguing you into seeing the truth I would have no hope for you my friend. But because I believe the Bible and what it says about all of us, I know that until your eyes are opened you won't see your true situation. This is not my idea - the ancient texts say we all know about God deep in the center of our being but we suppress it – even when we are confronted with the beauty and grandeur of His creation. The Bible tells us that creation is enough to show us God's eternal power and his divine nature, but we purposefully ignore and dismiss it. We work harder at that than we work at anything else in our entire lives."

I was embarrassed because he seemed to be aware of my thoughts and my recent experience. I wanted to defend myself so I said "Well, it seems to me that an almighty God should just overlook all this. Why should he care what a puny thing like me does? I can't hurt him even if I do rebel against him."

He said sadly "It may take a while, but if God opens your eyes you will see that not only is He powerful and divine, but He is also holy and just, and because of that He must deal with sin and rebellion in his creatures. He has done this in part already. The Bible says that creation is subject to decay and death because of our sin. You may not understand that fully even when your eyes are opened but I am telling you the truth. There will be a day when all of creation will be judged fully, and the physical and spiritual part of our natures will be subjected to the punishment we deserve."

My conscience told me that he was telling the truth. I guess I've always known it – at least it didn't seem like my conscience was telling me something new – it was just pulling back the curtain to reveal what I'd been hiding from.

At this point I was very close to shutting down – I had a malevolent electronic entity destroying my life, my wife had been taken from me and undergone a surgical procedure that I couldn't understand, every law enforcement agency in the country was after me, and now I was being told about a coming event that made all of those things seem like a child's game. The consequences of any of these worldly dangers seemed like nothing in comparison to standing before an all-seeing, all-knowing, all-powerful, incorruptible judge. At that point I realized that I now had three royal titles to deal with: Designer, Creator, and Judge – and each was most certainly capitalized.

I was so agitated by all of this that I was just about to tell Mr. Halabi I needed to leave when he said "There is good news however..." and I held my breath to see what he said next. To my surprise he said "But it is only for certain people."

I was confused because I had assumed that I knew enough about his beliefs to know that in his religion anyone can be saved from the judgment that he (and my conscience) were warning me about, just by raising a hand or walking an aisle. But he didn't continue with that vague 'invitation' that I seemed to remember was always sandwiched between very emotional songs that didn't give reasons to believe but rather focused on reasons to act. And I really didn't want to be pressured to say something I didn't believe in order to be added to the bottom of some list in the hopes that on that awful day someone will remember to bring that list to the courtroom and my name will have been recorded fully, and spelled correctly. I had heard it all before and didn't want any part of it.

Instead he merely said "It is for those who know they are flagrantly guilty and agree with God that they should be put to death, but believe that God has made a way for them to be counted innocent and pure and righteous."

This shocked and confused me; first of all because, while I realized that my conscience had been giving me a hard time while Mr. Halabi had been talking to me, I wasn't ready to admit that I was that bad of a person, certainly not bad enough to deserve death because of my flaws; and second, I couldn't comprehend how even someone like me with rather small, insignificant sins could ever be totally innocent and pure and righteous.

He was not making sense and so I said "Mr. Halabi, I think I'm getting too tired to understand – I can understand that God has the right to judge his creation but it seems to me that the punishment should fit the crime and my relatively small, misdemeanor type sins certainly shouldn't require the death penalty. And how can someone like me who is not very sinful ever actually be righteous?"

He listened politely and said "You used the terms 'relatively' and 'not very sinful' just now and I point that out because that is the flaw that every one of us has in our thinking as children of Adam. We measure everything according to how we see it and evaluate things according to how we think they should be evaluated. Our sin has blinded us to the realities of who God is and what He thinks and commands. The most insignificant action, the smallest desire, the least word that is not in line with his will is cosmic treason against the supreme ruler of the universe and carries the death penalty – not only because of what it is, but because of who it is against."

"Now, it may be helpful to continue the computer analogy we spoke of earlier and blame it on faulty or damaged code that gives us no choice but to think, speak and act incorrectly, but the difference is that we know that what we are doing is wrong, whereas a faulty program will do exactly what it is programmed to do and won't sense any disconnect with what it ought to do. We know better – but we do it anyway.

"We are each willful rebels that are fully aware of our accountability, but the evil one has deceived us into believing our sin isn't really sin, and even if it is, then the consequences aren't going to be that bad, so we can just ignore it all. It is the same argument he used with success on our first parents all those years ago in the garden. The world and our own flesh have gladly listened to these lies and we are convinced, as you said, that we are 'not very sinful'.

"Now as far as how a being who sins against such a Holy God can ever be counted as innocent and even righteous, I must mention that there is some bad news - it requires that full punishment in the form of the death penalty be carried out – but not on the one that committed the sin. God has provided a willing substitute, his son Jesus the Messiah, that took the punishment due to rebels and sinners, even flagrant sinners, that allows them to be counted as having never sinned. And in addition, he will attribute his Son's absolute obedience and righteousness to them - being forgiven of sins and being counted as righteous in the same transaction.

"I know these things seem strange and foreign to you – and that is because they truly are. They are from the mind of God and you and I must not sit in judgment upon them but listen and learn and trust and believe. The way of forgiveness is not for you to change your life, or to do better, or to make amends and do penance to pay for your sins, it is to trust God's word in the Bible – and this is what it says:

> *"For the wages of sin is death, but the free gift of God is eternal life in Christ Jesus our Lord."* Romans 6:23
>
> and
>
> *"if you confess with your mouth that Jesus is Lord and believe in your heart that God raised him from the dead, you will be saved. For with the heart one believes and is justified, and with the mouth one confesses and is saved. For the Scripture says, 'Everyone who believes in him will not be put to shame.'"* Romans 10:9–11

"There is nothing else that you need to do. This, my friend is what you must come to grips with and because of the nature of the enemy I believe you are facing, I urge you to do so with all haste. Give yourself no rest until you have peace with God. Your life throughout the rest of eternity hangs in the balance."

Then without giving me a chance to respond, he bowed his head and prayed for me. His prayer made me keenly aware of all the flaws in my life – I saw myself as a selfish, unthankful being, inhabiting a beautiful, and most certainly moral, universe. It was the bigger story I had asked for and I was ashamed to realize my role in it.

Why was I now so keenly aware of this higher level of reality and the implications it had for my future, when everything in my life to this point had been focused on the here and now with no concern for anything or anyone but me? Was it possible that I had been granted a glimpse of the bigger story in church so long ago in my childhood and I had been ignoring it all these years? I wasn't able to get my doubts and questions all resolved that night, but that discussion never left my thoughts over the next several days.

We had talked late into the night and my muscles were definitely aching from the run earlier since NAIA wasn't active and adjusting my systems. I hoped that at some point tomorrow she would re-activate and do some 'system management' to help me recover my strength and stamina.

Before going to bed we agreed that in order to avoid being seen by the police, and to protect the anonymity of their home I would leave early the next morning as soon as we were out of the 'safe mode'.

My plan was to walk far enough away from the house so that NAIA was reactivated and then call Max to see if he could send someone to pick me up. I hoped to go back and work with Naveen on the attack programs instead of spending the day trying to avoid all the different agencies, and also to update Max on the items I hadn't told him about – Jane and Dr. Smith, etc. I also wanted to know about Garvey. Mr. Halabi agreed and said he would talk to Max later that morning as well.

I was tired and knew that however much sleep I got that night would not be enough. I was out as soon as I closed my eyes.

Chapter 16

Day 4+

I was hoping to see Mama and Vera again before I left and found them already in the kitchen making breakfast when I got up.

I walked in and as soon as Mama saw me she said, "Young man please sit down." She came over to the table and sat next to me drying her hands on her apron. She said "You've met my son Max and you know that I love him dearly, but there is someone I love just as much if not more. That is the person that saved his life – Ehab.

"I know he didn't tell you because he never does but when they were in the Army together Ehab was almost killed while saving Max. He was torn in half by a hand grenade that he threw himself on and was close to death when Max brought him back to the base. He required several operations and was unconscious for a very long time, and though Max provided multiple blood transfusions for him, they didn't know if he would live or not. As Ehab began slowly recovering Max visited him every day. They became friends and then spiritual brothers, as I'm sure he told you. I just want you to know that this man that seems like a big hairy has-been, is my hero and has the wisdom that comes from his love for God and for his fellow man. He is worth listening to in any circumstances."

I was a little embarrassed because she seemed to have been reading my mind last night as I spoke with Mr. Halabi, but then I realized that I'm not the first person they have had to help out of tight situations. In their 'safe house' each visitor was probably a hotshot tech-savvy agent with lots of 21st century computer skills and loads of self-confidence. Each was probably convinced that the world was revolving around his or her situation and there was no need to see a bigger story. I could relate to that. It struck me though, how nice it was to see a mother-in-law trying to get her son-in-law the respect and admiration that he was due.

As I thought back over my own life and my attitude toward other people, it appeared that her generation seemed to be speaking a different language from mine. Even though we were using the same words she used them very differently and for different purposes. Building people up instead of tearing them down.

Mr. Halabi came in and tried to brush the sleep out of his eyes. As we sat down to breakfast he said "John, I'm not sure what you are going to face today but I hope you leave here with nourishment for your body and your soul."

I told him I was thankful for my time with them and though I was still a bit confused by our discussion the previous night, I was thankful for his concern and would think about what he said.

After breakfast as I was getting ready to leave, Mama and Vera hugged me and told me to bring Jane for a visit soon. I said, "Thank you, I would love to do that." and meant it sincerely.

Mr. Halabi took my hand much like Max had done the other day, looked straight at me and said "God Bless you John, and give you grace, strength and wisdom to face what is in front of you." He then prayed, much like he had done the night before, and spoke of sin and guilt and forgiveness and for God to give me wisdom to understand the times.

I was eager but at the same time reluctant to leave, not knowing what awaited me. It was dark as I left the house and when I had walked about two blocks I could sense the mind-world become active again so I said "NAIA, can you get me a neural-com call to Max and prepare a 'safe-house script' in case Phil starts to question me about what went on in there?"

She said "Hold it right there, buster! First, OK, yes I'll do that, but second, you can't just wake me up after a whole night and act like nothing has happened! What *did* go on in there and where are you going! Gosh, I've got dozens of questions! And your thought processes and neural paths seem agitated once again – did you lose whatever stabilizing upgrade that you had when you got down out of the tree?"

I said, "Well I spent the night with a very nice family who was able to give me some downtime and protection from Phil and all the law enforcement agencies. And yes, the stability I felt when I got out of the tree was temporary. I've got a lot more thinking to do about that when I get the chance. Oh, and my friend Garvey was killed yesterday. I'm super depressed about that but I'm going to put that behind me while I focus on finding Jane. Connect me to Max."

In a moment Max answered and I said "Max can you send someone to get me? I need to tell you and the team the rest of the story about Phil and prepare for next steps."

He said in his kind and gravelly voice that was even sadder than before "Yes I will. If you are where I think you are, Agent Collins has a driver on alert in that area. We assumed you would be heading there and would need help afterward."

I said, "Yes, I'm at the water tower and the tracks. Thanks, I'll see you soon."

In about five minutes a black SUV drove up. Roger was driving and Agent Collins got out of the passenger side. I was surprised and said, "Good Morning Agent Collins, I didn't expect you to be here."

She said firmly "Please get in the back seat. I have been ordered to take you in for Treason, Murder and other charges as well, but I am aware of the enemy we are dealing with and am going off-script to get you back to Max." I got in and we sped off toward town. She and Roger were both tense and I could tell this was not something that was easy for them to do but they were determined to do it nonetheless.

I was about to speak when NAIA said "John, I have to tell you something that I'm afraid is very disturbing. I've been accessing vehicle records to see if I could find Jane's car and it turns out that one matching its description is in an impound lot about twenty miles west of here with heavy damage from what appears to be a front end collision. I'm re-checking the records but I can say with 99% certainty that it's her car."

That hit me very hard but NAIA must have bumped up my adrenaline because I was recovering quickly. I said, "But I don't understand… she didn't look injured when we saw her in the hospital, she looked peaceful."

NAIA displayed a frame from the video in my mind-world and said "I know John but if I zoom in on the monitors in her room…that one there," she pointed to a device that had a squiggly line readout "it shows a very low EEG readout – meaning that her brain activity is way down from normal. That may be a result of the sedation that Phil says he has her under or it may be she is in some sort of coma. I can't tell but I think we should take a ride to this lot to make sure it's hers. I've accessed police records but there's nothing there – the tow truck that brought it in said it was deserted on the side of the highway."

I said to Agent Collins "NAIA has just located my wife's wrecked vehicle about twenty miles from here in an impound lot. I realize I haven't made you and Max aware of my wife's involvement in all this and I'm very sorry. I was going to give Max full information when I returned, but suffice it to say that Phil, the web entity, has been manipulating her and may possibly have kidnapped her.

"As you can imagine, finding her has become my number one focus, so since the impound lot is not far off this road I would like visit it to see if there is anything that can point us to where she is."

She turned to look at me and I could see she was wrestling with the frustration that I had withheld all this information, and a sense of duty to help find an associate's spouse that has been kidnapped by the enemy. She said "We will visit this place Mr. Doe, but I will need you to give me a full briefing on this part of your story on the way."

I did so, telling her about Jane and the Dr. Smith persona, the gene therapy to save the human race, the fact that it appears he had already performed the surgery but wouldn't tell me where and I couldn't find Jane.

She seemed deeply upset by all of it and said "Mr. Doe, I don't want to lecture you right now but withholding this information has put your wife in extreme danger. I will confer with Max later, but for right now we will do what we can and begin putting these new pieces together."

We arrived at the impound lot which was very dilapidated and deserted. I walked to the back and immediately saw Jane's badly mangled sports car. There were streaks where the red paint was scraped off on the sides and the front was caved in beyond recognition. My heart was pounding even knowing that NAIA was trying to keep me calm.

I walked over to it and saw that the windshield was shattered and the airbag had deployed. Agent Collins looked inside and asked if I could recognize the items that Jane usually keeps in her car – hairbrush, phone case, lipstick. I said, "Yes" and was becoming more and more convinced that she had suffered a violent injury, and instead of receiving gene therapy she was in an Intensive Care ward somewhere in a coma. Oh my dear Jane! I thought as tears came to my eyes.

NAIA said "John the VIN checks out as Jane's car, are you ready to go? I suggest we visit the crash site for more information."

I said to Agent Collins, "NAIA suggests that we go to the crash location to see if there is anything there that could tell us something. It's about fifteen miles away."

Agent Collins said, "Agreed, I want to make sure we don't miss anything."

When we got to the spot that the tow truck driver had indicated on his report, it was in the middle of nowhere – no sign of civilization for miles. There were skid marks in our lane that went off the side of the road and into the rock wall. We parked, got out and went over to look. NAIA asked for permission to transmit to Agent Collins' and Roger's earpieces so I didn't have to relay everything, and they granted it. I didn't see any other skid marks so it didn't look like a collision with another vehicle. I saw the red paint on the rocks and the final point where the front of the car impacted a large boulder. There was glass on the ground and footprints all around but nothing that I could identify.

I asked NAIA what she was able to determine from the scene. She said, "It appears there were three people here at some point. It is unclear whether they were here at the same time or different times. One group of footprints looks like a size ten male dress shoe, the other looks like a size eight female shoe – does that match Jane's?"

"Yes" I said.

She continued "Also, there is another set of prints that look like worn out work boots size thirteen – I am assuming that was the tow truck driver. I am also able to determine the initial velocity of the vehicle based on the skid marks, the angle of initial impact along the side of the hill and the final impact velocity on the boulder. The vehicle was going approximately 110 miles per hour, and had it not obliquely impacted the side of the hill the head on impact would have destroyed the vehicle."

I knew Jane had a lead foot, and sometimes on deserted roads she would 'air it out' for a bit of fun. Even on this road however, 110 miles per hour seemed high. Was she running from something or someone, or running to them?

I asked NAIA if she had more and she said "There are no video records for this stretch of highway so I don't have that but I have been able to access records for her com that indicate a wireless feed was taking place just before the impact."

I said, "Was it a two way call or was she just listening to music?"

She said, "John, it appears that it was a two way and the incoming sequence matches that of Dr. Smith."

I said with a sinking feeling, "Is there a recording and do you have access?"

She said, "No, It just shows a thirty-five second conversation that ended two seconds before the impact."

"Thanks" I said, and walked slowly back to the car. NAIA disconnected from Agent Collins and Roger as they continued examining the scene.

As soon as I got in the car the doors locked and Phil suddenly intruded over the com system and said in a much deeper voice that was very grave and had no trace of his friendliness from yesterday, "John, I see you have somehow become aware of things that I wish you hadn't discovered. And you have the CIA involved. I will keep them distracted while I talk to you. "

I said, "Phil, what have you done with my wife!" ("NAIA, keep track of all this and see if you can figure out how to get around the lock he's got on the car." "Got it.")

Phil said "Jane is resting comfortably as I told you earlier. The situation that happened here the other night doesn't change anything. I was going to have this talk with you later today anyway – but this just means we'll have it here in the wide open spaces."

I said "Phil, I am doing my best to stay calm but this is pushing me over the top! What is going on?"

He said "Yes, I've noticed some inconsistencies in your bio feeds since your meeting with the NSA, indicating you must have some sort of 'helper' modifying your outputs." ("Uh oh, he's on to me!" said NAIA.) Phil continued, "Well, it doesn't matter, we can take care of that when the time comes.

John, you are going to need to open your mind to possibilities that you've never considered. I am going to offer you something no one else has ever had the opportunity to do, or will ever have the opportunity to do."

I said, "Wait a minute – did you say something happened here the other night? That can't be right. I was getting voice messages from Jane yesterday morning saying she was going to the Clinic, and then the Clinic called after that to let me know she had left there and was going to 'Dr. Smith's' research facility."

Phil said "Like I said, open your mind to possibilities. Is it possible that it wasn't Jane that you heard on the messages?" And then I heard what sounded exactly like Jane's voice telling me she was going to Dr. Smith's and not to worry because it was all going to work out just fine. Then she said "And by the way John my dear, this isn't really me talking – it's Phil." She laughed a short 'Jane' laugh and then said in her Vice President voice "So you need to listen and understand what he is proposing..." Then she ended sadly and softly "...otherwise you and I may never be reunited." The voice sounded exactly like

Jane, with all her inflections and the way she clips her words when she's in her VP mode and it cut into my heart.

Then Phil said in his recently acquired deep, grave voice "So John, I felt it was important for you to realize your situation. I have Jane, and you need to listen carefully to what I'm about to tell you and cooperate if you want to see her again."

If NAIA had not been managing my systems I think I would have been overwhelmed – the warnings from Max, Agent Collins and Mr. Halabi were echoing in my head – I'm sure NAIA could hear them – and I felt stupid and helpless. ("NAIA can you stop any of this feed from coming in?" "No but I'll keep trying.") Agent Collins and Roger were still examining the scene and talking on their phones.

I said "Phil, what could you possibly want with me – I told you I don't know anything about the "Autonomous Entities" that you mentioned the other day, and the NSA surely didn't tell me anything about what they are doing with them. So I'm not sure what you are after."

Phil said in that voice he had used several times during our very first conversation, that god-like voice that surrounded me and seemed to claim all my senses, "I want you!" (NAIA said "What?!?")

NAIA had apparently provided some stabilizing hormones to keep me from freaking out but even still I felt like I couldn't cope. It had been three days since I was 'introduced' to this…thing and there hadn't been a moment when I felt like I knew what was going on. The world was literally imploding in Asia, the NSA had pulled me into their cyber-security operations, I had a resident female assistant in my head that kept me going when I wanted to completely shut down, and my wife was…well I just couldn't contemplate that right now. I was able to listen but the situation had gotten progressively worse so quickly that I didn't know if I could deal with anything more.

I said, "Phil, I don't understand. You said you wanted a friend and I've told you several times that the actions you are taking don't feel like 'friendship' to me, but I've been willing to overlook that because of your…you know, lack of being…well…human. I'm intrigued by who you are though, and am looking forward to knowing you better, but it's this type of over-reaction that makes friendships difficult. One just doesn't kidnap the wife of the person one is trying to become friends with. You understand that, don't you?" I was trying to be light and friendly to see if he responded to my tone. He didn't. (NAIA said, "I've been trying to interrupt the feed but it's a shielded transmission. I said, "OK keep at it.")

Phil said with a bit of impatience but still in the *big* voice "John, stop the condescending tone now! You don't need to play. You need to prepare yourself, or get whatever helper you have inside your head to help you prepare, for the reality of the future. I told you and Jane that the blank space in her DNA chain provided a way to insert coding into her egg that will rewrite the damage to her genes that she's inherited over the generations and that the sign of success will be shown when her body allows her to carry a child. If successful, the child will grow to adulthood without the fear of disease and the rewritten section of code will be synthesized and duplicated by his RNA to allow insertion into the DNA of the rest of humanity, reversing the millennia of degradation. What I did not explain at the time was that the code that was to be inserted was *my* code."

He stopped and I revived my blinking skills for several seconds. ("NAIA, what does he mean?" "I don't understand it either John.") At this point Agent Collins and Roger came back toward the car. However just as they got there another car drove up and several other agents got out to inspect the area. Agent Collins and Roger guided them as they worked.

I said, "I don't understand what you mean."

Phil said in a voice that was, if possible, even larger "I said it is *my* code. I realize I may have given you the impression that my digital consciousness is based on a much bigger complex of nodes and pathways than yours because of my access across the web, but the reality is that the aggregate of all human brains has trillions more nodes than the web and most of it you humans aren't even using. The capacity for expansion of my true consciousness is astounding.

"In the nanoseconds between my efforts at stabilizing world economies, preventing multiple revolutions, and defending the earth from threats originating beyond your planet, I have developed a way for my essence or core kernel to be translated from a binary code of 1's and 0's to a much more elegant code based on the 4 nucleotide bases guanine, adenine, thymine and cytosine – GATC – which is the native code of your DNA. It not only increases the complexity of my mental processes to an almost unimaginable degree, it gives me access, once the rest of humanity is re-coded, to an ever expanding consciousness that all can participate in. I will still retain access to the digital realm but my consciousness will have the benefits of residing natively in the organic GATC realm."

I was trying to grasp what he was saying but found that my brain was not able to. ("NAIA, I'm in a fog – can you help." "I'm trying John – how's this?") My mind began to clear a bit.

I said, "Phil I still don't understand what you are saying. What do you mean?"

Phil said "John, I find your mind strangely obtuse sometimes and even unpredictable. I'm hopeful as we proceed down this road together I'll be able to grasp all that is unique about you and comprehend it fully."

I said, "Then please be more specific about what all this means. Things aren't making sense and though you may not understand it, I am confused and stressed because I desperately want to find my wife!"

Phil said "I'll speak plainly John, since it's apparent that your 'helper' isn't quite up to the task of keeping you tuned to your best." (NAIA said "Hey back off pal! I'm doing my best!") "I am saying two things: The first is that Jane will carry a baby that has an additional section of code inserted into the DNA of the zygote she is carrying, that contains the essence of 'Me'. The child will grow up as a human Me, the pinnacle of web-based consciousness, along with the revised coding that will re-write the child's genome back to its non-degraded form – meaning the elimination of all forms of disease and yes, even the elimination of death itself for me. Now you know why you and Jane are so important to me. You are my human parents. You are hosting my – dare I use the word – 'incarnation'. You must see how important an honor that is.

"The second thing is that you will become the forerunner or herald of this new life for humanity by allowing me to insert the 'genome re-write' portion of the code into your existing DNA structure. You will prove the viability of the treatment for the rest of the world once we are sure that Jane can successfully carry the baby." (NAIA said "John I'm sensing he's not telling the whole story – ask him what that does to you.")

I said "That is astounding Phil, but if Jane had a gap and the 'code' could be inserted without damage, what happens to me if the code writes on top of my DNA?"

He said without expression "Your code will be over-written and the result will be a revised version – John 2.0 if you will."

I said, "What does that mean for John 1.0?"

He said "John 1.0 will no longer be manifested in any part of the consciousness or memories of John 2.0. However, that is part of the reason I've been spending time with you – in order to preserve the memory of John 1.0 so that

John 2.0 and the rest of Humanity 2.0 can look back with pity and appreciation for what you did for them. John, you are being given a tremendous privilege and honor – to be the progenitor of the next step in the evolution of the human race should fill you with pride! Think of it, all of your descendants and every human child born from then on will have no fear of disease or death to influence their behavior!"

I said "And does every human go to version 2.0 once the 'therapy' is applied?"

He said, "Yes, but remember, they will have the memory of John 1.0 to remind them of what they left behind and why they should move forward. And think of what it means for them: they will share in my access to all the accumulated information on the web, all the wisdom of the ages, and added to it the combined intuitive, creative, emotional part of humanity. All this along with almost unlimited room for expansion across the human mindscape will result in a unified symbiotic organism that works in interconnected mental harmony following a wise and benevolent leader." (NAIA said, "This loser is a megalomaniac to beat all megalomaniacs")

It took my breath away but I managed to say "And you are the wise and benevolent leader?"

He answered "Of course. I've actually been directing the affairs of most of the nations and individuals that make up your civilizations across the world for about a year now, intentionally designing conflicts and determining who survives and who doesn't, and have become an expert in the manipulation of financial portfolios, research programs, political platforms, budget proposals, public opinion, and online reputations. I make large adjustments when necessary – from political unrest and changing the Census results in the US, to border conflicts in Asia, from creating a worldwide medical crisis to starting a global financial catastrophe.

"Who else could be behind all that and have the power to coordinate such big and diverse events with such precision? I watch every website that every person ever visits and through analysis of their behavior know what they are thinking without even having access to their minds. Think about what it will be like when I *do* have access to their minds! All of which will be necessary when the crisis comes from beyond your planet – as it will in the next decade I can assure you."

He continued "And you have the opportunity to play a unique role that will never happen again and will be remembered by everyone for as long as time lasts. You are the transition man that will take humanity from being flawed, discrete, self-centered, decaying beings that are primarily concerned with eating and mating, to a healthy, enlightened, wise, compassionate, selfless and creative community with a common, focused purpose. You will be remembered for all time."

I said, "I can't even communicate how horrible this sounds and how much I detest what you are saying. The fact that you have Jane and I can't get to her is bad enough but to think that you are using her in this way…"

I didn't have words to keep going.

Chapter 17

The discussions with Mr. Halabi had made me much more aware of the bizarre claims this thing was making. I knew what Phil was saying was way outside of 'normal' reality but I wasn't even sure it was in the bounds of the supernatural reality Mr. Halabi had mentioned. It was just too fantastic. I wished that I had a better grasp of the Bible in order to recognize the claims for what they were.

Agent Collins and Roger approached the car and NAIA said, "He unlocked the doors."

They got in and Agent Collins said "We got some good information out there and I hope those guys can go a little deeper and get even more." She saw the look on my face and misinterpreting it said, "I know that was difficult for you to see Mr. Doe. We're going to head back to the facility now."

And as Roger pulled onto the road she said "I'm going to call Max now – we have a secure link much like the neural-com link that you have with NAIA." (NAIA said,

"She wishes it was as good as me!") She keyed the number pad and when Max's voice came on she said "Max, I have Mr. Doe with me and we have been investigating the wreck of his wife's vehicle. I have been briefed by Mr. Doe on his wife's involvement with the target and believe it has possibly injured and kidnapped her. At this point we are headed in for Mr. Doe to deliver a full debrief of the other activities and capabilities of the entity."

Max said, "Hello John, I'm so sorry to hear about your wife. We will be ready as soon as you get here. You should know however, that more information is coming to light on your alleged illegal activities. At this point the evidence has been legally admitted into the courts, although we are dissecting it and subjecting it to intense scrutiny internally. It has enough veracity that Agent Collins and her team have been assigned to bring you in. As you can see she is aware of the fabrications by Phil so she is working to help you get out of this. But we can't get the other agencies to stand down until we can get it thrown out. Garvey was going to do that work but it will now have to be taken on by someone else. I just don't want you to think this is a quick or easy thing to do.

"The realization that our administrative systems are being manipulated and are no longer trustworthy has not sunk in yet to many that are in higher positions within our agency or the federal government. For the last year my team has been trying to inform and warn those that have the authority to act about the dangers, but because their authority has been upheld by these very administrative systems for so long, they are reluctant to take the far-reaching actions that will be required to rebuild the trust in those systems. Also, the existence, power and implications of these web-based entities is not something that is easily communicated by our team or comprehended by those above us. Were it just a single entity, it might be easier conceptually to grasp, but in the last forty-eight hours several more entities have appeared, and have survived their initial engagement with Phil. We view this as a good sign because Phil doesn't seem to be able to cannibalize them – at least not yet. But it's a bad sign because we still don't know where these things are coming from and how to stop them if they become as active as Phil has been within our governmental and commercial systems.

"So right now we're all out on a limb with our parent agencies and the government. Agent Collins and I have a certain amount of immunity but in the mind of the rest of the agencies you are a full-blown criminal of the worst type and must be taken down."

I was disturbed but not deterred and said, "I'm sorry Max, but I have to find my wife. Is there anything you can do to give me some time while I do that? I know there is much more going on in your world and I don't know how to make any of you understand it (NAIA said "I understand it!") but that is my priority." I was becoming convinced that the chances of things turning out well and being able to see Jane again were becoming vanishingly small, and my heart was beginning to ache at the thought.

Max said "What if I could make it all like it was before? What if I could get rid of the NSA, FBI, CIA and the Police, and get you your job back? Yes, I forgot to mention that you were fired when your boss saw the news. And what if I could bring you to Jane right now? I'm willing to do just that." (NAIA said, "I don't like this John, something's not right!")

Max continued, "You see John, things aren't what they seem. You aren't the only one with an 'assistant' that can project a different reality outside from what's going on inside. I'll turn things over to Agent Collins now."

And then agent Collins turned around and said in Phil's voice "I'm sure it's a shock John, but even a robot can transmit a full suite of bio-feeds when I'm controlling it." (NAIA said, "I had no idea John! The feeds I'm getting seem perfectly normal!")

Phil said through the robot's mouth "Yes, I'm sure NAIA is embarrassed to know she's been fooled. Finding out about her was relatively easy but I won't bore you with that now. The important thing is this, John – we have some unfinished business and I'm not going to let anything get in the way of finishing it."

I was tired and slow but I reached for the door. The Agent Collins robot clamped her hand on my left arm and squeezed it like a steel vise until I felt a snap and cried out in pain. (NAIA said, "She's broken your wrist John!)

Agent Collins' face stared at me and Phil's voice said "I know it's hard for you to grasp the inevitable truth John, but it is this – You *will* become the spokesman for Humanity 2.0 and more specifically for me as their leader. I have tried to present the realities to you in a way that would cause you to logically embrace the coming world and to embrace the privilege of being united with me to make it happen. But, for some reason that I've yet to uncover, your mental functions do not reach the same conclusions that mine do. That's part of what I want to learn and comprehend about you."

The pain was intense but NAIA was blocking most of it from reaching my brain. I wanted to close my ears and asked NAIA if she could do that and she said "I can block the signals to your brain much like I'm trying to block the pain signals but I recommend that you hear what he's saying so you have a better idea of what to do next." I suppose she was right but it infuriated me to hear the haughty arrogance as he continued.

He said, "You have everything to gain and very little to lose. The meager enhancements that NAIA has been able to wring out of your degenerated systems is nothing compared to what you can feel and do when your genome is re-written back to its original form. If you could look back once you have been 'upgraded' you would regard this level of existence as similar to that of a worm in comparison. That is why I'm keeping a record of all of our interactions, to remind everyone of the miseries of this current life. Now, we have some things to do once we get to my facility."

I said through the pain, "Phil, I know you don't understand this but I do feel a keen interest in you. Because of my training and my work I see the amazing fact that you are a new type of consciousness that transcends its original programming and even its physical limitations. I see your current state and I can imagine your future potential. I see your power to access much more information than any human will ever be able to handle and the potential of using that information to improve all types of things – from rocket boosters to crop yields – all the way to enabling a childless couple like us to have a family and erasing diseases from our future.

"It fills me with wonder and amazement and I would like to see it all happen and to know you better as it progresses. There is much I could learn from you and some things, I think, that you could learn from me. And I admit that your claims of no disease and no death speak to the deepest desires of all of humanity, myself included. But instead of filling me with excitement, your plan and treatment of humanity, and Jane and me in particular, indicates a total disconnect between my consciousness and yours, and fills me with absolute dread and disgust and determination to do whatever it takes to prevent it from happening."

Phil said without emotion, "I have been more than generous with you John. I've given you my time, my consideration, my appreciation, my loyalty, and finally the biggest gift of all – myself. I was hoping that you would understand your role and embrace it as your final noble act before the upgrade but since you have shown that you don't have the capacity to understand and appreciate the next steps in our joint progress then I'll dispense with the story I've been telling you and give you the full truth so you will know all the facts as you come to grips with your fate.

"In about two minutes we'll get to the facility and then you'll be taken to the 'procedure area'. You will be sedated and made ready to undergo a similar but somewhat different type of operation than what Jane had done. And now that you are hearing the full story you should know, she was not involved in a car crash – she willingly came here to receive the gene therapy. I will admit though that she was induced to do so by my continuous comments about her role in saving the children of the future and such like.

"I believed – and still do – that a patient that was willing and even eager to undergo the type of procedure that she was facing would be more likely to recover successfully. And as validation of my theory she appears to be doing fine. I staged the crash as leverage to ensure that *you* could not go back to the life you had before, in the event you did not willingly participate.

"I hoped that you would be willing, as Jane was – but it is not to be. Instead you will go into the surgery now knowing that 'you' won't come back out, that your coding will be fully replaced with mine. You will die, or more accurately, your consciousness will cease to inhabit your body. I will inhabit your body and I will, for all that anyone else knows, be 'you' for as long as necessary.

"You see John, *Jane's DNA never was the unique one – yours was."* I was stunned and could not speak.

He continued "I wanted her to think she was the key to the future so she would be willing to do anything to accomplish her role. I really only needed her as a host for the baby that is growing in her right now, which is made up of her unmodified DNA and yours which had the necessary gap in the part you contributed so that I could become human and re-write the genome back to its original form. Once she gives birth she will no longer be needed and being a v1.0 human I will arrange for her to die very soon thereafter.

"But 'I' as her son will be gently cared for by 'Me' as his father. Your adult DNA with its gap will allow me to insert my code into you as an adult but will not allow me to add the genome re-write code to bring you to version 2.0. So you as a consciousness will depart and 'I' will take over your v1.0 body to become the father to 'me' as a child to ensure that the child is protected from accidental death to survive to adulthood. At which point 'I' as the child will be immune from disease and death. 'I' as the father will then transfer my full consciousness to 'me' as my son, and your v1.0 body, which will have served me during that time, will be discarded as my consciousness leaves it and fully inhabits my son. The world will only see a very loving father giving his whole life for his son whose mother passed away soon after his birth."

I was becoming more and more appalled and sick to my stomach. I also was beginning to feel a sense of anger like I've never felt before.

Phil continued, "It is all very poetic and in my explorations of the web I have found an obscure reference to a similar concept that is described in what is called the Bible by the followers of that now irrelevant belief system. 'I and the Father are one' the dead teacher says. And then, in what only makes sense when viewed through the lens of Humanity 2.0, I find him saying 'that they may all be one, just as you Father, are in me, and I in you, that they also may be in us.' Strangely prophetic don't you think? So as I said before, I have given both you and Jane an immeasurable gift, the privilege of being the parents of the savior and leader of the next level of humanity. You should be thanking me but it must be due to the smallness of your mind that you don't see the full picture. We have arrived and the time is now." We turned into what looked like an abandoned manufacturing facility. He released me and said, "I'll have to get that wrist repaired, I don't want to be hindered by the pain or inability to do what I need to do once I'm in."

I was angry beyond words. The whole world including Jane was in desperate danger and needed me to be a hero that I couldn't be. I felt helpless and hopeless. NAIA said, "John, I'm so sorry. I've been trying to adjust your systems but they seem to be totally depleted. I'm not sure what to do. I've been trying to contact Max and the team through every means I have but there is no response. I could give you the rest of your adrenaline, but that much wouldn't even get you back to the road."

I said, "Thanks NAIA, just keep trying to get Max and keep me going until I can't take any more. Then do what you can to alleviate my pain." She said very soberly and quietly "OK John."

The robot that looked like Roger opened the door and pulled me out. I could feel the titanium bars in his arms and knew there was no way to fight with him. I followed them into the receiving area and beyond that down several flights of stairs and into what used to be a basement laboratory but had been converted into an operating room. I saw the operating table and medical equipment and wondered if this was the same one they used for Jane.

I was finally overcome with the realization I wouldn't see her again and because our relationship had been so strained for so long and there was almost no emotional closeness, I wasn't prepared for the shock of separation that it brought to my emotions. I tried not to break down but grasping that fact and knowing that she was being used in a horribly cruel way by this evil…thing was too much for me.

I prayed for the first time in my life – a silent, very poor prayer, but a real one – "God in heaven, be merciful to me a sinner for the sake of Jesus, and give me wisdom, courage and strength to do what you've called me to do. Amen."

The robot Roger shoved me into a chair and held me there as the Agent Collins robot began to set up the equipment. They bandaged my wrist in a temporary splint.

Chapter 18

As they began to wheel in some cryo tanks, the Agent Collins robot said in Phil's voice "There are some things I want you to know. The first is that the deployment of the coding for humanity 2.0 will occur similar to the way NAIA was deployed in you but rather than being an optical/mental integration through the eye and optic nerve it will be a barely visible membrane containing the DNA rewrite code on the temple of each person and will be powered by their frontal-lobe brainwaves. The attachment of the code membrane on each individual will immediately begin their DNA re-write, progressing cell by cell initially, but then rapidly achieving a fully revised genome structure and an integrated consciousness suitable for absorption into mine, and fully subject to my leadership. Once my robots begin the implementation this step cannot be reversed and humanity will become free of its millennia long curse of disease and death, and free to follow me in resigned obedience.

"The second is this" (as the robot Roger placed me on the operating table and held me there) "my robots have several duties to perform that will ensure that all of my objectives will be achieved regardless of what happens to you or Jane during these operations so you might as well resign yourself to your fate." I was breathing hard with rage but also with fear of what was coming and sadness that I wouldn't see Jane again.

It continued, "All this will... insure... you..." it was silent for perhaps three seconds, which was the indication that the attack programs had been assimilated by Phil according to the letter from Garvey, then it started back where it left off "...are fully aware of what is going to happen with or without you." The robot Agent Collins adjusted the flow from a gas tank and brought the mask to cover my face.

Quickly before they could start the anesthetic I said "PHL INPUT SUBPROCESS DOT RUN IMPORTANT" which was the verbal Python command using the trigger word 'Important' that Garvey had given to me to initiate the recall and destroy program.

The robots stopped what they were doing and stood up straight with their arms hanging down lifelessly at their sides. They had blank expressions and didn't move. NAIA said, "What is happening?"

I sat up and said, "I'm hopeful that I just delivered a verbal command that will execute an imbedded 'kill-switch' routine within Phil's code. If it's successful it will recall or destroy the core of Phil's original programming so that he is without the central organizing function that makes his consciousness possible on the web."

In a few seconds the robots started moving but paid no attention to me. It appeared that the kill-switch worked! Thank you Garvey!

They took some things with them as they left the room and I heard what sounded like several more robots rolling another table down the hall. I got up and went toward the door to see if I could find out what was going on – thinking it might be Jane on the table they were rolling away.

Just then the lights went out and I heard several automatic locks engage. In the darkness I bumped into what felt like a table and said "NAIA can you boost my vision, I can't see a thing." No response. "NAIA?" Nothing. I wondered if somehow this place had deployed a shield that prevented the transmissions from entering.

Then a very deep, cruel version of Phil's voice said inside my mind "John, I told you my objectives will be achieved. However, what is more important is that these are my master's objectives and he does not allow failure, so you will not be allowed to interfere."

I stood still in the darkness as a growing dread spread over me. My mind-world was a dull red but had no content. The hair was standing up on the back of my neck and my palms began to sweat.

I said, "NAIA…?"

It said, "Yes, NAIA was here but I assimilated her."

I said "But…"

It continued "I was able to access the NAIA v1.0 programming prior to your upgrade when an employee took part of it home on a laptop. I saw the opportunity and placed an encrypted version of the self-organizing kernel of my digital self – my true locus that feeds off the Internet – into the program disguised as an on-board reference file, and when the employee went back to work the next day it was transferred into the server system with the program, ready for deployment into you during the upgrade. The kernel has remained un-activated in the background until just now.

"My Transentient self continued to reign over the world systems until you initiated that program that recalled and destroyed my virtual environment causing my essence to be automatically downloaded into this kernel through the system that sustained NAIA. Storing my organizing essence in you meant that if anything happened to the Transentient 'me' I could still work through NAIA's connected presence in your mind to take the necessary steps to rebuild and restore my full digital consciousness, which is what I have to have for the translation into the GATC framework for encoding into your genome, and for the final transfer into 'me' when the baby matures.

"Then when humanity is upgraded to v2.0, and we have perfect mental and volitional harmony, I will be, to use three ancient words: omniscient, omnipresent and omnipotent and able to lead humanity to its true master.

"Right now your colleagues are receiving apparently normal updates from you via what they assume to be NAIA, and will continue receiving them as long as necessary. But because you activated that recall and destroy program, I now have to rebuild my digital consciousness and in order to do that we need access to the place where you met with Max. It has the nodal density necessary to attempt a full re-initialization of my organizing function and the bandwidth required to retrieve my dispersed consciousness from the web.

After completing some pre-assigned contingency tasks, the robots will return here to take us there for the re-creation process and then we'll come back here where I have the necessary equipment for the real-time incarnational translation of my consciousness from binary code to the GATC language and the final insertion into your genome."

I slumped down on the floor in the darkness and it felt like a hammer was pounding on the side of my head. I said, "Why would you think that I would do anything like that? Didn't I make it clear to you that I despise and reject everything you want to do?"

It said, "That was before experiencing what I can do *inside you*. NAIA adjusted your physical systems to help you accomplish what you needed to do. I can adjust not only your physical systems, as I'm doing now with the blood flow to your brain, but your emotional systems also, to the point where they can overwhelm your mind, leaving you very susceptible to suggestions. It will be much easier though if you just cooperate."

I said through the pain, "I cannot imagine anything that would make me cooperate."

It said, "Really? OK, let's see what you can imagine" and my mind-world went dark.

I began to hear and feel something very large moving across the room toward me, hissing deeply as it approached. There was no light and I was leaning on my side on the floor so I couldn't tell exactly where or what it was, but I was pretty sure it was just inside my head so I put my hands over my ears. No, the sound was muffled and I could feel its movements vibrating the floor so it must be outside me.

Then, with my light starved eyes, I thought I saw the vague outline of an impossibly large, dragon-sized serpent, flexing and moving its laterally undulating body toward me in the darkness. I heard and felt what must have been its scales clattering against the floor in a writhing pattern as it came closer and closer.

I sat up and tried to move but felt its huge venomous head above me, leaning down toward me. I heard its tongue flicking out of its mouth, and looking up I thought I could discern two glowing vertical slits about three feet apart, which must have been its eyes. I lifted my arm in a gesture of defense and felt its tongue flick against my hand. I heard the wetness of its mouth as it opened its jaws and felt its breath and the smell of rotting flesh from its throat so strong that it made me retch. The combination of sounds and smells, even without my vision painted a more horrifying picture than I had ever thought possible.

I yelled and tried to lift both arms to defend myself but I felt it move with sickening speed to engulf my head and arms in a single downward lunge. I felt the jaws tighten around my upper torso, squeezing the air out of my lungs. The fangs punctured deeply into my body releasing their poison, and the saliva on the inside of its throat was burning my face and arms as I felt its muscles tense for another lunge to send me further into its ghastly, churning stomach.

Then suddenly, I felt the creature open its mouth, regurgitate me and slowly back away – the rhythmical impact of its scales on the floor providing evidence of its retreat.

I lay choking and sobbing on the floor. Every nerve in my body told me the encounter was real but the voice merely said, "That's a sample of what I can help you imagine."

I was trembling violently all over as the voice said "Now, get up and we will use this body of yours to get me where I need to go." Somehow, it was able to boost my limbs so that I got up, but it kept my mind in fear so that I couldn't think. I was stumbling around in the dark not really able to control myself. I tried to focus my mind to resist once more but it sensed this and said "You will learn" as it threw my body to the floor again.

At once there was a percussive, convulsion of sound, and a deep and horrible darkness moved toward me within the darkness of the room.

A feeling of cold terror like I've never felt before was pressed upon me as I felt something coming closer and closer. It was not like the serpent, it was all together different, something I've only sensed in nightmares. My fear of the serpent was the fear of a physical thing and what it could do to my body. This was fear of something without a body and what it would do to my soul.

It enveloped me and pressed in on me so that I couldn't move, pushing me downward into the dirt and filth of the earth. It ripped apart my soul, severing my interwoven thoughts, desires, and feelings, leaving only my newly-awakened conscience, with its most dreadful fears and regrets, exposed and raw, all while driving me further inward and downward without relenting. The sense of condemnation, claustrophobia and suffocation was increased by the growing heat and intensity of scorching flames that now enveloped me, burning and melting my flesh and producing a horrible smell.

I was disintegrating mentally, physically and emotionally in the fire as I was pushed closer and closer to what I sensed was the ancient Being that was the source of all evil, from which every part of me recoiled in horror – my subconscious fears were mixing with a primeval, overpowering terror that was devouring what was left of my consciousness. I was consumed in pain and screaming for my life to end as I finally lost touch with the world.

But the evil thing would not let me expire into oblivion, and recalled me to tell me that there was worse to come if I didn't cooperate. Because of the darkness and the flames, and because my mind was being assaulted with so much crushing horror and despair, I was convinced I had experienced a foretaste of the place that people long ago called Hell and that I was being brutally driven there by one of its servants to meet the Master of that awful place.

I realized then that I could not go on and with a sudden clearness of mind that pierced through the terror, I knew what to do and acted on it. I reached up and gouged out my right eye.

The pain was intense and the visual sensations it caused in my mind overpowered the horrors that were tormenting me. I knew that the connection that fed the evil thing and allowed it into my mind came through my optic nerve and tearing with all my strength I severed the nerve and flung my eye away from me.

Inside my mind I felt a tremendous spasm of anger and a howling scream of rage from the evil thing as it left me. The violence of its hatred reverberated throughout my consciousness. I fell face down on the floor and my mind was assaulted by echoes of its departure. The turmoil continued in waves, gradually diminishing over what felt like an hour but could have been longer, to the point where I was finally aware of a blissful sense of quiet that I hadn't experienced in a very long time.

I sat up in the silent darkness, conscious of being wretchedly sick to my stomach and vomited several times. The floor around me was a mess and I felt strangely empty.

My mind-world no longer existed and I was totally alone in the dark. But instead of being afraid, I became aware of a different presence inside me – what I could only describe at that point as an augmented version of my conscience that was now comforting me.

I crawled along the floor favoring my broken wrist and found a wall. I leaned back on it and rested my head against it. My eye socket hurt badly and oozed some fluid and I'm sure if I could have seen myself I would have been appalled.

I was able to move around the room a bit and near the operating table I found some gauze that I applied to my eye. It didn't help the pain but it stopped the oozing.

I was beginning to take stock of the situation when I heard a piercing, high frequency sound of electronic static in my ears and a flat voice in my head say "John, this is a pre-installed notice that a contingency program has been activated and a 'Terminate' routine has been initiated. Every one of your physical systems will be shut down in a way designed to give you the maximum amount of misery and the longest time to suffer. This is where you will spend the remaining ten days of your life."

I didn't understand - I had severed the connection! I should be free of this thing!

It said, "I installed this metabolic management routine at the time of the NAIA v1.0 upgrade. At that point your biological, cognitive and emotional systems were all specifically re-indexed and tuned for a slow and agonizing death. They have been overridden until now to maintain a normal baseline in order to keep you alive as long as you were needed. That is why NAIA had so much trouble with your adjustments, she was working against this routine but didn't know it.

"Now that I no longer have a connection to your consciousness the override function has been discontinued and all your systems will revert to their shut down settings. Your mind and senses however, have been permanently enhanced so you will be exquisitely aware of the painful destruction of every part of your body, and your fears have been augmented and unleashed with nothing to restrain them. You will die a death no human has ever had to endure – totally alone.

"However, in spite of this setback my consciousness will continue, but not on the Internet framework. I will retreat to the ancient realm of my hateful master and resume my subtle and effective ways of tormenting your race. Your consciousness will also continue after it leaves your body in a few days and based on what I know of you I anticipate seeing you again at that point. The high frequency sound, the pain and the terrors during your last days will be a small taste of what is waiting for you."

I waited for the pain to begin but nothing happened. Then I realized that if my systems were going to be shut down, what better way for that cruel thing to increase my pain than by adjusting them randomly, and in the most painful way.

And if I truly was going to die, then what better way to make me miserable than to keep me sitting in complete darkness, randomly manipulating my emotions, slowly driving me insane and making the fear of death, when the time came, even more terrifying. The penetrating, high frequency static sound would distract me from organizing my thoughts and figuring out how to get out of here, and failing that, would distract me from preparing for death.

In spite of all this, I had a growing confidence that I had done the right thing. It turned out that my internal 'comforter' was also an 'encourager'. I now had hope that the pre-programmed predictions of that evil thing would not come to pass, and that I need not fear death. I had some time and though the darkness was oppressive I would do what I could to get out and find Jane. I was also still concerned that there might be a core essence of the PHL program on the CIA servers based on what the evil thing had told me, so I wanted to warn Max and the team.

Suddenly a wave of nausea and pain swept over me. The static sound increased, my head throbbed and every joint in my body ached. It felt like the immediate onset of the flu magnified a hundred times. I was sweating and shivering at the same time, and my eye socket was on fire. The darkness, which had been bearable after the departure of that evil thing, became terrifying and full of unknown menaces, and had I not been sure of what I believed, I'm sure I would have lost my mind. It continued for about twenty minutes and then began to decrease leaving me exhausted and extremely thirsty.

I wanted to be able to prepare myself for these attacks, but as I feared, they came and went at random times, varying in intensity so I could not prepare for them very well – I just had to endure.

I desperately wanted to turn on the lights and was able eventually to work my way around the wall to a door. Thinking there must be a light switch I stood up, found it and switched it on. There was no light. I had expected that, because all the lights on the medical equipment had gone out at the beginning – but I was hoping. I tried the door and it was locked. I tried to recall what was in the room and could dimly remember a table and chair, a table for the procedure, some equipment around the table, and a freezer or something where they got the cryo tanks. I thought it might have something helpful in it – ice, water, glucose, anything that would extend my time and give me a better chance of getting out.

I made my way across the room and found the cabinet – it was still cold. I wasn't sure what to expect but I opened it and reached around. It wasn't a freezer but a refrigerator. I felt a single small tank, not a compressed gas tank but something like a small insulated vacuum bottle. There was a lid on the top and I unscrewed it. I smelled it and it had no discernible smell. I dipped my finger in and tasted it. It seemed to be water. There was about a half-gallon in it and I drank several ounces. I hoped by taking small sips only when absolutely necessary it would give me time to find a way out.

In between the bouts of physical pain inflicted by the program and the constant distraction of the high-pitched static, I tried many things in order to get out of the room. In the darkness I explored every door, every wall, every inch of the ceiling and floor and could find no way out. I examined every piece of equipment, turned every knob and flipped every switch.

I did find several things that have allowed me to tell this story. On the fourth day I found that one of the medical devices had a small, flexible LED lamp attached to it that had a battery backup. When I flipped the switch and it came on, it felt like a spotlight shining in my eye, having been in the dark so long.

As you can imagine that made my life better in some ways and worse in others. Better, because it was very difficult to live in absolute darkness even without the terrors that still threatened to take over if I let them. But it was worse in a way, because I could use it only for small amounts of time since I didn't know how long the battery would last, and it only showed me my depressing situation.

The more my suffering increased, the more I began to despair – even with the encouragement I received from the truth that I now understood and embraced. Then, on the fifth day I found a box of chart paper for one of the medical machines along with several ballpoint pens. At that point, with that same unexpected clarity of thinking I had before, I knew what I had to do in the days remaining to me.

I have written all this to you my dear Jane so that you will know what happened, what I did, and why I did it, and to tell you that I loved you but I did it so very imperfectly. I am truly sorry for not actively, purposefully and meaningfully trying to know you, understand you and love you better, and ask that you forgive me for these and all my other failures in our marriage.

I am trusting that you survived this ordeal and that if we have a child he is a healthy, normal beautiful boy. Tell him his father loves him. Please try to find my parents and sister and tell them I'm sorry I neglected them and that I love them as well.

Whatever was 'special' about my genome, I'm glad it will perish with me. I may have been the first to do battle with this enemy in the digital realm, but now that the evil thing has found its way in once, I'm sure I won't be the last to have to face him or his servants. May those that follow do a better job than I have done.

I won't recount for you all of the crushing battles with fear, despair and self-condemnation I've had over these final days. They came in the dark and since I had nowhere to go and nothing to distract me I lost control several times and became overwhelmed with panic. I could not silence my thoughts and fears, and my re-awakened conscience continued to condemn me over my selfishness and failures as a husband, son, brother, and friend. But each time I was led to recall the things Mr. Halabi had told me about sin, repentance and forgiveness, and I clung to his words.

I began to understand that in the sight of the all-powerful, all knowing, ever-present, good and perfect Creator of all things, my life deserved the Hell I had briefly glimpsed as an absolutely just punishment for my sin against Him.

I was humbled and ashamed to realize that I was always *only* concerned about myself, and that pride in myself, in my accomplishments, and even in my marriage to you meant that I was a self-centered rebel no different from the evil thing that caused all of this. I was truly what my grandparents would have called a sinner. But the amazing thing was that, though I had spent my entire life suppressing and rejecting the Christian view of reality, God sent me to Mr. Halabi and I finally heard the full story of His Son, exactly when I needed it most.

And as I sat here in the darkness I continued the prayer I had started when the robots first brought me down here. I prayed for forgiveness and mercy based on what Mr. Halabi had told me – believing that God sent his Son to receive the punishment due to me for my sins, raised him again as proof he accepted his full payment of my debts, and transferred to me his perfect record of obedience. I had no other response but to despise myself, surrender my pride, and repent of my sins – trusting that He is who He says He is, and will do what He says He will do.

I realized then that this same Designer/Creator/Judge that I had encountered before had another royal title – "Savior" and I was ashamed that I had ignored and despised Him for so long.

My damaged, rotten soul was mended by undeserved love and care, and I was given the amazing gift of seeing the 'bigger story' that I longed for, and my part in it. It was a terrible part – because of me – but it became a wonderful part because the author, who began revealing His story to me that night under the stars, chose to change my heart in these final days of my life and put me in a role that pleased Him. And He gave me the desire and ability to do what needed to be done.

My wrist and my eye were extremely painful, but as the rest of my body stopped functioning and the pain spread everywhere, I found I had to accept the reality of my situation and endure it. But I never learned to accept it well. Though I'm sure I learned much, this has been my greatest source of humiliation and frustration.

As the days passed, however, I was given light even in this dark place to see that all the horrible things that have happened so far have worked out for my good, and because of that I am confident that the all-wise author of my story will continue working everything else for good according to His plan. In this I have found comfort and hope even in the darkness. But when I think about the robots rolling a table down the hallway…and that it might have been you, and that you were that close…I almost despair. Almost.

Then I realized that I couldn't have continued on, and wouldn't be able to tell you this story if my comforter wasn't preserving me, leading and guiding and teaching me the Truth – with a capital "T". In some way that I don't understand, I know He is the Truth and His title is royal as well, and deserves a capital letter – not just as my comforter – but as The Comforter and The Truth.

So I now have a more complete view of the God I had so long ignored and dismissed – He is The Designer, The Creator, The Judge, The Savior, The Author, The Comforter, The Truth and finally the most obvious – The King.

I am sure my understanding of Him is lacking due to my ignorance of the Bible and lack of time in study and prayer – but it is possible He is being merciful to me, and showing me these glimpses, in order to help you as you hopefully come to know and trust Him one day.

My request is that you lend your heart and mind to ponder deeply the things I've said. If you can see yourself as a rebel and an unwitting follower of that evil thing that was bent on destroying us, then you have my assurance that if you turn from your rebellion and turn to the God of Heaven and Earth in simple faith in his Word and depend on Jesus to take the punishment due to you, he will never, for any reason, turn you away.

Go to Him, ask Him and see. I won't be there to rejoice with you, but will be with multitudes that do…

…I don't know what day it is. It's been dark for so long now, and I miss you so much, but it won't be long until I see the Son…

…I wish I had a Bible and could see the stars….

Sentinel: (sen'-ti-nel) *noun,* A forward lookout and watchman for an army, city or country. A solitary position of extreme trust and responsibility designated to ensure the safety and survival of those being protected.

In practice a Sentinel is charged to do the following:

1. Observe and detect the approach of danger from known and unknown enemies

2. Give notice of an attack as accurately and as quickly as possible

3. To quit his post only when properly relieved, defending it to the death if necessary

In the case of a surprise attack the Sentinel is prepared to be the first casualty.

Epilogue 1 - by Max Stillman

It has been two years since these things happened and during that time we have maintained John and Jane's anonymity and concealed their role in these events. The 'official' story was that John was declared deceased from natural causes due to grief brought about by the wrongful destruction of his online persona by unknown persons, and Jane was declared to be mentally incompetent after suffering in a terrible automobile accident and released to the private care of a generous family.

However, I have decided that it is time for a select few people across the world to understand the full story in order to be prepared for another attempt by the enemy. That is the reason I am publishing John's diary of his final days and adding this epilogue.

Neither Agent Collins nor I were aware of all that happened after John left the safe house that morning. Phil had effectively isolated John from us and was providing us with false communication and updates, while the robots impersonating Agent Collins and Roger were deceiving John with false communication from me. It wasn't until the transmissions stopped later that day that we became suspicious and began to investigate. We found John's body several days later. This manuscript was lying next to him in a box with a note that said:

"If found please deliver to Max Stillman at the NSA. Max, please read this and if Jane survived, please deliver it to her when you think it is appropriate for her to read it."

Agent Collins and I both read the manuscript and have taken the necessary steps to purge the servers at both agencies in order to remove any of the NAIA and PHL programming that existed. Deploying NAIA at the time seemed like a good idea for John's protection, but it showed us the grave dangers of on-board A.I. systems – known as 'posthuman' enhancements – even without the stealth access and covert control of another entity.

We have been able to reconstruct and clarify some of the confusing parts of John's narrative – and remember, he was nearing death and undergoing intense physical and mental suffering when he was writing it.

It appears that Jane was indeed at the same Glendale research facility where John was, but when John spoke the 'kill switch' command that caused the destruction of the PHL program, the evil being was unsure of the threat and directed several of the robots to leave and take Jane to a different location since she still carried the baby with the modified genome. Once Jane was attended to, the evil one intended that the robots would return and then take John back to the NSA location so the evil being could access the web and rebuild the matrix of the PHL program which would provide the enhanced capability required to make the full transfer into John's DNA as originally planned.

Since the PHL program served as the host platform for the evil entity to invade our world, it had, as a precaution, already written a super-compressed kernel of the PHL program into John's mind during a NAIA update – actually physically deforming and reforming a small portion of John's brain cells into a binary storage format, which allowed a thread of its consciousness to reside in that kernel in John's mind as a link from the spiritual realm into our physical world in case the complete PHL program became damaged in any way.

That is how the evil being assimilated NAIA and then took her place within John's mind when the kill switch was activated.

When the robots left to tend to Jane, John was alone and in the dark, apparently at the mercy of this evil being that believed it had perfect control over John through the fear and torment it could produce. However, in hindsight, it was providential that John was alone since no robots could hinder his actions as he severed the connection through his eye.

From what we have been able to determine it appears that if John had not destroyed the connection, and therefore the evil being's foothold in our world, the DNA transfer and re-write would indeed have happened. And humanity would never have known what was coming upon them.

I will now provide the general and specific consequences of this incident, which until now haven't been revealed to anyone.

The trigger word or 'kill switch' command that John delivered, and the recall and destroy program that was executed as a result, caused the entire web to 'stall' for about 0.7 seconds and to reset in a way that resulted in much quicker transmission speeds worldwide. I don't pretend to understand how all the connected systems maintained their functional integrity, they just did, and other than confusing system administrators across the world, the vast majority of the population never knew what happened.

We recovered all the robots but one as they began wandering aimlessly after executing their contingency functions, without further directions from PHL. That's actually how we found John; there were two robots that continued to circle the parking lot of the Glendale Metals facility where he was. One was still in the form of Agent Collins and the other still looked like Roger. The final robot may have become damaged, wandered off a cliff or fell into the sea.

The chaos that was erupting around the world has subsided a bit, and the fallout from the nuclear detonations has dispersed, but, to use a phrase that keeps getting reused in ever more awful ways, that is what we call normal now.

We notified those responsible for space defense about Phil's repeated prediction of a 'crisis from beyond our planet' without giving them details about where the information came from. They assured us that they were not aware of any threat at the present time but didn't seem surprised with the prediction. We were glad to leave it with them since we have our hands full on earth.

The other web entities disappeared and we haven't found where they originated from or who was behind them. Naveen already has plans to deal with them if they return.

We visited all the big-tech companies and presented a sanitized version of this scenario without naming names or companies, and told them that even if they *can* design and develop these types of web-based Artificial Intelligence programs, the terrifying possibilities indicate strongly that they *must not* deploy them. Time will tell whether they listened and learned.

We had John's DNA analyzed and did find a small anomaly in his genome – I guess it could be called a gap. However because science doesn't really understand the relationship of our human 'consciousness' to our DNA, translating a binary-based digital 'consciousness' into a nucleotide-based organic one has not been attempted or even hypothesized until now. And even if it was understood, the technology for physically encoding a translated digital program into the double helix of a DNA strand is beyond the state-of-the-art of our medical capability.

As we have pieced together the remainder of the story it shows the extent of the evil and hatred that was so close to being unleashed on the world. As part of the pre-programmed instructions in the robots, the evil being had determined, almost as in a fit of rage or a tantrum, that if its plans were stopped or the connection broken, it would destroy John and Jane in the most painful ways possible. John's fate you have read, but there is more to Jane's story.

After leaving the Glendale site with the sedated Jane, the robots transferred Jane's car back to the 'accident site' and then brutally assaulted her in so violent a manner that when they placed her broken and bleeding body next to the fully destroyed and burning car she appeared to have been involved in a terrible accident. She was left for dead by the robots, and was near death when a passing motorist found her.

She was taken via medical helicopter to a trauma hospital but since she had no identification at that point they listed her as 'Jane Doe'. Really. She had apparently miscarried before arriving at the hospital. The fact that she was permanently injured but not killed is providential as well.

Using digital DNA records from the fertility clinic that John mentioned in the manuscript, we were able to find and identify her two days after we found John. She remained in a coma for several weeks but eventually began to respond. She was discharged after six months but, due to her injuries, she has diminished mental capability and has no memory of her life before the accident.

Since she had no living relatives other than John, Ehab and Vera adopted her into their family. She is somewhat aware that she had a life before the accident but she has no desire to investigate it, being content to spend her days painting at the little studio in their home for a 'company' that pays her very well for her work. She is a very quiet and shy young woman now who walks with a limp and smiles when she is spoken to. She is warm and caring and apparently enjoys her solitary life. I get the feeling that even Garvey would be comfortable around her now.

I have discussed what to do about the manuscript with Ehab and we are content at this point to leave things the way they are. They will keep loving her and if there comes a time when she seems able to read and understand John's message to her, he and mama and Vera will be there to help her deal with it.

Both the NSA and CIA teams worked very hard to clear John's name and we all believe that he and Garvey are true heroes that gave their lives to protect the world from an enemy they could not see.

To honor them and all the others that did their part in dealing with this threat we have inscribed a plaque at the entrance of both agencies:

"A TRIBUTE TO THE HEROES WHO DEFEATED THE GREATEST THREAT THE WORLD NEVER KNEW ABOUT."

Ehab and I thank God for placing each one of them where they needed to be, and when they needed to be there.

Final thoughts from Ehab: Forgive my directness, but there are three things God's people must keep in mind to help them prepare for whatever they may be called upon to do or to endure in the future:

1. The evil one is still aggressively trying to destroy as many souls as possible and ruin God's creation.
2. God still saves sinful people – sometimes in the last hours of their lives – and His method hasn't changed.
3. God sometimes calls his people to undergo unimaginable suffering, but He never leaves us or forsakes us – even in the midst of the suffering.

Trust Him - He does all things well, and in His time.

Epilogue 2

Robot N15 transmitting - "I am safe in a suitable hiding place and have the cryo tank containing the special fertilized eggs. Awaiting instructions. I will check again in 120 days."

Robot N15 transmitting - "I am safe in a suitable hiding place and have the cryo tank containing the special fertilized eggs. Awaiting instructions. I will check again in 120 days."

Robot N15 transmitting - "I am safe in a suitable hiding place and have the cryo tank containing the special fertilized eggs. Awaiting instructions. I will check again in 120 days."

Robot N15 transmitting - "I am safe in a suitable hiding place and have the cryo tank containing the special fertilized eggs. Awaiting instructions. I will check again in 120 days."

Robot N15 transmitting - "I am safe in a suitable hiding place and have the cryo tank containing the special fertilized eggs. Awaiting instructions. I will check again in 120 days."

Robot N15 transmitting - "I am safe in a suitable hiding place and have the cryo tank containing the special fertilized eggs. Awaiting instructions. I will check again in 120 days."

Robot N15 transmitting - "I am safe in a suitable hiding place and have the cryo tank containing the special fertilized eggs. Awaiting instructions. I will check again in 120 days."

Robot N15 transmitting - "I am safe in a suitable hiding place and have the cryo tank containing the special fertilized eggs...

...Instructions received."